# *Instead of starting, his car exploded.*

The force of the  explosion knocked her ... to the ground. She felt dazed ... what had happened. The ... heard screams, runni... then another, smalle... d.

Then Eric was t... supporting her as he helped her to her feet. "Are you all right?"

"I think so." She glanced up and gasped when she saw the jagged gash on his cheek. She couldn't look away from all the blood.

"You're bleeding..." Swaying, she clutched at him.

"Easy. I think you're going into shock," he murmured.

"What exactly just happened?" she asked, her voice hoarse.

"Someone blew up my car. If we'd been inside when it started, we'd both be—"

"Dead."

And then the seriousness of the situation slammed home. Someone was after her. Someone who, for whatever reason, wanted her dead. But why? Who was she?

\* \* \*

Be sure to check out the next books
in The Coltons of Oklahoma miniseries.

The Coltons of Oklahoma: Family secrets
always find a way to resurface...

\* \* \*

If you're on Twitter, tell us what you think of
Harlequin Romantic Suspense!
#harlequinromsuspense

Dear Reader,

In over forty published books, Eric Colton was my first doctor! I truly enjoyed learning about the world of trauma ERs, and as always, I love visiting the Colton family. This story is also set in Oklahoma, which is a state I've visited often and where I have many friends. Throw in cattle ranching and I was thrilled to write this story. A cowboy doctor! Who could resist?

And the heroine MW (Mystery Woman) has amnesia! This made me happier than you know, as years ago one of my first published books had a heroine with amnesia and I haven't written one since! What fun, though not for her.

Add in danger and a huge family, and I have to say this book was very entertaining for me to write. I hope you love reading the story as much as I enjoyed writing it!

*Karen Whiddon*

# THE TEMPTATION
# OF DR. COLTON

## Karen Whiddon

HARLEQUIN® ROMANTIC SUSPENSE

Special thanks and acknowledgment
are given to Karen Whiddon
for her contribution to the Coltons of Oklahoma miniseries.

ISBN-13: 978-0-373-27930-2

The Temptation of Dr. Colton

Recycling programs
for this product may
not exist in your area.

Copyright © 2015 by Harlequin Books S.A.

Printed in U.S.A.

www.Harlequin.com

**Karen Whiddon** started weaving fanciful tales for her younger brothers at eleven. Amid the Catskill Mountains, then the Rocky Mountains, she fueled her imagination with the natural beauty surrounding her. Karen lives in north Texas and shares her life with her hero of a husband and three doting dogs. You can email Karen at KWhiddon1@aol.com or write to her at PO Box 820807, Fort Worth, TX 76182. Fans can also check out her website, karenwhiddon.com.

### Books by Karen Whiddon

#### Harlequin Romantic Suspense

*The CEO's Secret Baby*
*The Cop's Missing Child*
*The Millionaire Cowboy's Secret*
*Texas Secrets, Lovers' Lies*
*The Rancher's Return*

#### The Coltons: Return to Wyoming

*A Secret Colton Baby*

#### The Coltons of Oklahoma

*The Temptation of Dr. Colton*

#### Silhouette Romantic Suspense

*The Princess's Secret Scandal*
*Bulletproof Marriage*

#### The Cordiasic Legacy

*Black Sheep P.I.*
*The Perfect Soldier*
*Profile for Seduction*

Visit the Author Profile page at Harlequin.com, or karenwhiddon.com, for more titles.

To all the wonderful and patient medical professionals who answered questions about trauma surgeons, especially Heather Rodriquez, thank you for your insight. I also learned a lot about Oklahoma cattle ranches from the website of Ree Drummond, AKA The Pioneer Woman. Any mistakes about either are my own.

## Chapter 1

Despite the steady, light rain, Dr. Eric Colton plowed forward, chin up, his stride brisk. After a long, hot Oklahoma summer, any rain in August was a cause for celebration, though the slate-gray sky matched his mood. Walking home had become his own form of therapy, a way to clear his head after another exhilarating, stress-filled day as a trauma surgeon at Tulsa General Hospital.

The sound of tires squealing on slick pavement made him look back. A black Lincoln Town Car came barreling around the corner, engine revving. The light had just changed and a woman carrying a purple umbrella stepped into the crosswalk. The vehicle never slowed.

With his heart in his throat, he shouted a warning. Too late. As if in slow motion, he watched the car hit the woman, sending her into the air, umbrella and all. The Town Car kept going, taillights flashing red as it disappeared into the distance.

Eric ran, pulling out his cell phone and dialing 911. The woman lay in a crumpled heap on the pavement. He knelt and checked her pulse. Good. Since he knew better than to move her, he grabbed her umbrella and held it over her while he waited with her. As a small crowd gathered, he motioned them back. The same eerie calm he always experienced when he was working had settled over him, though adrenaline still pumped through his veins. Mentally, he assessed her possible injuries, already thinking ahead to types of treatment.

Siren sounding, lights flashing, an ambulance arrived. Still holding the purple umbrella, Eric identified himself as a doctor and explained what he'd witnessed. He watched as the EMTs used the scoop stretcher to get the woman up and he informed them he would be going to the hospital with her.

Once she'd been safely secured inside the ambulance, he climbed in, too. Though careful to stay in the background and not interfere, he kept a sharp eye on them as they worked on the woman. A bruise had begun to form on one high, exotic cheekbone. Even banged up, he could tell she was pretty, maybe even beautiful.

A few minutes later, they pulled up at the ER. While the EMTs got everything ready to bring the patient in, Eric took her small, delicate hand. To his shock, she opened her eyes—they were a startling light blue.

"Walter?" she asked, her husky voice weak. Before he could respond, she drifted back into unconsciousness.

Eric strode ahead, barking out orders, as they brought the woman in. Though his shift was over and Dr. Gina Patel was now on call, he wanted to be kept fully apprised of this patient's progress. He also figured the police would be around soon to question him, since he'd witnessed the entire thing, so he might as well hang around.

He stepped back and let the staff take care of the woman. When Dr. Patel came running around the corner, she stopped short at the sight of him.

"I thought you'd left."

"I had. But I saw someone get run over, so I came back with her."

Dr. Patel raised one brow. "I see. I imagine that's the patient they're paging me on."

"It is." He dragged his hand through his wet hair, surprised to see he still held the purple umbrella. "Please keep me apprised of her status."

"Will do." With a brusque nod, the other doctor hurried off.

As Eric had predicted, the police arrived shortly after. Since Eric's brother Ryan was an officer for the Tulsa PD, they recognized Eric's name. After Eric relayed everything he'd seen, which unfortunately didn't include the license plate on the Town Car, they thanked him and left.

"Dr. Colton, you should go home." Dr. Patel again, leaving the woman's room and stopping directly in front of him. "You look exhausted and clearly need some rest. You've done your civic duty. I think this patient is going to live. We'll let you know her status once we finish running all the tests. I've asked the neurologist on call to stop by as well."

Standard protocol. Nodding wearily, Eric exhaled. "Okay, thanks. Keep me posted." He knew he sounded abrupt, but if anyone would understand, it'd be the ER doctor.

He turned and headed toward the front door. Suddenly the process of trudging home in the rain—even with the woman's umbrella—seemed unbearable, so he hailed a cab instead.

Once he arrived at his town house—five blocks away from the hospital—he overtipped the cab driver and dashed inside. Once there, he eyed the purple umbrella and realized he would need to return it to her.

Leaning it against the wall in his foyer, he changed out of his drenched scrubs and toweled off his short brown hair. After pouring himself a scotch—neat—he grabbed the remote and turned on the TV. Then he poured the scotch out and opted for water instead. He expected the hospital to call at any moment, telling him they were prepping the woman for surgery. He figured she probably had a traumatic brain injury, despite what Dr. Patel thought. After all, the other doctor hadn't seen the woman get hit.

Too restless to sit, he paced in front of his floor-to-ceiling windows as dusk settled over the city.

That woman. He kept seeing the moment of impact over and over, like a video recording set on repeat that he couldn't seem to turn off. While he dealt with traumatic injuries every day, from gunshot wounds and stabbings to car accidents, he was used to seeing the patient *after*.

Surely after being hit like that, she'd have some

sort of issue. Hopefully not a brain injury, or something internal.

The physician in him itched to be the one to heal her. The man in him wanted to find out more about her. When she'd stepped out into the crosswalk, she'd moved with a jaunty stride, despite the rain. Her purple umbrella had white cupcakes printed all along the edge.

She'd had short brown hair with reddish highlights. Even soaking wet, it had still managed to retain its curl, framing her heart-shaped face nicely.

And her eyes… Something about them, maybe the unusual light blue color, intrigued him. Who was Walter? When she'd briefly regained consciousness, she'd managed to say his name, which meant he had to be someone important to her. A husband or lover?

Sipping the water, he rolled his neck and shoulders. Though his body felt exhausted, he couldn't shut off his mind. He needed to unwind, somehow.

His building had a gym, but after being on his feet for the better part of twelve hours, the last thing he felt like doing was working out. Even though intellectually he knew it would be good for him, tonight he'd take a pass.

It was Friday night. He could call one of his brothers and see if they wanted to meet up to shoot some pool or drink a few beers, even though he'd have to stick with something nonalcoholic, just in case. But— no surprise here—he'd rather be alone.

Clicking the TV off, he turned on his Bose stereo, with his iPod set to play classical music—Bach, Beethoven, Mozart—and let the music wash over him. His taste in music had been the source of much amusement growing up on the family ranch, where everyone listened to Garth Brooks, George Strait, or Willie Nelson. One or two of his brothers had secretly listened to rock, but no one, not even his sister, Greta, understood Eric's musical choices.

He didn't care. The soaring notes and perfect melodies were the polar opposite of the often violent cases he saw each day.

Tonight though, even his favorite music couldn't soothe him. He reached for his phone, tempted to call the ER and find out the mystery woman's status. But he didn't. After all, he was on call through the weekend and if anything happened with her, they'd page him. He expected this at any time. Sometimes, waiting really was the hardest part.

The woman opened her eyes, fighting back panic. Where was she? What had happened? Machines beeped, and she realized she had an IV in her arm. A hospital? She tried to remember. Had there been an accident? Had she been ill? Her head hurt. No, more than hurt. Throbbed. Pressing against her forehead with her hand, she wondered if she could make it stop.

As she struggled to sit up, she set off some kind of an alarm. A nurse came running. "You're awake," she said, as if being awake was something special.

The woman nodded, then winced. "My head hurts," she said. "Actually, my entire body is in pain."

"That's to be expected. You were in a pretty serious accident, though you were lucky. Nothing is broken."

Processing this, she squinted at the other woman. "Where am I?"

"Tulsa General." The nurse bustled around her,

silencing the screeching machine, checking various things. "How are you feeling?"

She had to think about that for a second. "I'm...not sure. Dizzy? Hungry? Thirsty, maybe?"

The nurse smiled. "We can fix that. But first, can you tell me your name? We couldn't find any ID on you."

Her name. She tried to recall, to think, battling through the pain, hating that her head felt so muzzy. Finally, with a grimace, she admitted defeat. "I don't know. I can't seem to remember. I just don't remember *anything*."

"That's okay," the nurse soothed. "Don't worry about that right now. I'm sure it will come to you. Meanwhile, how about I see what I can do for you in the food department."

As it turned out, not much. The attending doctor had ordered a liquid-only diet until all the test results were in. She was given some tasteless broth, and unsweetened tea. Which turned out to be okay, since an attempt to drink the broth had her gagging.

What on earth had happened to her, and why couldn't she remember even her own name? After racking her brain, the woman closed her eyes and went to sleep.

Despite Eric's certainty, a call didn't come that night. He fought the urge to phone the hospital himself, well aware that he needed to force himself to have a little separation from work. His colleagues had been telling him that for months now. Heck, even the nursing staff had taken to asking him when he'd take a vacation.

Time off. Such a concept was for other people, not him. He'd worked too hard to perform his life's work just to chuck it for a week or two. There probably existed a healthy balance between work and personal life, but for him such a thing was an abstract concept. A couple of guys he knew from back when they'd done their residencies had all complained about the eighty- and ninety-hour workweeks, but Eric never had. The more time he worked, the more he thrived.

Being a trauma surgeon was all he'd ever wanted to do. If not for his siblings' insistence that he spend the occasional time hanging out with them, he figured he'd probably devote every waking hour to the hospital.

His three brothers, one sister and one half brother had made it their mission to ensure he saw his family. Even if Eric never found time to visit the Lucky C— the Colton family ranch—they all drove in to Tulsa to spend time with him. He appreciated this more than they knew. He valued his family connection and loved his siblings.

Their closeness helped Eric live with his parents' distance. His mother and father never came to see him. Despite Eric's oldest brother, Jack's, dedication to the family business, Big J—as they called their father, John—had never gotten over his second son's defection to another line of work. At least the man had an excuse, unlike Abra, his mother.

All through his youth, Eric's mother had always been too self-involved, too busy with her travel and her shopping to care about her children. Only once her friends had begun commenting on how fortunate she was to have a doctor in the family did she begin to make noises of approval about his career. By then, it had been too little, too late.

Eric told himself he'd gotten used to the fact that neither of his parents had even seen his town house. He even wondered what it said about him that his parents' lack of interest in his life rarely bothered him anymore.

And then the unthinkable had happened. A few months ago someone had attacked Abra and she'd been transferred to Tulsa General. Eric had been on call, and seeing his mother's beaten, comatose body had made him realize how foolish their stubborn feud had been.

Her condition had been stabilized and there'd been nothing to do but wait. The neurologist had said in cases like hers, there was a fifty-fifty chance.

Months had gone by and Abra remained in a coma. Big J had hired a private nursing firm and had her moved to the Lucky C. Though the waiting seemed agonizing, Eric knew only time could heal her. She'd wake when she was ready, or not at all.

He hoped she woke. The two of them had a few fences to mend. Never again would he let his hurt pride get in the way of what mattered.

Thinking about his family finally lulled him to sleep.

The next morning, even though it was a Saturday, he woke at five, his usual time. Once he slugged back a glass of water, he dressed and hurried downstairs to the building's gym. He pounded out ten minutes of cardio, worked his upper body with free weights and then did another ten on the treadmill.

Satisfied and sweaty, he returned to his town house, downed a protein shake and showered. He'd promised to meet his sister, Greta, for lunch later since she was in town, but he still had enough time to run up to the hospital and check on the mystery woman. Surely by now they'd moved her to a regular room.

When he arrived, the nurse on call, an older woman who always seemed disgruntled, frowned at him. "Dr. Colton? Are you doing rounds today, too? I show you're off for the weekend."

With a shrug, he slipped behind the counter and checked the computer. "I witnessed a woman hit by a car and brought her into the ER last night. What's her status? Sorry, I don't know her name."

"Jane Doe?"

"That's her name?" He crossed his arms. "Or is that what you're calling her until you learn her real name?"

"The latter. She's been admitted for observation."

"Observation?" Which explained why he hadn't gotten a phone call.

"Yes." She handed him the chart. "Take a look yourself."

Flipping through the pages, he barely noticed when the nurse bustled off. Unbelievably, all Jane Doe appeared to have suffered was a concussion and some bruised ribs. No broken bones or internal injuries. Wow. As far as he could tell, she was the luckiest woman in Tulsa.

He might as well take a look at her while he was here. Chart in hand, he hurried down the hall toward her room.

After tapping briskly twice, he pushed open the door and called out a quiet "Good morning." Apparently, he'd woken her. She blinked groggily up at him, her amazing pale blue eyes slow to focus on him. He couldn't help but notice her long and thick lashes.

"Doctor?" Pushing herself up on her elbows, she shoved her light brown curls away from her face. "You look so familiar."

"That's because I rode with you in the ambulance last night."

"Ambulance?" She tilted her head, giving him an uncertain smile. "I'm afraid I don't know anything about that."

Amnesia? He frowned. "How much do you remember?" he asked.

"Nothing." Her husky voice broke and her full lips quivered, just the slightest bit. "Not even my name or what happened to me."

He took a seat in the chair next to the bed, suppressing the urge to take her hand. "Give it time. You've suffered a traumatic accident. I'm quite confident you'll start to remember bits and pieces as time goes on."

"I hope so." Her sleepy smile transformed her face, lighting her up, changing her from pretty to absolutely gorgeous.

Unbelievably, he felt his body stir in response. Shocked, he nearly pushed to his feet. This kind of thing had never happened to him, ever. He'd learned to maintain a professional detachment.

Yet something about this woman was different. She seemed more…helpless, or something. And cute. Despite her bruises and the road rash on her cheek and neck, she reminded him of a flower, delicate and fresh.

Again, not appropriate. But, he reminded himself, he was not her doctor. He'd only witnessed her accident after his shift.

When he went silent, her long, silky lashes swept down over her eyes, making him wonder if she'd fallen back asleep. But then she sighed, and raised her gaze to give him a long look. "The nurse said I was in an accident and then you mentioned an ambulance."

"Yes." He decided not to elaborate, feeling it would be better if she remembered on her own.

"Was I in a car crash?"

"Sort of." Eyeing her, he remembered something else. "When you were hurt, you called out for Walter. Do you remember who that might be?"

"Walter?" she said, overenunciating, almost as if trying to sound out a word in a foreign language. "Walter."

"Husband?" He didn't like that idea, but it was a possibility. "Friend? Brother? Coworker?"

"Stop. I honestly have no idea." She held up her hand, turning it to study her ring finger on her left hand. "I don't see a wedding band, so I don't think I'm married."

The rush of gladness he felt at her words shocked him at first. "I wouldn't think so," he agreed.

"Me either." A faint hint of hysteria had crept into her voice. "Hopefully I couldn't forget my own husband."

Now he did give in to temptation and touch her, lightly squeezing her shoulder, overly aware of the smoothness of her skin under the thin hospital gown. "Don't stress. Believe me, you'll remember in time."

When she exhaled, she seemed deflated. "Thank you, Doctor." The slight shine in her cornflower eyes told him she was fighting back tears.

This made his chest tighten. Immediately, he stood,

slightly confused at the tangle of emotion she invoked in him. "You'll be fine," he repeated. "I'm sure Dr. Patel will be by to check on you soon."

"Dr. Patel? You're not my doctor?"

Unbelievably, she sounded…hurt. Even more unbelievable, he had to hide a grin.

"No, I'm not. I'm sorry." On the way to the door, he turned back to glance at her. First mistake.

Her light brown curls looked windblown, and the perfect bow of her lush mouth made him want to kiss her. The stab of desire hit him low in his gut, completely unexpected and unwelcome.

He dragged his hand across his face, aware he needed to go but unable to pull himself away.

"Even though I can't recall anything about what happened to me, for some reason I recognize you," she mused. "How is that possible? Why would I remember one thing and not the others? What happened to me, exactly?"

"Probably because your memory is coming back in bits and pieces," he told her, aware he hadn't answered her question. But he didn't want to reveal to her how she'd been injured; he'd rather give her the chance to remember on her own.

She blinked, her gaze both sleepy and seductive. His instinctive response to this slammed into him, so powerful he took a step back.

*Dangerous.*

Clearly, he'd lost his mind. He had to get out of there immediately, before he did something he'd regret. "Feel better soon. Take care," he said, dipping his chin in a quick nod before he left her room.

He didn't slow down until he reached the nurse's

station, which mercifully was empty at the moment. Taking a seat, he tried to calm his racing heart. Since work usually absorbed him, he took another look at Jane Doe's chart.

Everything confirmed what he'd been told. Mild concussion and some bruising. Which meant, under any other circumstances, she'd be released to go home soon.

But she didn't know where home was. So what were they going to do with her?

His cell phone vibrated. His brother Ryan. Since Ryan worked for the Tulsa PD, maybe he could help find out who the mystery woman was, and who exactly Walter might be. He really needed to know if Walter was her husband, for reasons he didn't even want to consider right now.

Stepping into the hallway, Eric answered.

"I heard you got involved in a hit-and-run last night," Ryan said by way of greeting.

"Yes, as a witness. As a matter of fact, I just left the victim's room. I'm hoping you can help me." Briefly, he outlined what little he knew. "I've already told most of this to the guys who came out to investigate last night. Though I know they're busy."

"Like I'm not?" Ryan laughed, taking the sting off his words. "How about we discuss it over lunch?"

"I'm meeting Greta. She's in town and I haven't seen her in a while." And they both knew their sister frowned upon any "shop" talk when they got together.

"Dinner, then?"

"It'll have to be a late one. You know how Greta likes to talk."

They both laughed. Lunch would no doubt turn out

to last at least two hours. Which was fine with Eric. He didn't get to see his sister as often as he'd like. Since she'd gotten engaged, she'd moved to Oklahoma City, and didn't come back to Tulsa as often. Her wedding had been postponed when Abra got hurt. Greta refused to get married without her mother. She continually said she'd wait until Abra was out of the coma.

"Dinner it is. I'll call you when I get off work." With that, Ryan ended the call.

Eric had just started to walk toward the elevator when his phone rang again. Thinking Ryan must have forgotten something, he answered.

"This is Nurse McPherson from Tulsa General. Dr. Colton?"

Immediately every nerve ending went on full alert. Phone calls like this usually meant he was needed for trauma surgery. Adrenaline pumping through him, he answered in the affirmative.

"I'm here, at the nurse's station on the fifth floor," he said, heading toward the elevator so he could get to the ER. "What's the case?"

"I'm sorry." She apologized for the misunderstanding. "I should have made myself clear. I'm not calling you to bring you in for surgery. I'm phoning about Jane Doe."

Putting the skids on, he frowned. "What about her? I just saw her."

"We're discharging her today."

"Discharging her?" he repeated, letting his tone reflect his disbelief, though he'd expected this. "To where?"

Now the nurse sounded apologetic. "That's why I called you. I thought you'd like to know. It's wrong, but you know how it is. There's nothing medically wrong enough with her to keep her here. Plus, she has no insurance—"

"She doesn't even remember who she is," he exploded quietly, keeping his voice down and remembering that none of this was the nurse's fault. "Where will she go? What will she do?"

But he already knew the answer.

"I'm sorry, but you're aware of how this works," the nurse replied. "We can't hold anyone who isn't injured or ill. We'll give her a card with directions to one of the homeless shelters."

Homeless shelter. Eric thought of the woman, with her cloudy blue eyes and sweet, sexy smile. Who knew what would happen to a woman who looked like her if they placed her on the streets with no memory?

He couldn't let that happen. "Don't discharge her yet," he said. "Let me find Dr. Patel. Do you know where she is?" But he hung up before the nurse could reply.

Striding down toward the emergency department— a place that seemed more familiar than his own town house—Eric refused to consider the hundred reasons why he shouldn't get involved. After all, it was just a matter of time until her memory returned or Ryan figured out her identity. Once that happened, Eric could return her safely to her home and consider a good deed done. Especially since he knew he couldn't live with himself if he let a woman who had temporary amnesia be put out into the street to fend for herself.

If there was more to it than that, he refused to think about it. He had to protect her, no matter what the cost.

## Chapter 2

When Eric arrived back at the mystery woman's room, a nurse was with her, messing with the controls on one of the monitors. She now sat on the edge of her bed, her wavy hair tied back in a neat ponytail. Rather than the hospital gown, she wore some ill-fitting clothes that obviously had come from the lost and found. Considering whatever she'd been wearing had probably been cut off her, the nurses hadn't had a choice, but the sight still offended him.

When her unusually colored eyes met his, he again felt a sense of connection and attraction.

"Back again?" she asked, her generous mouth curving in a smile.

"Hey, there," he said softly, trying like hell to maintain a professional demeanor under the watchful gaze of her nurse. "I hear you're well enough to go home."

The misery in her expression spoke louder than words. "That's what they've told me. Unfortunately, I have no idea where home might be." She couldn't quite disguise the terror in her voice.

He cleared his throat, pretending not to be affected.

"Well, then, it's a good thing I'm here." He kept his voice light and carefree, as if speaking to a child instead of a beautiful woman. "I'm going to take you to my place. You can stay there until your memory comes back."

The nurse gasped, then scowled at him, her silent disapproval making him want to ask her to leave.

"Your place?" Her frown deepened. "Are we friends, then?"

"Sort of." He didn't want to lie, but he also didn't want to frighten her. "I brought you in here. I can't let them send you out into the street with nowhere to go."

He looked at the nurse, who still stared at him. "Could you please find Dr. Patel and send her here? She and I need to talk."

With a curt nod, the woman left the room. He turned his attention back to the patient—not his patient, he reminded himself. "I promise you'll be safe with me."

Considering him, her gaze serious, she lifted her chin. He was prepared for her to argue. Relief filled him when she simply nodded. "You're a doctor. I have to believe you wouldn't take advantage of me."

"I won't." He took a deep breath, well aware that as far as the rest of the world was concerned, he walked a fine line. Since he took care to be meticulous, he'd be exceedingly careful now. "Are you about ready, MW?"

One arched brow rose. "MW?"

"Mystery Woman. I refuse to call you Jane Doe."

Regarding him with a bemused expression, she finally nodded. "All right. And what should I call you?"

He almost said Dr. Colton, but at the last minute changed his mind. "Eric. My name is Eric."

"The nurse said Dr. Patel had to sign my discharge papers. Even though you asked the nurse to send her, I don't have any idea how long that will take."

Eric knew, depending on how busy the attending physician might be, that a discharge could take hours. But not with him expediting things. "Let me check on those. Will you wait right here until I get back?"

A brief flash of humor sparked in her eyes. With a graceful motion, she shoved the wisps of her unruly hair that had escaped her ponytail away from her face. "Sure. After all, where else am I going to go?"

The nurse had disappeared. Whether to find Dr. Patel or attend to other patients, he didn't know. After locating the discharge papers at the nurse's station, he hunted down Dr. Patel, and got them signed. He sidestepped his colleague's questions, keeping his answers purposely vague.

Snagging one of the available wheelchairs on the way, he went to collect his new houseguest. When he got to her room, he was surprised to find her standing, clutching the bed frame.

"Hospital protocol," he said, gesturing at the wheelchair. "Let me help you get seated."

"I can do it." Waving away his offer, and moving slowly, she made it to the end of the bed and then took the necessary steps to reach the wheelchair. Even in this, her movements were graceful.

Feeling inordinately proud, he grinned at her. "Are you ready?"

After a moment's hesitation, she smiled back. "Let's rock and roll."

Bemused and glad she couldn't see his face, he began pushing the chair. When they reached the lobby, he hailed a cab, bundled her up into it and gave the cabbie his address.

She glanced around her in curiosity as they headed toward his town house.

Once there, he had MW sling her arm around his shoulders and supported her on the short sidewalk to his town house, despite her protests that she could walk just fine. He liked the way she felt, all lush and curvy, not a bony toothpick like some of the women he'd dated in the past.

"Hungover or injured?" a feminine voice drawled. He jumped. His sister, Greta. He'd managed to completely forget their lunch date.

"Injured," MW replied, her mild tone at odds with the arch look she gave him. "Though I kept insisting I can do this, Eric here refuses to believe me. I'm sorry, Mrs....?"

"Miss," Greta corrected with an inquisitive smile. "I'm Greta. Eric's sister."

His heart sank. Realizing Greta would spin an entirely innocent occurrence into a fantastical story to entertain his family and anyone else who would listen, he hurriedly recounted the events of the night before.

"So I have no memory," MW put in when he'd finished. "And your brother was kind enough to offer me a place to stay."

Despite her casual attitude, Greta appeared as if she'd been punched in the stomach. He shot her a look, telling her not to say out loud whatever she might be considering saying.

"Oh," Greta managed weakly. "That's nice of him." The look she gave him back told him he had some explaining to do later.

He didn't care. He'd done what he felt had been right, and that would be the end of it.

"What's your name?" Greta asked.

"Right now, we're calling her MW," Eric put in smoothly. "For Mystery Woman."

If anything, Greta's hazel eyes got rounder. "I see."

"About lunch…" he began.

"I can run out and get a few sub sandwiches," Greta managed. "If you don't want to go out. I can bring them back here."

Glancing at MW, he nodded. "That would be helpful."

"No, that's okay. I don't want to disrupt your plans," MW said. "I'm pretty tired anyway, so if you could direct me to your guest room, I think I'd like to take a nap."

Ignoring his sister's eagle-eyed stare, he took MW's arm and led her down the hallway to his spare room, which thankfully his cleaning service kept ready for guests.

Despite everything that had happened to her, and his insistent hold on her arm, she carried herself confidently. He noted the top of her head came up just underneath his chin.

Perfect.

"Here you go," he told her, swallowing hard as he released her. "We're going to need to get you some toiletries and clothes, too."

Consternation turned her eyes the color of storm clouds as she blinked up at him. Helpless to move, he again noticed the sensual rosebud shape of her mouth and the luxurious sweep of her dark brown eyelashes.

"I have no money, no way to pay you back. At least, not right now."

Clothes. They'd been talking about clothing.

"Then it's a good thing I have plenty." Unable to resist the urge to touch her again, he squeezed her shoulder. "Right now I don't want you to worry about anything but getting better."

"Thank you, then." And she moved away. Her yawn as she settled onto the bed told him she'd be out in minutes.

He almost asked her if she wanted to take off the ill-fitting and ugly clothes, but the realization that she'd be naked if she did stopped him in his tracks. Once summoned, the image wouldn't leave him. He had to throttle the rush of desire racing through him.

Crud.

Without saying another word, he left.

After he closed the guest room door, he went into his living room, where Greta still waited for him, fairly bouncing up and down in her agitation. Today she wore her wavy dark hair in a ponytail and her usual jeans and cowboy boots, even though the temperature was pushing a hundred.

"What the heck are you doing?" she whispered loudly. "If she's your patient, aren't you going to get into all kinds of legal trouble for doing this?"

"She's not my patient," he told her back. "And I'm just helping out a fellow human being."

"A fellow…" She gave him a sidelong look. "I think I get it. This is an extension of your job to you, isn't it?"

Since his entire family all knew Eric lived and breathed for his work, he nodded. "Yes. I was there, I saw the car hit her. I can't just turn her out on the street with no memory and let her fend for herself. I've asked Ryan to personally work on finding out what we can about her."

Greta's skeptical expression told him she still wasn't entirely buying into his story. "Okay. Couldn't you have turned her over to adult Social Services or something?"

"Not without knowing her identity."

"What if she's a criminal? She could be a bank robber or a murderess, for all you know."

He laughed. "When you hear the sound of hooves, don't look for zebras. It's usually a herd of horses."

"What?"

"It's an old medical school saying. What seems obvious usually is. MW was just a very unlucky woman. Some idiot was in a hurry and ran a light and hit her. I believe it won't be long until she's back to normal. Until then, she's welcome to stay here."

Continuing to study him, her hazel eyes dark, Greta finally nodded. "Okay. Then tell me how I can help," she said.

Relieved that he'd managed to sound convincing, he nodded. "Let's go grab some lunch—we'll bring something back for MW—and I'll tell you."

"Okay."

Grinning, he took his sister's arm. "What are you in the mood for?"

She gave him a second sidelong glance. "We can go to the deli. I've been craving a panini."

They visited the little deli a block from his place. It wasn't fancy, but the interior felt homey with the blue-and-white-checkered tables. Inside, the smell of cheese and pastrami and marinara made his mouth water. Eric loved their meatball subs. He exchanged a grin with his sister.

Greta ordered a chicken pesto panini, which arrived perfectly cooked and smelling like heaven. If not for his own meatball sub, Eric might have stolen hers. "I'll have to try that one next time," he said, even though they both knew he wouldn't. He always said he'd try something else, but stuck to the same sandwich. How could he resist perfection on a hoagie roll?

All talk ceased while they both dug in, eating fast so they could get back to MW.

When Greta had gotten engaged and she and their mother had started planning her wedding, his sister had been the happiest Eric had ever seen her. Then their house had been burglarized and Abra attacked, and the entire family had been thrown into a tailspin. Greta more than anyone else—as the only daughter, she and Abra had been particularly close.

Now that Abra had been placed in a medically induced coma, Greta had put her entire life on hold. She and Abra had been in the middle of planning the wedding. Despite her fiancé's pleas, Greta refused to move forward without her mother at her side.

As a result, Greta's usual zest for life had dimmed somewhat. All of her brothers worried about her and did whatever they could to cheer her up. Feeding her always seemed to work for Eric.

As if she'd read his thoughts, Greta's gaze studied him. "As far as distractions go, this one's a biggie," she commented. "You bringing a strange woman to stay in your town house. I know she's pretty, but still…"

He didn't bother to pretend not to understand. "I know," he answered. "I can hardly fathom it myself. But something about her… I couldn't let her get put out into the street with no memory."

"They really do that?"

"We treat a lot of Tulsa's homeless population," he said, blotting his mouth with his paper napkin. "There's a limit to what we can do to assist them, especially if it's not medical."

She frowned. "I didn't think of that."

"Most people don't. It's a sad fact of life in the city."

"I'd like to help, too," Greta said. "Is there anything I can do?"

Eric didn't even have to think before answering. "Are you available this afternoon?" When she nodded, he continued, "Good. Then take her shopping. She needs everything."

Greta's eyes widened. She loved shopping. Next to training horses, shopping was her favorite activity. "Seriously?"

"Yes." Removing a credit card from his wallet, he handed it to her. "Use this. And buy yourself something, too."

Her eyes lit up, making him smile. Growing up, Greta had always been a tomboy. She hadn't gotten into what he thought of as girlie things until she'd gotten engaged.

At his smile, she shook her head, though she still accepted the credit card. "What's your budget?"

"Within reason. There's no need to take her to fancy department stores. Just get her a few comfortable outfits that fit. A couple of pairs of shoes, pajamas, et cetera. You know better than I do what kind of things a woman needs."

Her grin turned wicked, warning him she was about to tease.

"What about *lingerie*?" she drawled, drawing the word out so that it almost became four syllables rather than three.

"Don't." He could still shut her down with a glare. Relenting, he softened his tone. "Don't try to turn this into something it's not, all right?"

"Sorry." Clearly unrepentant, she turned his credit card around in her hands, her hot-pink nail polish gleaming. "When you say to buy myself something nice, are you talking about a T-shirt or an entire outfit?"

With pretend annoyance, he sighed loudly. "Fine. An outfit. Just don't be too extravagant, okay?"

"Yes." She gave him a fist pump, then quickly tucked his credit card into her purse. "Do you think MW will feel up to shopping this afternoon? I mean, she just got out of the hospital today. I can't do it tomorrow, because I have to go back to the ranch tonight and say goodbye to everyone. I'm heading home to Oklahoma City in the morning."

Hearing "home" and "Oklahoma City" in the same sentence sounded weird, though he didn't say so.

"All we can do is ask her. She should, since the only thing wrong with her is a slight concussion. I'm hoping she'll be feeling much better when she wakes up from her nap. If not, then find out her size and go shopping without her. She has nothing but the clothes she's wearing, and those apparently came from the hospital lost and found."

"That's awful." Greta grimaced. "But honestly, she didn't look in too great of shape. You were practically carrying her to your front door."

He felt his face heat. "That's my fault. She insisted she was fine, but I didn't want to take a chance."

Narrow eyed, she watched him as if waiting for him to say more. Instead, he concentrated on finishing the last of his meal.

Once every crumb had been devoured, instead of wanting to sit and chat like she normally did, Greta fidgeted.

"I'd like to go back and check on MW," she finally confessed. "If I'm going to be back at the ranch by suppertime, we need to get started on shopping."

After getting an extra meatball sub in case MW was hungry, he paid the bill and they headed back to his town house. Usually, Greta enjoyed strolling at a leisurely sauntering pace. Today, she moved with an unusual briskness in her step. Shopping, he thought. A lure she couldn't resist.

"You know," Greta mused on the walk back, "I can finally see why you like living downtown so much."

He stared. For her entire life, his sister had loudly professed her love of the country to anyone who'd listen. When she'd moved away, everyone in the family had wondered how she'd survive life in Oklahoma City.

"You do?" he asked. "How's that?"

Ducking her head, she gave a little shrug. "I don't know, but I never thought about how nice it would be to be so convenient and close to everything. Sure, I miss the horses and the land, but this has its benefits, too."

He laughed, resisting the urge to say "I told you so." "You're preaching to the choir."

Back at the town house, the guest room door was still closed. "Let me go talk to her," Greta said, shaking her head when he moved to follow. "Alone. Woman-to-woman. She might be slightly embarrassed over all this."

With a shrug, he acquiesced. "I'll be out on the patio. I've got a few calls to take care of."

Lying in a soft bed, MW smiled and stretched. Pure luxury. She had decided to use the moniker the kind doctor had given her, and the sheer bliss of the silence instead of constant hospital noises felt like heaven. She only hoped Eric was right about her memory returning soon. She had the constant niggling worry that it might be important she remember something, though she wasn't sure what exactly.

After dozing off, she must have fallen into a deep sleep, because she dreamed of cooking. She was working in a kitchen, a huge, modern, professional place, and whipping up some kind of risotto. Lobster risotto. The task involved a lot of stirring and just the right heat, but in this dream she was an old pro at this sort of thing.

After the risotto finished, she had a beautiful beef Wellington cooking, waiting to be sliced.

Bemused, she went with the flow. Just as she'd gotten the entire meal together to be served, a firm tapping on her door woke her. Blinking, she yawned and stretched. After a moment of panic as she tried to orient herself, she realized where she was. "Yes?"

"May I come in?" Eric's sister, Greta. Which meant they must be back from lunch. Her stomach growled as she remembered the sandwich Greta had promised.

When MW answered in the affirmative, Greta bounced into the room. "How are you feeling?"

Blinking, MW sat up, pushing her thick, wavy hair away from her face. "Hungry," she answered honestly.

"Oh." Greta rushed out of the room. She returned a moment later carrying a brown paper sack. "Here you go."

The smell of marinara and meatballs made MW's mouth water. She pushed herself up from the bed, relieved when the room didn't spin. "This isn't the kind of thing one eats in bed. Can you point me toward the kitchen?"

Still smiling, Greta led the way. While Greta watched, MW devoured the sandwich, stopping just short of licking her fingers—it was honestly that good. She washed it down with bottled water.

"Better now?" Greta asked. She'd been jiggling one leg up and down the entire time MW ate, as if she had something else she needed to do.

"Yes, thank you." MW looked around. "Where's Eric?"

"Out on the patio." Greta pointed. "He needed to make some phone calls. I was wondering, do you feel good enough to go shopping?"

"Shopping?" Bewildered, MW wasn't sure how to respond. "I can't. I have no money."

If anything, Greta's smile widened. "That's okay. I have a credit card with a very high limit."

Appalled, MW shook her head, feeling almost frantic. "No. I can't take your charity."

"Not mine." Greta laughed. "My brother's. Eric asked me to take you. He'd like you to have something to wear."

"But—"

"I'm sure you can pay him back once your memory returns. Either way, I'm going to buy you some clothes. It'd be a lot better—and more fun—if you came with me."

MW considered. Did she enjoy shopping? And did that even matter? Eric was right, she needed clothes, at least until she could remember. "I'd like to go," she decided, but looked down at the ill-fitting and ugly sweat pants she wore. "But I don't think I can go out like this."

"Greta, don't you always keep workout clothes in your car?" Eric asked, startling them both.

Hand to throat, MW spun around. He stood just inside the sliding glass door, watching them. Her entire body tingled at the sight of him, his light brown hair backlit by the sun, his green-eyed gaze intense.

Greta looked from one to the other. "Yes, I do." She sized MW up, her gaze considering. "And I think we might be close in size, but I'm a lot taller."

"Even so, anything is better than what she's got," Eric said, smiling softly at MW to lessen the sting of his words.

Nodding, Greta hurried away while MW burned from shame.

Eric caught sight of her face. "What's wrong?" he asked, coming closer. "Are you feeling all right?"

She tried for indifference, but instead her eyes filled

with stupid tears, which she hated. "Physically, I'm fine," she replied. "But I have to say, I might not know who I am, but I know enough to realize I hate being a charity case. Borrowing an outfit is bad enough, but borrowing money to buy more clothes, when I'm not even sure I can repay you…"

"Then don't." He seemed supremely unbothered. "One thing's for sure, you've got enough to worry about without stressing over whether or not you can repay me. So let it go."

She opened her mouth, and then closed it. Because he was right. She had few options right now. Luckily, Greta reappeared, carrying a bright pink gym bag.

"Here you go." She shoved it at MW. "Go ahead and try something on." Pointedly glancing at her watch, she sighed. "Then we need to get going. I'm on a pretty tight schedule."

Though Greta's tone had been friendly, MW still flushed with embarrassment as she retreated to the bathroom. Catching a glimpse of herself in the mirror, she realized not only did she stand shorter than Greta, but was quite a bit curvier as well. As she opened the gym bag, she wondered if anything would actually fit.

Luckily, the workout clothes were made of stretchy material and she was able to pull them on. She didn't have sneakers—the battered pair of flip-flops she'd been given by the hospital would have to do. Either way, this was a huge improvement on what she'd worn before. However, the tight workout outfit highlighted every curve. Almost embarrassingly so.

Feeling oddly shy, she emerged from the bathroom.

"You look great," Greta crowed. "Doesn't she, Eric?"

He let his gaze rove over her, his eyes darkening. "Much better," he finally said. She couldn't make herself look away. The vitality he radiated drew her like a magnet.

"Ahem." Greta cleared her throat. "Are you ready?"

Face heating yet again, MW nodded. "I am."

"Then let's go. I've got to be back at the ranch at sundown."

MW quickly learned that shopping with Greta was an endurance event. For the next three hours, Greta dragged her from store to store. MW was shocked when she found herself imagining Eric's reaction to each outfit she tried on. Pushing away those thoughts became as difficult as trying to examine the price tags and mentally calculate the cost. Each time she tried to broach the subject with Greta, Greta refused to discuss it.

In the end, they purchased two dresses, three pairs of jeans, an assortment of T-shirts, blouses, bras and panties, socks, sneakers and two pairs of heels. Each time MW tried to protest, Greta just grinned and purchased the disputed item anyway.

By the time Greta pronounced them done, both women were loaded down with bags and MW had begun to stagger with exhaustion. Greta glanced at her and did a double take.

"I think we might have overdone it a little bit," she muttered.

"Just make sure and give me the total," MW replied tiredly. "I'm going to keep track of everything so I can pay it back."

By the time they reached Eric's street, MW's stride was seriously lagging. The late-afternoon August heat made her feel dizzy. She also realized she hated to perspire. One more thing she remembered, which under normal circumstances would have energized her. Now she just longed for a cool shower.

"Are you all right?" Greta asked, her voice sharp. "You look like you're about to pass out."

Straightening her shoulders and lifting her chin, MW concentrated on putting one foot in front of the other. "I'm fine." They were nearly there. She prayed she could cross the last fifty feet and get through the door. Then she planned to find the closest available chair and plop herself into it.

A white panel van with dark tinted windows pulled up alongside them and slowed, matching their pace.

"Keep walking," Greta said, her voice sharp. "Faster."

MW pulled strength from somewhere and increased her stride.

The van stopped just ahead of them. A man with a baseball cap and dark sunglasses jumped out of the passenger side. He lunged for MW, grabbing her arm. She struggled, using her shopping bags as weapons, albeit ineffectually.

Shouting for someone to help them, Greta came to her aid. Somehow, she managed to wrench MW free, just as two Good Samaritans emerged from inside the coffee shop and chased after the men.

One would-be assailant cursed and jumped back into the van, which sped off.

It all happened so fast. Numb, heart pounding, MW watched the vehicle go while Greta and the two strangers picked up the spilled packages. She couldn't seem to catch her breath, standing there frozen and shell-shocked.

"Hon?" Greta touched her arm. "You look like you're going to pass out. Do you need to sit down, maybe put your head between your knees?"

Blinking, MW slowly shook her head. "I want to go home." Except she didn't know where exactly that might be.

"Hang on, okay?" Greta turned to assist their rescuers in picking up the scattered clothing.

Once everything had been collected and placed in neat little piles, Greta thanked the two men who'd helped them.

"Are you all right?" Greta asked, putting her arm around MW.

Despite the fact that she'd started trembling and felt very unsteady, as if she might pass out at any moment, MW nodded. "I think so," she answered, pleased that her voice came out strong and sure.

"We need to hurry up and find out who you are," Greta said firmly. "And why so many people are out to get you."

# Chapter 3

Right after Greta and MW left to go shopping, Eric's cell rang. Seeing Ryan's name on the screen, he answered immediately.

"We've run everything we can think of on any missing women as well as anyone named Walter," Ryan told him. "We've checked missing persons, warrants, and people who have been recently incarcerated. We even checked black Lincoln Town Cars registered in Tulsa. The traffic cameras were too blurry due to the rain. We've come up with absolutely nothing. Not on her or on the person who hit her."

"Thanks for trying. It wasn't a lot to go on." Eric had known it would be too much to hope for this to be so easy. For the first time ever, he considered himself lucky the hospital hadn't paged him to come in and do some sort of emergency surgery today. Next to medicine, there was nothing he liked more than a good mystery. And MW certainly presented one.

"How'd your meal with Greta go? Or are you two still at lunch?"

Eric laughed. "No, we finished in record time. Greta was in a hurry. She took the mystery woman shopping."

The total silence told him how much he'd stunned his brother. Quickly, he explained. "MW—Mystery Woman—has nothing. No clothing, no toiletries, nada. I figured the best person to get her the basic things women need would be Greta. I gave her my credit card and let her get busy. She was thrilled. You know how she loves to shop."

Ryan groaned. "You're sure asking for it. At least I know you can afford the bill when it comes in. You should have plenty of money since you never buy a damn thing for yourself."

Eric made a noncommittal sound. Ryan knew him well. He liked to work, didn't have many hobbies, and aside from making his student-loan payments, paying the hefty premium for his malpractice insurance, his office space rent and employees' payroll, his personal needs were few. After purchasing furniture and a sweet sports car, he banked most of his salary. Which was much less than most people realized.

"Are you still on for dinner?" Ryan asked.

Eric found himself wondering if his impromptu houseguest would be all right. "Can I get back to you on that?"

Ryan swore. "Sure. But I don't have to tell you how much I've been looking forward to barbecue."

"What is it with you and Greta and your food?" As

far as Eric concerned, he ate to fuel his body, nothing more. It helped if it was something he truly enjoyed, like the meatball sub earlier, but he never obsessed about it. "She was craving a panini earlier."

"Whatever. Like you don't. I know you enjoy Red's Ribs," Ryan prodded. "Because as far as I can remember, the last time we were there, you ate an entire rack of them by yourself."

Grinning, Eric conceded maybe he had. Growing up, with all of them crammed together on the ranch, he'd sought any means to escape his siblings. These days, he enjoyed their company. Maybe absence really did make the heart grow fonder.

"Most likely, I'll be there," he told his brother. "I want to make sure my houseguest is going to be all right by herself."

"If not, just bring her with you."

Eric frowned. "Why would I want to do that?"

"For me. I want to get a look at what kind of woman can get past my big brother's defenses."

"It's not like that," Eric started to protest hotly, and caught himself, aware his brother loved to tease him. "Both you and Greta like stirring things up, don't you?"

"Maybe." Ryan chuckled. "Give me a call as soon as you know if we're on for dinner."

"Will do." He had some investigating of his own to do. Back in medical school and during his residency, he'd become a master of the internet search. Once he got started, he could lose hours of time without realizing it, but usually was pretty successful at getting results.

Right now, he planned to find out anything he

could about the mystery woman who'd landed in his town house, and her connection to someone named Walter and a speeding Lincoln Town Car.

As MW tottered along behind Greta, who urged her to hurry, she nearly groaned out loud in relief when Eric's town house came into view.

"We're almost there." Turning, Greta flashed her an encouraging smile. "At least once we're in the atrium, you'll be safe."

MW couldn't keep from looking behind her. "As long as they—whoever they are—don't see where I'm going."

Eric opened the door before Greta could knock, which was a good thing considering how many shopping bags she carried.

His vivid green eyes widened. "What the..."

Sweeping past him, Greta flashed an unrepentant grin as she dropped all her bags on the floor. "Your guest is now fully outfitted. You can thank me later."

Ignoring them both, MW staggered past them and sank into the chair, dropping her shopping bags in the pile with Greta's. She leaned forward, putting her head between her knees, willing the dizziness to abate.

Immediately, Eric crouched down next to her, taking her wrist to feel her pulse. "What's wrong?"

She managed a weak smile. "I think I just overdid it a bit, that's all."

When he gave her shoulder a light squeeze, she had to fight the urge to lean into him. His big hand lingered on her wrist, making her aware he could completely encircle it with his fingers.

"Are you going to tell him or shall I?" Greta demanded, twin spots of color high on her cheeks.

MW swallowed.

Eric went tense, suddenly alert. "Tell me what?"

Gently rubbing her wrist where his grip had tightened, MW exchanged a glance with Greta. "You go ahead," she said.

"Some men in a white van—just like in the movies— pulled up alongside us as we were walking. A guy got out of the passenger side and tried to grab MW. I screamed for help, but we were able to fight them off. Two guys came out of the coffee shop and chased them away."

Both Eric and Greta stared at MW. She wanted to shrink into the chair. Inhaling deeply, she shrugged. "I know what you both are thinking, but I have no idea."

"First someone tries to run you down, now someone else tries to grab you," Eric said, echoing his sister's earlier words. "We have got to increase our efforts and find out who you are and why someone is after you. As quickly as possible."

Feeling slightly dejected, MW nodded. "I agree."

"Until then, you both need to be super careful," Greta said, her cool gaze sliding from one to the other. "Right now, I've got to go." She walked over to Eric. "Here's your credit card."

"Thank you." He tucked it away in his wallet.

Greta rummaged through the mountain of bags until she found the ones she wanted. "One outfit for me, including shoes, and thank you very much."

She gave her brother a quick hug and rushed out the door.

After Greta left, Eric turned his emerald gaze on

MW. Alone with him, suddenly she felt self-conscious. Why, she had no idea. At least the room no longer spun and she could catch her breath.

"Other than the attempted abduction, did you have a good time?" he asked. "I know my sister really enjoys shopping."

"I did. But honestly, I didn't need all of that," she said, waving her hand at the pile of shopping bags. "We can return most of it tomorrow."

Dragging his hand through his close-cropped hair, he shook his head, his mouth quirking. "Yes, you did. Keep it. You had nothing. Now you have something. Consider it my gift to you."

Immediately, she shook her head. "Not a gift. I barely even know you. I want to pay you back as soon as I can."

As their gazes locked, she realized the inherent strength and compassion in his rugged face appealed to her on many levels. His aquiline nose and the sensual curve of his mouth, combined with the intelligence shining in his eyes, drew her with an intensity she couldn't explain.

Which might not be a good thing, especially if she was married. Or even involved. For all she knew, Walter could be her significant other.

Or her brother. Until her memory returned, she had no way of knowing. And while she wasn't wearing a wedding ring, that meant nothing. Until she realized if she was someone's wife or girlfriend, she needed to rein in her attraction to this handsome, kind doctor.

"We'll see," he finally said. "If it makes you feel better, I'll pull all the receipts and figure out the total. I'll hang on to it until your memory comes back."

Relieved, she nodded. "Thank you. Now what?"

"You're welcome to hang out here. Rest, recuperate, do whatever makes you happy. I work a lot, so we won't bump into each other much."

Both appalled and fascinated, she swallowed. "You and I are strangers, correct? We didn't know each other before my accident?"

"Right."

"Yet you trust me alone in your beautiful home?" She glanced around, noting the polished wood floors, the perfectly matched accessories. Either the sexy doctor had impeccable taste or he'd hired an interior decorator. "How do you know I'm not a criminal? What if you were to come home one night after work and find I'd cleaned you out?"

His sensual mouth twitched, an obvious attempt not to laugh out loud. "Okay. Do you plan to do that?"

"Well, no. But…"

"Then there's no problem. Don't worry so much." The warmth in his voice echoed in his smile. "I promise you, I really don't mind."

"As long as I don't interfere in your life," she continued stubbornly. As if she had some other place to go. "I'll stay here if you give me your word you'll let me know the second I become a burden."

"Deal." He held out his hand, making her notice his long and graceful fingers. A surgeon's hand.

Taking a deep breath, she clasped his hand, surprised when he wove his fingers in between hers and held on. She found herself gripping his big yet elegant hand, at a total loss for words, but not wanting to let go. Inexplicably, this small kindness made her throat ache and her chest feel tight. She wondered if he could feel her heartbeat through her touch.

Again, her body tingled at the thought. Somehow, she managed to gently extricate herself before she got into trouble.

"I think I need to rest," she finally managed, her voice a hoarse whisper.

"Let me help you." Taking her arm—why did he have to keep on touching her?—he lifted her from the chair and supported her as they headed toward her room. Though she knew she could walk, she couldn't bring herself to refuse his assistance, secretly enjoying the hard masculine feel of his body.

Once they reached her room, he held on to her while pulling back the covers to her bed. "Good thing you didn't make the bed after your nap," he said, his voice as husky as her own had been earlier.

A shudder of unadulterated wanting ran through her. Trouble, that was what he was. If she wasn't careful, she could lose herself in him and possibly betray someone who might mean the world to her.

Struck dumb, heart pounding, she managed to nod. Despite her effort to shore herself up against her attraction to him, a sudden mental image came to her of the two of them, naked, sliding beneath the sheets. Skin on skin… Her entire body flushed as she realized the direction her thoughts had taken. Sex. Which was the last thing she needed to be thinking about when she didn't even know her own name.

Luckily, Eric didn't even notice, which was a good thing. How mortifying if he detected her unwarranted attraction and it made him pity her even more.

"Here you go." He helped her onto the bed, finally

letting go of her. She nodded, keeping her gaze averted. She couldn't even look at him, afraid he'd somehow recognize the need burning in her eyes.

To her relief, he waited a moment before telling her to get some rest.

"Thank you," she muttered, head still down, heart still racing.

"Oh." At the doorway, he stopped. "I'm meeting my brother tonight for dinner. Barbecue. You're welcome to come with us. He asked me to invite you."

The idea terrified her. Thinking of the abduction attempt earlier, she couldn't suppress a shudder. "I don't know if that's safe. Until I—we—figure out what's going on, it's probably best if I stay hidden."

"Your choice." He shrugged. "But you should know, my brother is a police officer. If anyone can keep you safe, he can."

Despite being tempted—barbecue!—she shook her head. "I'd rather not risk it. I'm still recovering from the accident and this afternoon shopping zapped my energy." She finally forced herself to look at him, hoping her smile seemed impersonal enough. "I feel like a loaf of bread someone tried to make but forgot to put in the yeast."

"That's an odd sort of comparison." His gaze slid over her, delivering a flash of heat to her belly. "Do you like to cook?"

Did she? She shrugged to hide her confusion. "I don't know."

For the space of a couple of heartbeats he watched her, as if waiting for her to say more. When she didn't, he reached to close the door. Before he did, he looked back at her. "You'll probably be hungry later. Do you want me to bring you something?"

"I don't want you to go through any trouble."

A muscle quirked in his jaw. "We need to get something straight. If I offer, then it's no trouble. Understand?"

Considering, she finally nodded. "Then thanks. I'd love a sliced-brisket sandwich." She frowned, a memory tickling the edges of her mind. The more she tried to access it, the more it seemed to dance away, just out of reach. Aware he still watched her, she managed a smile. "Enjoy your night out. I'm going to get some rest."

Finally, he left, closing the door behind him. She let out her breath, willing her racing heartbeat to slow.

For the first time since bringing her home, Eric realized MW might have the power to completely disrupt his orderly existence. Something, some reaction or emotion he glimpsed in her light blue eyes, had practically brought him to his knees. Damned if he understood what it was about this woman, but she made him feel things he shouldn't. For one thing, she didn't seem to realize how extraordinarily beautiful she was, which might be totally due to her amnesia.

For another, if he had a type—and until now, he hadn't—MW would be it. He liked her generous curves, her perfect proportions. And her hair. Those wavy, thick strands had him longing to tangle his fingers in them.

Then there was her mouth. If ever he'd seen a mouth made to be kissed, hers...

*No. Stop.* Dragging his hand across his chin, Eric

stared at her closed door and walked back into the living room. He didn't know what was wrong with him, but he wasn't the kind of guy to take advantage of a woman with no memory. As a physician, he'd sworn to help, not hurt. Just because his libido had finally decided to wake up and take notice didn't give him a valid excuse to act like a fool.

Maybe the hospital board was right. Perhaps he should consider taking a vacation. Possibly once all this was over.

Again his thoughts returned to MW. How long could one woman take to regain her memory? In all his years of study, plus his five-year surgical residency and one year of medical fellowship, he hadn't seen a single actual case of true amnesia. Brain trauma, yes. Stroke, yes. But MW had only suffered a mild concussion, definitely not something bad enough to cause her to forget her entire existence.

Glancing at his watch, he saw he had thirty minutes before he needed to meet Ryan. Since getting to Red's Ribs would require him to drive, he'd better get a move on.

His little sports car could use an outing. He'd made the wildly impractical purchase after careful consideration, weighing his love of speed with the steep cost of a Porsche. He'd gone to the dealership one weekend just to look and had ended up becoming the proud owner of a brand-new Porsche Cayman GTS.

Though he rarely drove, every time he did, he was glad he'd made the purchase. At 340 HP, his car could do zero to sixty in 4.5 seconds. He should know, he'd tested it a few times.

Once he reached the restaurant, he parked, noticing that Ryan had beaten him there. Eric recognized his police cruiser parked one row over. He practically bounded from his car, not an easy feat since the sleek sports car sat so low to the ground.

Inside, he spotted Ryan, his dark brown hair as short as Eric's. Ryan was out of uniform since he was off duty, and he'd already snagged a table. Pulling out a chair, Eric straddled it, quickly filling his brother in on everything that had happened.

"Her memory still hasn't come back?" Ryan sounded skeptical. Eric didn't blame him.

"Not yet. I'm hopeful it will soon, especially since there have been two attempts to harm her."

"Except you don't know that the hit-and-run was on purpose," Ryan pointed out.

"It was. I have no doubt. I was there. I saw the Town Car gunning for her. And since two men in a van tried to grab her when she was shopping with Greta…"

"Again, they could have just been pervs out to grab the first woman or women they saw. You don't know for sure that she was their specific target."

Eric shook his head. "Don't you think that's a bit coincidental?"

"In my line of work, I learned early on never to jump to conclusions."

"Point taken." Eric looked around for the waitress, but since the dining room appeared packed, and all the servers seemed busy, he figured she'd stop by eventually.

"So what are you going to do now?" Ryan asked.

"I'm hoping her memory comes back quickly. At least once we know what we're up against, I can come up with a better plan to keep her safe."

At Eric's words, Ryan stared. "Keep her safe? I'd think you'd contact her family."

"Depends on the situation. I'm not going to allow her to be placed in danger."

"Not going to… What does this woman look like?"

Immediately understanding where his brother was going, Eric shrugged. "Brown, shoulder-length hair. Wavy with reddish highlights. Light blue eyes. She doesn't look like a fashion model, if that's what you're getting at."

"No." Taking another sip of his beer, Ryan grinned. "I'm asking if she's pretty."

Eric pretended to have to think about it. "Well, she's not ugly. Why does that matter?"

"Because you are always so laser focused on your job, you barely have time for family, never mind some strange female who you don't even know."

Refusing to let his brother needle him, Eric finally managed to catch the attention of a waitress and ordered a diet cola. "I'm on call," he explained. Which, as Ryan knew, meant he couldn't drink in case he got called in for surgery.

He waited for Ryan to say something like he usually did about how badly he needed a vacation, but the other man only shrugged and took another pull on his beer.

When the waitress reappeared, they ordered their meals. While waiting for his barbecued ribs, Eric couldn't understand why he felt so antsy. He couldn't stop thinking about MW, all alone and probably frightened, and he realized he probably shouldn't have left her by herself. He decided he'd eat as quickly as possible and hurry home.

Of course Ryan, with his detective's powers of observation, noticed his fidgeting. Luckily, their food arrived, which distracted him, though Eric knew it wouldn't last for long.

Digging in, he tried to shrug off his fascination with his temporary houseguest and focused on the delicious meal.

Ryan ate heartily as well, though he kept shooting Eric questioning looks while he ate. Finally, he shook his head. Putting down his ribs, he licked his fingers before wiping his mouth with his paper towel. "All right, spill. You're superdistracted. What's wrong?"

Since there was no way Eric wanted to give his brother more ammunition with which to tease him, he shrugged and said the one word that always made Ryan change the subject. "Work," he lied, and went back to devouring his meal. When he could eat no more, he used the finger wipes and cleaned his hands.

"That was good." He leaned back in the chair and gave a sigh of contentment. Even now, in the back of his mind, he could picture offering MW a plate of ribs and watching her eat. Then he remembered she'd asked for a sliced beef sandwich, and got lost again contemplating her charms.

"There you go again." Ryan's sharp comment brought Eric out of his reverie.

"Sorry," Eric apologized, meaning it. "I don't know what's wrong with me."

"Working too hard, probably."

Because he had been and he hoped that was the reason for his unexplained preoccupation with his pretty houseguest, he nodded. "Probably."

"You been home lately?" Ryan asked quietly, meaning the Lucky C ranch.

"No." Eric refused to feel guilty. Both brothers had escaped the family ranch as quickly as they could— Eric because he'd never fit in, Ryan because of the never-ending drama. "How about you?"

Ryan sighed. "I've had to run out there a few times. I'm still investigating the attack on Mother. Since she's unconscious, she can't tell me anything. And there have been a couple other instances of vandalism, mostly minor."

Eric grimaced. While he loved his mother, Abra Colton had always been one of those women who always seemed to be on edge. Everything made her nervous, including her children. Thus a series of nannies had raised Eric and his siblings. None of the Coltons had felt particularly close to their mother growing up, though not from lack of trying. Greta in particular. Eric had hated watching how often Abra's careless indifference hurt his sister.

But these past several years, Abra had begun to mend the fences. She and Greta had become close. She'd even reached out to Eric, hoping to try to forge a tentative relationship. Unfortunately, this had been right before she'd been attacked, and Eric and she hadn't made up.

"How's Dad holding up?"

Ryan shrugged, his expression grim. "Oh, you know Big J. He's devoted to making sure Mother is comfortable, as long as the hired nurses take care of her."

Lately their father had been showing signs of early dementia, though he refused to see his doctor and get tested. Big J had always been larger than life, with his booming voice and his raucous laugh. Though he never spoke about it, all his sons understood he wouldn't go down without a fight.

"Some days he seems better than others," Ryan continued. "Jack's keeping an eye on him."

Their oldest brother, Jack, managed the Lucky C. Nothing mattered more to him than family, especially his son, Seth. The ranch came in a close second, though.

"You need to try and pop out there when you can," Ryan said. "Even though Abra won't know you're there, I know Jack and Seth will be thrilled to see you."

"I will," Eric promised, meaning it. He adored his five-year-old nephew, Seth, and hadn't seen him in too long. He couldn't remember the last time Jack had brought his son into Tulsa.

Once they'd finished, Ryan announced he'd decided not to order his customary peach cobbler. Instead, he kept checking his watch. "I've got to run," he said. "I've got a couple of reports I need to fill out and email in."

Even though turnabout would be fair play, Eric resisted the urge to tease his brother about his own work. Truth be told, he felt relieved Ryan wasn't inclined to chat. He wanted to get home and make sure MW was okay.

He ordered the extra sliced-brisket sandwich, paid for it as well as his own meal and gave his brother a quick hug goodbye before taking off.

The Porsche begged to be driven fast. Sometimes he had to force himself to travel relatively close to the speed limit. With all the afternoon traffic, this was one of those occasions. Nonetheless, he made it home in less time than it had taken him to go the opposite direction, mostly because rush-hour traffic went out of the city rather than in.

After parking in his private garage underneath the townhome, he grabbed the bag and hurried outside. He winced as the late-afternoon August heat blasted him the instant he left the garage. Sadly, the cooling rain of the previous day had turned into a distant memory. Oklahoma summers could be tough. The relentless sun and constant wind sometimes made him feel like dust coated everything, even mixing with the blood inside his body, turning it sluggish. Fanciful, certainly, since as a physician he knew such a thing wasn't possible. He gave himself a mental shake. It was just a typical Oklahoma summer, and he wasn't often given to such flights of abstract fancy.

Again he had the nagging feeling that taking in this mystery woman might change his life in ways he never could have anticipated.

## Chapter 4

Anticipation at seeing her again quickened Eric's footsteps. Using his key, he entered his town house, trying to be as quiet as possible so if MW still slept, he wouldn't wake her.

But when he stepped into the living room, she rose gracefully from the sofa to greet him. She'd opened the blinds, and the western sun streamed in so brightly it silhouetted her in a halo. Stopping short, he caught his breath, struck dumb by her beauty.

"You're back early," she said, smiling.

Blinking, he took another step forward.

"Ryan had to go back to work. But I brought your sandwich." He held up the now grease-stained bag. "It's pretty big, so I hope you're hungry."

"Starving," she told him, her soft voice matching her smile. She followed him into the kitchen, taking a seat at the bar while he located a plate for her. Handing her the sandwich and some paper towels for a napkin, he asked her what she wanted to drink.

"Water is fine," she answered. "But you don't have to wait on me. If you'll point out the cabinet that holds the glasses, I'll be happy to get it myself."

Unfortunately, he needed to keep busy to refrain from touching her. "Just sit. I can take care of this, so let me. Maybe after you're feeling better, but for now, rest and relax."

Once he got her water, he leaned against the counter and watched as she devoured her sandwich, trying not to eye her too intently while he attempted to figure out what exactly about her so entranced him.

As a physician, Eric believed in logic, in cold hard facts. He knew physical attraction could be due to pheromones, or physical appearance, or a combination of these things and more. Whatever the reason, he desired this woman, whom he'd just met, with a fierceness that should have shocked him. The fact that it didn't made him wonder if he was losing his mind.

The sandwich disappeared, and MW sighed, blotting her lush mouth with the paper towel. He couldn't help but follow the gesture with his gaze, feeling as if he might be drowning. She took a deep drink of water, then smiled at him. "Thank you so much. That was absolutely delicious."

He swallowed tightly. "I'm glad you liked it."

"Thank you so much for all you're doing for me." Impulsively, she pushed to her feet and enveloped him in a tight hug. His arms came up of their own accord, holding her close. He could feel every soft, rounded curve of her as she pressed herself against him. His body stirred, his arousal immediate and strong. Not wanting to frighten or horrify her, he quickly extricated himself from her embrace.

"You're welcome." Struggling to sound normal, he cleared his throat. He spied her purple umbrella, still in the stand near the doorway. "Do you recognize that?" he asked, pointing.

Frowning, she walked over to it and picked it up. "Purple with white cupcakes. Very cute. Is it mine?"

"Yes. You were carrying it the night you…had your accident."

"Oh." Dropping it back in the umbrella stand, she sighed. "I think I need to get some more rest." She gave him a wobbly smile that made his chest feel tight. "I'll talk to you in the morning, okay?"

Still battling a fierce and persistent need, he nodded. And then, feeling like a fool, he watched her walk away, all the way down the hall until she closed her bedroom door behind her.

Only once she'd vanished from view did the tightness disappear from his chest.

Some things couldn't be analyzed, he knew, and if he'd been prone to flights of fancy, he'd think MW had been brought into his life for a reason. He'd been in the right place at the right time, and knew his quick call to 911 would have saved her life had she been badly hurt.

Imagination, wishful thinking, was as foreign to him as modern medicine might be to a witch doctor. Eric had never been anything but honest with himself. For whatever reason, he found MW attractive. His desire for her made the space around her seem electrified. Had she been anyone else, in any other situation, he'd have pursued her.

But until she had her memory back, until she knew who she was and the details of her life, he needed to keep himself under control. Somehow.

Frustrated, he considered heading down to the gym and working out, but didn't want to leave her alone again.

Instead, he unwound by watching television, falling asleep to the ten-o'clock news. At some point near midnight, he roused himself and headed off to his own bed.

Always an early riser, the next morning, for the first time in his life, Eric tried to move around quietly so he didn't wake his houseguest. Growing up on a ranch, he'd learned to wake before sunrise most mornings, a habit he'd temporarily abandoned in college, then taken back in medical school and residency. Out of necessity, these days he got to the hospital bright and early, sometimes even before the sun was more than a hint of light on the Oklahoma horizon.

When he walked into the kitchen for his first cup of coffee and flicked on the light, he stopped short at the sight of MW sitting hunched over a mug at his countertop bar.

"Hey." She flashed him a weary smile. "I couldn't sleep. I hope I didn't wake you."

Since she looked brittle enough to crumble, he kept his movements slow. "Nope. This is when I normally get up."

Now her eyes widened as she glanced from him to the wall clock. "At four-thirty?" She said the time with horror. "Seriously?"

"Yep." He crossed to the Keurig coffeemaker, put his coffee pod in and pressed the button to brew. While he waited, he turned to study her. "Maybe today you'll start to remember something."

Her nod didn't contain any real enthusiasm, which told him he hadn't imagined her mood last night. "Why does that upset you?" he asked.

"I have no idea. I simply can't remember. But for whatever reason, just thinking about it ties my stomach up in knots. That's why I couldn't sleep."

Snagging his coffee, he took the bar stool next to her. "How long have you been sitting here?"

"I don't know." The downturn of her mouth fascinated him. He had the strangest urge to see if he could make it curve up in a smile.

Instead, he sipped his coffee. "What would you like to do today while I'm at work?"

She thought for a moment. "Do you have any cookbooks?" she asked.

Surprised, he nodded. "I can probably rustle up one or two. At one point I thought I might teach myself to be a better cook."

"Did you?"

"No." He grinned at her, mentally urging her to smile. "I don't have the aptitude for it."

Finally, one side of her mouth lifted, then the other. "I guess we can't all be gifted in the kitchen."

A hint? Careful not to show his excitement, he focused on his coffee. "Are you a good cook, then?

He looked up in time to catch her slight frown. "I... Maybe. It's possible. Either way, while you're at the hospital, I'd like to try."

"Great." Pushing to his feet, he dragged his hand through his hair and tried not to notice the way the frilly, brightly colored pajama shorts Greta had bought her showcased her legs. "I'll find the books and leave them on the counter for you. Right now, I've got to get ready for work."

He hurried out of the room, more flustered than he'd like to admit, even to himself.

After Eric left for the hospital, MW sat in the kitchen, lost in her own thoughts. The two cookbooks Eric had been able to locate sat in front of her, untouched. She didn't understand why the idea of finally knowing her own name terrified her, or why a heavy weight of depression settled over her every time she thought about her memory returning. Had something bad happened to her? Or worse, what if she'd committed a horrible act? What kind of person would she turn out to be?

She didn't know. Eric had said her memory could return at any time, but she shouldn't try to force it. Since he hadn't known precisely how long that would be, she had no choice but to try to be patient, even if she felt as if she were about to jump out of her own skin.

Finally, after her second cup of coffee, she reached for the first cookbook. Flipping through the glossy pages, she tried to figure out what she'd like to try making. Of course a lot of that depended on what supplies Eric had on hand.

Why this strong urge to cook, to make something with her own hands, she didn't know. Maybe some vestige of who she really was. Either way, the idea brought her comfort.

After checking in Eric's fridge and cupboards, she settled on a simple apple crisp. After all, she didn't really know if she had any cooking skills.

Peeling, coring, slicing the apples she'd found in a bowl on the kitchen counter, she didn't try to overthink anything. Her hands seemed to know what they were doing, so she let them. Measuring out the ingredients, she found herself adding a pinch of this and that, some extra cinnamon and a bit of nutmeg. When she finally placed the dessert in the oven to bake, she felt such a happy sense of accomplishment that she wished for music. Since she didn't have any, she danced around the kitchen anyway.

She'd always loved to dance and sing while she cooked.

Stunned, the certainty of that knowledge made her freeze. An actual memory? What else could it have been?

Desperate, she tried to see if she could recall anything else. Evidently, she tried too hard, because all she came up with was a blank slate.

Meanwhile, the kitchen filled up with the fragrant smell of the apple crisp. It might have been the wrong thing to make in August, but for whatever reason it seemed like comfort food to her.

A quick glance at the clock showed noon had come and gone, and she needed to eat something for lunch. She fixed herself a salad, enjoying the selection of fresh greens she found in the refrigerator crisper. Dr. Eric Colton might be a busy man, but he sure knew how to stock a kitchen.

While she ate, she flipped through the second cookbook, wondering if she should make him something for dinner. Though she didn't have any idea what time he actually came home, she guessed she could always keep warm whatever she prepared.

The idea energized her. She checked to see what kind of proteins he had. Once again, his freezer was well stocked. She took out a pork roast and put it in the fridge to thaw for tomorrow, and took out a packet of hamburger meat. She'd thaw it in the microwave, and whip up some kind of pasta casserole. That would be easy to reheat.

Grinning—listen to her, thinking she could just *whip up* a casserole—she started assembling the necessary components.

To her surprise, once she'd followed all the steps in the cookbook, again she found herself intuitively adding a pinch here and there of different seasonings. Just like with the crisp, it felt like she somehow instinctively knew they'd enhance the dish. Humming happily, she conceded the fact that since she had no idea of her past, she just might be a very good cook indeed.

Once she'd put the casserole in the oven, she decided to keep herself busy by concocting another dessert. A cake? Pie? In the end, she realized Eric had enough ingredients for her to make a delicious cheesecake. Since it would need an hour baking time, plus time to cool, she needed to get it going. What on earth they were going to do with two desserts, she didn't know, but surely the sweet treats wouldn't go to waste.

Quickly, she pulverized graham crackers, melted the butter, located a pie plate and made a crust. She put that in the oven for a few minutes, then got busy making the cheesecake itself.

Whipping the cream cheese and other components felt strangely satisfying. She again found herself performing steps by rote, as if from the memory of doing this before so many times the actions had become habit.

Since the oven temperature for the casserole was 350, she slid the casserole over and placed the cheese-cake next to it. She set the microwave timer for that.

And then she sat back and waited while everything cooked.

By the time she removed the ground beef, pasta and mushrooms, all in a creamy cheese sauce, from the oven, she knew she'd made a winner. First, the fra-grant smell made her mouth water, and secondly, the dish looked fit for a photographic spread in a cooking magazine—it was that beautiful.

A quick glance at the clock showed several hours had passed. She couldn't believe the time—six-fifteen. She had no idea when Eric got off work at the hospital, but since he'd gone in over twelve hours ago, surely it would be soon.

Her stomach growled. Should she eat? Or wait? She decided to let the casserole cool slightly and if Eric wasn't home, go ahead and have her meal. She knew he'd understand, especially if he didn't return until much later.

Thirty minutes later she pulled out the cheesecake, pleased with the way it looked. She placed it on a rack to cool and opened a bottle of red wine. After pouring herself a glass, she walked to the window, gazing out at the busy city streets below.

The sound of the key in the front door lock made her jump. When Eric came inside, her heart skipped a beat.

"Wow." He stopped, sniffing appreciatively. "What-ever that is, it smells great."

His comment made her beam. Glad she'd waited, she hurried to set the table. "I made dinner."

His green eyes twinkled. "You know you didn't have to, but you wouldn't believe how glad I am that you did. I barely had time to eat an apple today, so I'm starving."

Happiness and pride hummed inside her as she placed the casserole in the center of the table. She poured him a glass of wine and took her seat across from him, watching as Eric dished up a large serving on his plate. Though her own helping was a third of the size of his, she felt a jolt of alarm as she realized she should have tasted it before serving it. Every good chef knew that.

Every good chef? What did she know about that? Shrugging off the thought, she watched as Eric raised his fork to his mouth.

He rolled his eyes, making appreciative sounds. "I didn't know you were a gourmet chef," he said, once he'd swallowed.

Delighted, she managed a casual shrug. "Neither did I," she teased. "I simply followed a recipe I found in one of your cookbooks."

One silver brow raised. "Taste it."

After she complied, she made a pleased noise. "It is pretty good," she admitted, having another bite.

Too busy devouring his meal to comment, Eric merely shook his head. When he'd cleaned his plate, he had seconds, which gave MW a serious case of the warm fuzzies.

"Try and leave room for dessert," she told him, unable to keep from smiling.

"Dessert?" He followed her gaze to where the

cheesecake sat cooling next to the apple crisp. "Be still my heart."

This time, she laughed out loud. "You have a choice. I hope they're as good as they look and smell."

Eric opted for the cheesecake, promising to try the crisp in the morning. "Mmm. It's even better." Eric devoured his slice, then gave her a sheepish look as he got a second. "I'll gain weight if I keep eating like this," he said, sounding not the least bit repentant.

She laughed again. With surprise, she noted that despite everything, she was happy. She liked him. Not for the first time, she wondered if losing her memory gave her a much-needed opportunity to start over. A blank slate.

But that would only be needed if it turned out she had an awful past.

With that, she gave herself a mental shake. Until she knew the truth, why waste her time speculating?

When the meal was finished, she began clearing off the table. Rising, Eric helped. "We can eat these leftovers again," he told her, smiling. "I'll cover them and put them in the fridge for later."

The tableau felt so cozy and domestic, she blinked. Swaying, she felt as if she watched them both from a distance, as though viewing a show on television. "Is disassociation part of amnesia?" she asked, trying not to worry.

Eric went still, eyeing her carefully. "Why do you ask?"

His stillness scared her more than anything. "Nothing," she lied. "Just curious."

She didn't know him well enough to know if he believed her or not. "Do you get to take a lunch break during the day?" she asked, changing the subject while she carried the dishes to the sink.

"It depends." She couldn't help but notice he still watched her closely. "If there's a lot going on, then no. Today was one of those days. We had a shooting, a stabbing, a battered woman and two car crashes. And that was all before noon."

Stunned, she stacked the plates in the dishwasher, trying to imagine. She couldn't. "Were you able to help them all?" She prayed he'd spare her the gory details. Apparently, she had a squeamish nature.

"Of course." His casual assurance verged on arrogance. "I'm damn good at what I do."

Blinking, she realized she found his confidence attractive. Maybe because right now she had none of her own.

A bit flustered, she closed the dishwasher and changed the subject. "I know I keep asking this, but how long do you think it will take before I remember something about my identity?"

"I don't know. It might be a day or two. Has anything come to you?"

"Not really." She began covering the leftovers so she could put them in the fridge. "Small flashes of little things, here and there. Apparently I seem to have an affinity for cooking."

"Lucky for me." Crossing the room, he took the casserole dish from her. "I really appreciate the meal. But you don't have to do this every day."

When she looked up at him, her heart lurched. "What else am I going to do?"

He frowned. "Going a bit stir-crazy?"

Though she hadn't been, she could see where the

sheer blankness of her days could turn into boredom. "Even if I cook every day, there's no way to fill that many hours."

Again he flashed that überconfident, sexy smile. "I'm sure a switch will flick on in your brain soon. Until then, just rest and relax. I have a ton of books if you like to read, plus there's always the good ol' television. Oh, and this building has a wonderful gym, if you feel like exercising. I can show you where it's located."

She nodded, curbing an impatience that had come out of nowhere. "I can't help but feel like I'm supposed to do something, something really important."

Her own words shocked her. "I mean," she stammered, "I hadn't felt like that until I said it. I guess that's another piece of my memory coming back."

"Don't try to force it. Just relax and if something comes to you, let it. If not, don't worry. I promise, you'll be back to normal in no time."

Since he was a doctor, she chose to believe he was right. "Still, I don't know what to do with myself all day. Not complaining," she said, though she sort of was.

"There's a desktop computer in my office." He pointed toward the hallway. "Third door on the left. It's not password protected. Feel free to use it for anything you like."

She tilted her head. "How do you know I won't go shopping and use your credit card info?"

His short bark of laughter made her smile. "Because I don't store any of my credit card info on my computer. So knock yourself out."

At least she could check out Facebook. The instant the thought occurred to her, she realized she didn't know her real name, so she couldn't access her account. Though for once, that information seemed to hover just out of reach at the edge of her consciousness. Which felt like a minor breakthrough.

"Thank you," she told him. "I might even use your computer to find new recipes."

He only shook his head and chuckled.

After dinner, they watched TV together, which made her feel like they were a couple in a long-term relationship. When she took a seat on the couch, he went for the chair, almost as if he didn't want to get too close to her. She told herself her thoughts were foolish and waited to see what shows he'd put on.

He chose two related dramas that ran back-to-back. As she watched them, again she felt a nagging sense of familiarity, as if she might have seen the programs before. Or maybe because the self she'd forgotten had been in a relationship, maybe even married or living with someone.

This idea caused her so much anxiety she had to push it away. Instead, she struggled to focus on the story unfolding on the television.

Yet it seemed she couldn't. When she wasn't obsessing over her past, she studied Eric. One thing she wished she could turn off was her hyperawareness of him. While he watched the show, she found herself sneaking glances at him. Everything about him fascinated her, from his close-cropped brown hair, to the wide span of his shoulders and his strong and sensual features. Even his hands with his long, elegant fingers—a surgeon's fingers. Knowing they were capable of saving lives made her wonder how they'd feel caressing her skin.

No. She brought herself up sharply, trying to disguise the restless agitation that took hold of her when she got too comfortable with him. This could only mean one thing as far as she was concerned. Something or someone in her past gave her a reason why she shouldn't get close to Eric Colton, no matter how sexy he might be.

After the evening news, Eric turned off the TV. His guileless green-eyed gaze met hers, sending another bolt of heat to her belly. "Good night," he said, covering a yawn with his hand, obviously not similarly affected by her.

She rose, still unable to shake the strange combination of desire and unease. When she had taken a few steps to head toward her room, Eric switched off the lights.

As she watched him, the one thing she did know—how much she owed him—made gratitude well up inside her. Her chest ached over how much he'd done for her. She didn't know if she'd ever be able to repay him for the kindness he'd shown her, but she sure as heck intended to try.

Resolve straightened her spine as she got ready for bed.

The next morning, she began. Since she now had an idea of what time he got up, by the time he came into the kitchen for his morning cup of coffee she'd made him breakfast. Scrambled eggs, toast and two sausage links. Nothing fancy, and part of her knew she could do more, but for now it would have to do.

Eric stopped short when he saw she'd set two places at the kitchen bar. "What's this?"

"You need to eat, right? Making you something hot and nutritious before you head in to work is the least I can do." She gave a mental wince. She sounded as if she wanted to mother him or something.

For an instant, she thought he might protest. He opened his mouth to speak, then apparently thought better of it. "Thank you," he finally said, pulling out his chair and eyeing his full plate with obvious appreciation before digging in. "You know this is going to ruin me, though."

She didn't understand. Filling her own plate, she took a seat next to him. "How so?"

"I never have time to make this kind of breakfast." He made a sound of pleasure as he tasted the eggs. "Cheese and garlic?"

"Yes." She couldn't keep from frowning. "I would have liked to have added some spinach and mushrooms, but you're all out."

"This is just perfect." When he rolled his eyes, she laughed. "Really."

Since he cleared his plate in record time, she had no choice but to believe him. "Thank you."

Before she could help herself, she wondered if he made love with the same enthusiasm. Quickly, she banished the thought, trying to focus on eating her own breakfast instead.

She'd barely taken her second bite when he pushed to his feet. "Sorry to eat and run, but I've got a busy day ahead."

Her heart skipped a beat as she thought—for just a moment—he was about to lean in and kiss her cheek. But he had only reached for his orange juice, which he downed in two gulps.

"Thank you." Again the megawatt, impersonal smile. She watched as he poured a second cup of coffee, his thoughts already a million miles away. More proof her clearly unfounded infatuation with him could only lead to trouble for them both.

After he left, she showered and dressed. With a sense of excitement mingled with trepidation, she turned on the computer. She read the news stories that came up on the home page, and did a search for her own story, but she could find nothing. Apparently a woman getting run down by a car that didn't stop wasn't newsworthy since she'd lived.

Next, she did a search for recipes. Amazingly, she remembered how to use the Google search page. She lost herself poring over various recipes, delighted with the sheer variety of them.

She finally settled on what she wanted to make that evening for dinner, and she decided to go ahead and prepare the dessert ahead of time. While that baked, she began assembling a sandwich for her lunch. Part of her wished Eric got to come home for a quick bite, but she understood why he couldn't.

Meanwhile, she had a lot to think about. Such as, who was Walter? Eric had told her she'd said that name after she'd been hit. Obviously, Walter was someone very important to her.

But she wore no ring. No one had come looking for her or reported her missing. Eric's brother the detective would have notified them if someone had.

What did that mean? Again she wondered what kind of life she had led that no one even cared if she disappeared. What if—the thought horrified her, but she knew she needed to face it head-on—she'd been an awful person? Maybe even some kind of criminal? The idea that had seemed so outlandish at first became more and more probable with each passing day.

# Chapter 5

Right after MW finished her sandwich, she stood up, trying to decide if she wanted to eat something sweet. She just taken the newest dessert—a gorgeous flourless cake—out of the oven when a sound made her freeze. Glancing at the clock, she saw it was a little past noon. An intruder? Or had Eric decided to come home for lunch?

Heart pounding, she hurried out into the living room, unsure whether she should hide or not.

When the door opened and Eric came inside, the relief that flooded her felt so strong, she had to restrain herself from launching herself at him and hugging him.

She let her gaze drink him in. Full of a kind of virile grace, he moved into the room. When he saw her, he smiled, devilishly handsome and unintentionally seductive. How one man could be so attractive and sexy, she didn't know.

Though her knees went weak, she managed to act unaffected. "Has something happened? Is that why you're here?"

He frowned. "MW, you need to stop assuming the worst. Today was fairly quiet so I took your suggestion from yesterday and came home for lunch. I couldn't stop thinking about that casserole you made yesterday."

Pleased, she nodded. "I'll reheat some for you."

"Great." He followed her into the kitchen. As she got the casserole out and spooned a generous helping onto a plate, his bold stare seemed to assess her. "You look like you've been having a good day so far," he commented.

"I have." She flashed him a quick smile before turning and placing his plate in the microwave. "I've been baking a little, spent some time on the internet, and…"

"And?"

"Worked on trying to regain my memory," she admitted, aware he'd told her specifically not to try to force it. "I went to Facebook, Instagram and Twitter and started poking around. I hoped something would jar my brain, but nothing did. I couldn't find my accounts on any of those social media sites, which felt pretty disappointing."

He came closer. When she saw the intense look darkening his eyes, she froze. Every sense leaped to life.

The instant their gazes met, he smoothed out his expression, but it was a little too late. She realized whatever this thing blossoming between them might be, it definitely wasn't one-sided.

Which would make it that much more difficult to resist. Still, the knowledge filled her with a warm glow.

"Are you really hungry?" she asked, trying to pretend she didn't want to dance for joy.

One corner of his mouth quirked and the spell was broken. He looked around and sniffed. "What is that smell? Whatever it is, I bet it's delicious."

"I made a flourless cake for dessert after dinner tonight."

A slow smile spread across his handsome face. "Are you trying to fatten me up?"

The teasing glint in his eye flustered her. "No, not at all. I just…"

"You really do like to cook, don't you?"

"Apparently." The timer beeped on the microwave and she placed his plate on the counter. "Dig in."

"What about you?"

"I made myself a sandwich," she admitted. "And I've already eaten it."

"Ah, well." He shrugged, digging in. After his first bite, he moaned with pleasure, which made her pulse skip. "This is so good."

Clearly oblivious to his effect on her, he continued to eat, not stopping until he'd cleaned his plate.

"This is the first time I've ever come home for lunch since I bought this town house a few years ago," he announced. "I have to tell you, your cooking is so good, you ought to consider opening your own restaurant."

A pang went through her at his words. "That's a thought." Though she kept her tone light, something about the idea made her sad.

Blinking, she pushed away the thought and focused. "Do you want more?" she asked.

His eyes narrowed, as if he were considering, and then he shook his head. "Regretfully, no. If I eat too much at lunch, I'll be fighting the urge to take a nap all afternoon."

"How about dessert? We still have apple crisp and that cheesecake from yesterday."

His mouth twitched with amusement. "Sorry, I'm out of time." He glanced at his watch. "I've got to go back to work. I have a ton of things I need to clear up. We'll talk more tonight, okay?"

"Wait," MW said. When he hesitated, she grabbed some cellophane and wrapped him up a piece of cheesecake. "Take this for later."

Accepting her offering, he met her gaze. Something intense flared between them, the pull so strong she took an involuntary step back.

Just like that, his expression became shuttered. "I'll see you tonight." As he turned to go, someone knocked on the door. They both froze.

"Stay right here," he said. Crossing to the door, he looked through the peephole and shook his head. "It's my neighbor Dave." He kept his voice low. "Stay out of sight while I see what he wants."

She nodded and Eric opened the door.

Though she couldn't see the man outside, she heard every word.

"I just wanted to let you know that there have been several break-ins," Dave said, "all of them to town houses in our building and surrounding buildings."

"Robberies?"

"That's the weird thing. So far, nothing's been stolen. People are coming home to find their town house trashed, ransacked, like whoever broke in is looking for something."

*Or someone.* MW shuddered. She couldn't help but wonder if the break-ins were somehow related to *her*.

"Better get an alarm system," Dave continued. "I just had one installed. I'd be happy to give you the name of the company."

"Thanks." Eric sounded distracted. "I'll call you later. Right now I've got to get back to the hospital. I'll call my brother Ryan and see what he can find out."

"That's right, he's on the Tulsa PD."

Eric nodded. "Yep. He'll know what to do. Thanks again." And he closed the door, standing with his back to her, so still, MW knew he was thinking the same thing.

Panicked, she swayed.

A strangled cry made Eric turn. He took one look at MW's ashen face and rushed to her, enfolding her in his arms. "It's not because of you," he said, wanting to reassure her while he battled with the knowledge of how good she felt held so close to his body.

"How do you know?" She pulled away. "If the break-ins were robberies, than I'd have to say you're right. But since even your neighbor said the intruders appear to be searching for something, I don't think it's too much of a stretch to assume that something is me."

Her husky voice broke, ruining him. Muttering an oath, he pulled her back into his arms.

This time, she buried her face into his throat, clinging to him as if she thought him a life raft in a turbulent sea. He felt a jolt as her hip brushed his thigh, and he clenched his teeth.

Even her scent—whatever fragrant shampoo or lotion Greta had purchased for her—aroused him.

She didn't cry, nor did she move. Instead she stood as still as a statue, her expression far away as if she was lost in thought while she accepted the comfort he offered.

While he tried like hell not to let it become more than that.

Holding her had been a mistake. He never should have come home. He didn't take lunch or leave the hospital. But all day, she'd been on his mind, and he'd found himself thinking of her when he needed to be concentrating on something else. Plus that casserole... Still, he would have been better off if he'd remained at work.

"I don't like this," she finally said, sounding as if her teeth were clenched.

"Me neither," he admitted. Dave's news had worried him, though he truly didn't think the break-ins were related to MW.

Somehow, he managed to drop his arms and casually step away. "I need to phone Ryan," he managed. "I'll call him on my way back to work. Meanwhile, keep the dead bolt locked and stay out of sight."

She inhaled sharply. "Could I go with you?" she asked, wincing as she spoke. "I won't bother you while you work. I can sit with a book in one of the waiting rooms. I just don't want to be here alone."

Though he could hardly blame her, he couldn't have her just hanging out at the hospital all day. "That won't work," he told her. "I'm sorry. While I honestly don't feel you need to worry—they're not home invasions, just break-ins—what I can do is ask Ryan to have one of his patrol cars circle the area the rest of the day.

And I'll leave you his number. If you have the slightest worry, call him. Okay?"

Lowering her thick brown lashes, she nodded. "Sorry. I don't think I'm normally a big chicken like this, but since I have no idea what's going on…"

"It's understandable." Resisting the urge to hug her again, he gave her a reassuring smile instead. "Let me jot down the number before I go."

Once he'd done that, he turned to find her standing near the entrance to the kitchen, hugging her arms around herself. Her safe place, he realized. Where she felt most at home.

"You're going to be fine," he promised, even as he wondered if he should bring her to the hospital after all. "We're probably overreacting."

"Maybe so." Her calm expression fooled neither of them. "I'd be interested to see how many break-ins have occurred, though."

Conscious of the ticking clock and mindful he had a surgery scheduled that afternoon, he pulled out his cell phone. "Now, that I can find out."

Luckily, Ryan answered. As soon as Eric told him the information Dave had passed on, Ryan looked up the incidents. "Two break-ins," Ryan said. "The only thing unusual about them is that nothing appears to have been taken. No one was home. Both times, the place was tossed, vandalized. Windows broken. We're lucky no one was hurt."

"Do you think this is going to happen again?"

"There's no way to tell." Ryan didn't seem concerned. "If I were you, I'd install a burglar alarm."

"That's what Dave did. I'll get on that, but for right now I want to make sure my houseguest is safe."

Silence. When Ryan spoke again, he sounded serious. "Is she still there?"

With sheer effort of will, Eric avoided glancing at her. "Yep." And then he put in his request for a marked squad car to patrol the area.

"I'll see what I can do," Ryan promised. "Do you have any reason to believe she's in danger?"

"No, but we don't have any reason to believe she isn't either." Eric made the mistake of looking at MW. Shifting from foot to foot, she watched him, her cornflower-blue eyes wide. She looked so vulnerable that he ached.

"I'm sure she'll be fine." Clearing his throat, Ryan promised to send a car around every thirty minutes.

Thanking him, Eric hung up. He had to get back to the hospital, but he didn't want to leave MW. Not like this, trying so hard to be brave despite her obvious fear.

"I'll be fine," she said softly, looking anything but, despite the way she'd squared her shoulders and raised her chin in an obvious effort to appear strong.

Uncertain, he wavered. Finally, though, duty called. "How about I drop you off at the library? It's just past the hospital, and you could stay there until I get done. That way you'll be around other people rather than here alone in the town house."

"I'd love that." Visibly cheered, she hurried over and smiled up at him. "I'm ready whenever you are."

In that instant, as heat spiraled through him, he knew he'd do just about anything to keep that smile on her face.

As he opened the door and let her precede him, he took her arm. "Maybe tonight when I finish up at work, you and I could go out to dinner. We'll drive across town, in case whoever is looking for you is still in the area."

Her pale blue eyes lit up. "I'd really like that," she said, her mouth curving into yet another beautiful smile. He managed to continue walking, though his pulse had begun racing again. He wondered how this woman he barely knew could make him feel more alive than he had in years.

"All right," he said, clenching his hands into fists to keep from touching her. "Don't leave the library until you see me. I'll try to get there as quickly as I can and we'll walk back here and pick up my car to go out to dinner."

"Sounds wonderful." As she beamed up at him, he realized her light blue eyes had little flecks of silver in them. In fact, she had the most beautifully colored eyes he'd ever seen. His gaze fell to the creamy expanse of skin on her chest and he swallowed tightly.

"Are you all right?" Her smile had changed into a frown.

Quickly, he rearranged his expression. "Just trying to decide where we should have dinner. Do you like Mexican food?"

Too late, he realized she couldn't remember.

For a moment she wrinkled her brow, clearly trying to think. Finally, she shrugged. "I guess I'll find out."

They walked past the hospital to the library. Eric barely resisted glancing at his watch, aware he needed to get back so he could prep for surgery.

Made of the same color brick, the two-story building almost seemed an extension of the hospital. Only an alley separated them. Except the library had lots of windows and the bright light shining inside made the place appear cheerful.

Just outside the double glass doors, he stopped. "Here you are. You should be safe here. I'll meet you sometime after five."

MW nodded. She turned and wrapped her arms around him in a bear hug. "Thank you, so much," she told him. "This is so much better than staying inside your town house. I can find a lot to occupy my time here. And I have dinner out to look forward to. You have no idea how much that means to me."

He froze. Her lush body had all the right curves in all the right places. Though he moved his arms around her automatically, he had to forcibly stifle the urge to let his hands roam.

As his body stirred, he realized he might have to do more than keep her safe from the men who were after her. He might also have to protect her from himself.

"Go on, now," he told her. He stood and watched until she'd strolled safely inside before turning and hurrying back to the hospital, where he could lose himself in his job.

Inside the library, MW took her time looking around. The huge library was the kind of place she would enjoy exploring, and she thought the hours until Eric returned would pass very quickly and safely.

Somehow, she doubted whoever was hunting for her would think to search here.

Up and down row after row of books, she wandered. Once she happened upon the cookbook section, she felt like she'd found heaven. Pulling several from the stacks, she carried them over to one of the reading tables and began leafing through them. She didn't understand why she found herself so drawn to cooking, but she figured it had something to do with her past.

One of the books had a chapter on how to open a restaurant. As soon as she found that, her heart began pounding. Reading the first few paragraphs, she knew she'd seen this before. Studied it, in fact.

Did she own a restaurant? Or only dream of owning one?

Frustrated, she closed the book. As she did, something flashed in her memory. She heard a gunshot, saw a man jerk as he was hit. She got her hand to her mouth, barely stifling a scream. Had that really happened? A true memory? Or the product of an overactive imagination, fueled by the dramas she'd watched with Eric on television?

As her heart raced, she tried to think. What did this mean? Had she shot someone? Could she really be a criminal, a murderess as she'd wondered before? Wouldn't a person know if they were capable of such things?

Her head began to ache. She remembered Eric's words, telling her not to try to force it and not to jump to conclusions.

Standing, she gathered up the cookbooks and carried them back to the shelves to put them away. She sighed. Next, she thought she'd go peruse the fiction. Because until she got her memory back, that's all her past could be to her. Fiction.

After finishing up his last surgery for the day, Eric touched base with the ER. Things were relatively quiet there, the triage nurse told him cautiously. They both knew making statements like that could sometimes boomerang, and chaos would immediately ensue.

He hoped that wasn't the case today. He wanted to get out of there fairly early. All afternoon, the idea of having dinner with MW had exhilarated him.

Since overanalyzing her effect on him wouldn't accomplish anything, he'd reached a conscious decision to just go with the flow.

As soon as he could, he finished up at the hospital and, still wearing his scrubs, headed down the street to the library.

He found her totally engrossed in a book, her wavy hair reflecting red in the fluorescent lights. Standing still, he watched her, again admiring the graceful flow of her neck and shoulders, the lush swell of her breasts and her tiny waist.

When she looked up—apparently sensing his presence—and smiled, his heart began to sing. He wanted to kiss her right then, among the stacks of books and the scent of paper, just bend her over backward and claim her as his.

Of course he did no such thing.

"Hey," he said, speaking quietly since they were in a library after all. "Are you hungry?"

Cheeks pink, she nodded. "I could eat. I think you mentioned Mexican food earlier?"

"I did. There's a great Mexican restaurant a few minutes' drive from here."

"I've been thinking about that." Her light blue eyes lit up. "I adore Mexican food." She frowned. "Or at least I believe I do."

"Then, come on." Holding out his hand, he waited

for her to take it. Which she did, but as they began to walk toward the door, reluctance showed in her steps.

"What's wrong?" he asked as they neared the exit.

"I hate this, but I'm wondering if it's safe."

"It should be." In this he felt confident. "It's a short walk home and there will be tons of people out and about. My car's in the enclosed garage. We'll just get in the car, go eat and come right back. There won't be enough time for you to be in any sort of danger, I promise."

And there he went again, giving his word. Ever the omnipotent surgeon, he supposed. Old habits were hard to break.

Yet his absolute confidence must have finally convinced her. "I'd like that," she said, smiling up at him. "I confess I did enjoy getting outside and enjoying the sunshine on the walk here and back, even though it's hot enough to fry an egg on the sidewalk."

The warmth in her smile made his chest feel tight. Shaking off the unfamiliar feeling, he nonetheless continued to hold her hand all the way to the town house and his garage.

She stopped short when she saw his little black sports car. "That's yours?"

Not sure what to make of her frown, he nodded.

"It looks expensive."

He saw no reason to lie. "It was."

Turning to eye him, she appeared puzzled. "I didn't peg you for a Porsche guy."

Amused, he shrugged. "What did you think I'd drive, a Ford F150 pickup?" Since that's what they drove on the ranch.

"I don't know." Her frown deepened. "It's really frustrating, not knowing anything."

"I imagine. Go ahead and get in."

He enjoyed watching her climb into the low-slung vehicle. And as he took his seat behind the wheel, something felt right, watching her buckle herself in.

*His.*

This stopped him short. *Go with the flow*, he reminded himself. Tonight he'd treat her and they'd have a good time. No sense spoiling it by worrying about something he had no control over.

On the drive across town to Tres Hombres, he pointed out landmark buildings, even though if she had lived in Tulsa any time at all, she probably already knew about them. Or would, once her memory came back.

"That's the Ambassador Hotel." He slowed at the corner of 14th and Main. "Built in 1929."

She looked and nodded. "Pretty."

Since the old building was more interesting than pretty, he didn't comment. He couldn't blame her for being distracted. He couldn't imagine facing life with a blank slate, no idea of the past, present, or future.

Though the sun was a long way from setting, the sign for Tres Hombres already flashed its garish colors.

As he pulled into the parking lot, a space opened up on the side fairly close to the back entrance. He took it.

"Wow, you must be lucky," she mused, twisting back around after checking out the sign. "Parking-space luck. It's a rare and amazing thing."

He laughed.

She did, too. "But I'm serious. Look around. This

place is packed already. There aren't any other spots anywhere close to the building. You're lucky."

"I usually am, for whatever reason." Hurrying from the car and around to her side, he opened the door for her. "This restaurant is known for their brisket tacos."

Again that warm smile. "I can't wait," she said.

For a moment, he held her gaze. When he finally looked away, he felt giddy, like a teenager skipping school to meet a girl. Which, in a roundabout way, he was. Though technically this time was his to use as he wished, normally he spent the hours after his shift catching up on his files. If he ate dinner, he scarfed down hospital food at his desk or in the doctor's lounge. Going out to an actual restaurant would be a rare treat.

Especially with present company.

Several men eyed MW as the hostess led them to a booth, making Eric want to glare at them in warning. He restrained himself, well aware of her mesmerizing beauty and glad he got to show her off.

They ordered and while they waited for their meal, they munched on chips and salsa. MW chattered about some of the recipes she wanted to try, and he merely listened, not wanting to bore her with stories about his day at the hospital.

Most of it would be either routine or gory. Once he'd left for the day, he tried not to talk about it with anyone other than colleagues. War stories, they called them. Most times their black humor wouldn't be understood by anyone who didn't deal with what they did on a day-to-day basis. They knew it was one of the few ways they could let off steam.

The food arrived. They'd both ordered the brisket

tacos. MW studied hers, inspecting the meat and rice, the cheese and guacamole. Then she lifted one taco and sniffed, as though gauging the worth of a fine wine.

As he watched, amused, she finally took a bite. Clearly savoring the taste, she slowly chewed. The motion of her throat as she swallowed seemed both graceful and sensual. "Wonderful." Her voice vibrated with pleasure. "I think I can figure out the seasonings."

He laughed, already halfway through two tacos and ready to start on a third.

For dessert they had sopaipillas, another delicacy MW had to examine and nibble, as if mentally coming up with a recipe.

"I'd like to try to make this," she said, confirming his suspicions as she licked honey off her fingers.

He couldn't look away. He wondered if she knew how seductive her actions were, and if she'd intended to start a burning ache of need low in his gut.

Catching him staring, she blinked and colored. "I was thinking about cooking," she said, a bit defensively.

That, more than anything, broke the spell.

"You sure do like to cook," he managed to comment, using the moist towelette to clean their fingers.

She rewarded him with a shy smile. "I really do."

Again, the flare of desire. Still, he smiled back. "I'm glad. Because I like to eat."

Once he'd settled the bill, they walked to the door together, both full. He considered taking her hand, but decided against it. He already felt way too warm and fuzzy. Why make it worse?

"It sure is hot," she exclaimed as they stepped outside, stretching her arms out in the fading sun. "It must still be in the high nineties, even after seven at night."

"August in Oklahoma," he said, pulling out his car keys and hitting the button for remote start so the vehicle could begin cooling with the AC.

Instead of starting, his car exploded.

# Chapter 6

The explosion knocked them both to the ground. Dazed, at first MW didn't understand what had happened. Through the shrill whine of ringing in her ears, she heard screams, running footsteps and the roar of fire. As she struggled to catch her breath, there came then another, smaller explosion. Even so, the ground shook almost as badly.

The car. The car must have blown up when Eric remotely started it. Stunned, she realized she'd started shaking and seemed unable to stop.

As the smoke cleared, she rubbed her eyes, trying to see. "Eric?"

"Right here." Next to her, he pushed to his hands and knees and swore. "Are you all right?"

"I think so." Still too shaky to move on her own, she allowed him to help her up. Sirens sounded, which meant someone had called 911.

A group of people rushed up to them, all talking at once. MW winced, disoriented. Her head ached. Her body hurt. This felt a lot like when she'd first woke up in the hospital, except she wasn't alone.

Eric was there, his strong arm supporting her. She glanced at him and gasped. Horrified by the huge, jagged gash on his cheek, she couldn't seem to look away from all the blood.

"You're bleeding…" Swaying, she clutched at him. "Oh, Eric, your arm doesn't look good."

"Easy. I think you're going into shock," he murmured, supporting her easily. "Let's get you over to the paramedics so they can check you out."

Paramedics? Belatedly, she saw the ambulance, lights flashing. She didn't understand how she'd missed its arrival, but then again she remembered absolutely nothing about being hit by a car.

"And you, too. You need to get that cut looked at."

He nodded, continuing to move her toward the ambulance.

A fire truck hosed down the fire, and police cars had arrived. Dizzy, she thought the scene looked surreal, like an action movie or a television show.

But no, this was real life.

"What exactly just happened?" she asked, her voice hoarse. At least she had her shivers under control.

Expression grim, Eric met her gaze. The gash on his face gave him a dangerous look. "Someone blew up my car. If we'd been inside when it started, we'd both be dead."

Dead. As Eric spoke, even if MW's dazed look told him it hadn't yet registered with her, the seriousness of the situation hadn't slammed home.

Someone really was after her. Someone who wanted her dead, for whatever reason, and would stop at nothing to kill her.

In that instant, Eric knew what he needed to do.

No backtracking now. He thought of all the patients who might need his talented hands to operate on them, and again wondered how he could even consider doing what he'd just decided to do. Take time off from his job. For the first time ever. To keep MW safe. He couldn't think of a better reason.

He didn't expect too much resistance, since everyone and their brother, from the hospital administration to the nurses, including his own office staff, had been telling him for months that he needed to take a vacation. So had his family. They'd practically begged him on a regular basis to take a break from his admittedly demanding job and spend some time at the ranch.

Now he'd do exactly that, since there was no way to keep MW safe here in Tulsa. And the chief of surgery could breathe a sigh of relief. According to him, when doctors were overworked and stressed, they started to make mistakes. Since surgeons couldn't afford that luxury, Eric's boss had ordered him to schedule some vacation days soon.

Now Eric would put in his request for two weeks off. He'd take care of it the next afternoon, once he knew MW was all right. As soon as he could, he needed to get her out of town.

She'd be safe at the Lucky C, his family's ranch. He knew the rest of his family would be delighted. They'd better be careful what they wished for, he thought with a grimace. He wondered how they'd feel when he— along with a mystery woman who didn't even know her own name—showed up on the ranch for an extended stay. But where else could he go? What better place to hide her than his family's sprawling cattle ranch?

After helping MW to the ambulance to be checked out, at first Eric declined when they offered to look him over. But at MW's worried insistence, he let them clean and bandage the cut on his arm and another on his cheek. Then he called Ryan, and got his voice mail. Leaving a quick message, he relayed what had happened.

The paramedics finished checking MW out and offered her the choice of going to the ER for observation or going home.

Eric gave a minute shake of his head. Right now, he wasn't even certain she'd be safe in the hospital.

Her light blue eyes came up to study his face. "I'd really like to go back to the town house," she said, getting the message.

Eric glanced at the EMTs. One nodded. "She seems fine. A little scraped up, but nothing too bad."

Though every instinct urged Eric to get MW out of the parking lot, he knew he had to give a statement to the police.

Leaving their squad cars' lights flashing, two uniformed officers began to disperse the crowd. Two more approached Eric and MW.

"You again?" The tall one asked.

Eric recognized him from when MW had nearly been run over. "Yeah. Sorry."

"Does Ryan know about this?"

"I left him a message," Eric said, dragging his hand across his jaw, unsurprised when it came away bloody.

Despite the EMT cleaning his larger wounds, he had several smaller ones all over his face and neck.

Speaking slowly and succinctly, he gave them the details on what had just happened. "I think we need to notify the ATF," he said when he'd finished. "They handle bombs, right?"

The two policemen exchanged glances. "Give us a minute." And they moved away, one of them already on his phone.

"Can we go now?" MW asked, sounding just short of desperate. Eric glanced at the policemen, still on their phones, and nodded. "Yes. Let me see if we can get a ride with them."

Since they knew his brother Ryan, the officers readily agreed. On the short drive back downtown, they bantered back and forth, apparently trying to distract MW, who'd gone silent and appeared shell-shocked.

Back at the town house, Eric thanked them and they drove off. He hustled MW inside, noting the way she kept glancing back over her shoulder as if she expected a sniper to start taking potshots at her any moment. This broke Eric's heart and angered him. Especially since he couldn't really blame her.

"Why don't you go clean up?" he told her gently. Her heart-shaped face had grime and blood on it, and he thought a hot shower might make her feel better.

Locking the front door, he called Ryan again. This time, Ryan picked up. His brother had already heard what had happened and promised to immediately dispatch a patrol car to watch the town house.

"I need to cook." MW sounded desperate. "I know we just ate dinner, but I have to keep busy."

He understood. "Shower first," he said. "Doctor's

orders. Once you are in clean clothes, then you go right ahead and knock yourself out in the kitchen."

He couldn't imagine what she was going through. To be under attack and have no idea why.

"I'm sorry," she told him, her chin coming up as she angrily brushed away the tears shining in her large blue eyes. "I've done nothing but cause you trouble."

Before he could reconsider, he went to her and pulled her into his arms. "Don't even think that. None of this is your fault."

"You don't know that." She raised her chin and met his gaze. "You don't know what kind of person I was—am—or what I may have done to make people want to kill me."

"Shh," he soothed. "There's nothing rational about any of this, so stop blaming yourself. Whoever is behind this is the bad guy, not you."

Twisting in his arms, she moved away. Back to him, she shook her head. "Neither of us really know that. And until we learn the truth, I think you'd be a lot safer far, far away from me."

It took a minute for her words to sink in. "You want to leave?" He couldn't believe it.

She turned to face him again. "Don't you think that would be for the best?"

"No. Not at all. First off, where would you go? Second, how would you stay safe?"

"I—"

Not giving her a chance to answer, he continued on. "I have a plan. I just need to take care of a few things to set it in motion. I'm going to get you the hell out of Tulsa."

At his words, she visibly deflated. "You are?"

"Yes. But until I've finalized everything, I need you to be patient and sit tight."

"Here?" She gestured around the room. "With someone breaking in to surrounding townhomes? How will that be safe? What if someone tosses a bomb into the window?"

Normally, he would have refuted such a preposterous claim. Now, he knew it could be entirely possible, and winced.

"True. Maybe you can go back to the library," he offered.

"I don't know..." But her resolve had begun to waver, he could tell. "For how long? I don't think anywhere in this immediate area is free from danger."

Realizing her terror lurked just beneath her skin, he knew the wrong choice of words could destroy her fragile composure. Best to try to act normal, as if they hadn't been a few seconds away from dying.

"I agree. We'll leave here together and I'll keep you safe. I just need a few hours to take care of some loose ends before we can go." He knew he had at least one surgery scheduled for tomorrow. He'd have to perform that one, and then try like hell to find a replacement surgeon so he could spirit MW out of town.

"A few hours?" she repeated, hollow-eyed.

"You know what?" he heard himself ask. "I think you can wait in my office at the hospital tomorrow while I do the surgery I have scheduled. I won't be able to concentrate if I'm not certain you're safe."

The look she slanted at him contained equal parts disbelief and gratitude. At least the terror appeared to be banked. "Thank you. I promise I won't disturb anything."

"Perfect." He pointed toward the bathroom. "Now shower. I want to have a turn, too."

"All right." She moved woodenly, probably still in shock. A moment later he heard the sound of the shower starting.

He wanted to punch something. As a surgeon, he was used to being in control, taking charge and fixing everything that had been broken. But this…this was beyond the scope of his control. He'd never forgive himself if he failed to protect MW.

After they had both showered and changed, he found her in the kitchen, whipping up a batch of cookies.

"What are you doing?" he asked gently.

"Keeping busy," she said. "I thought I'd make cookies to take with us wherever we end up going."

Her hollow expression worried him. All along, despite the horrific things that kept happening to her, she'd managed to smile and have a positive attitude. This explosion seemed to have been the final straw.

Once the cookies were cooling, he tried to get her to eat. When she refused food, claiming she wasn't hungry, and then told him she wanted to go to bed early, he knew she needed solitude to try to come to grips with everything that had just happened.

He'd have given much to be able to be there for her, to hold her through the night and kiss her and chase her fears away. Instead, he'd simply nodded and told her to sleep well.

Later, alone in his room, the decision he'd reached earlier still rattled around inside him. He, a man who didn't believe in indecision, struggled to make up his mind. Even though he knew what he had to do, part of him—the rational, type-A, focused surgeon—fought it.

But every time he closed his eyes, he relived the explosion, and knew he had to keep her safe, no matter what it took.

The next morning, he got up, showered and headed toward the kitchen for his coffee. There, instead of finding MW with a hot, home-cooked breakfast, an empty kitchen greeted him. At least the Keurig coffeemaker brewed quickly, so he made himself a cup of strong coffee.

Struggling to contain his worry, he drank, the hot liquid scalding his throat. Despite having had this exact same scenario every single morning except for the past couple days, he felt MW's absence keenly.

Was she all right? Still locked in fear? Or had she simply overslept? As he sipped his coffee and tried to rationalize checking on her, she walked into the kitchen and gave him a tentative smile.

"Morning." She wore jeans and a navy T-shirt. The slight circles under her eyes attested to a rough night.

But at least she was okay. He too had spent the entire evening reliving the awful moment when his car exploded.

Relieved, he saluted her with his mug. Better not to discuss any of that. "Are you about ready to go?"

"I must be used to rising before sunrise, because I am." Taking a large container out of the refrigerator, she filled two small bowls, and placed one in the microwave. "Steel-cut oats," she told him. "I made them ahead of time since they take so long to cook. All we have to do is nuke them, and we have a hot, nutritious breakfast."

He nodded, glad he hadn't made toast or something. "Sounds great."

After they ate, she left their dishes to soak in the sink and smiled at him again. He was relieved to see her fighting spirit had returned. The spark of excited light in her eyes made them a vivid shade of sky. Much better than the dull terror from the night before. "Thank you for taking me with you. I'll definitely feel much safer. Plus, I think this is going to be interesting."

He laughed, holding out his arm. As she took it, he shook his head. "You might find it excruciatingly boring sitting around in my office for several hours. Perhaps you should buy a magazine or book at the gift shop."

Her smile widened. "Maybe I will."

Eric managed to keep walking toward the door. MW entranced him; he had no other word for how she made him feel. She'd awakened a new sense of life, of endless possibilities, of hope. She made his heart—and his body—sing.

Once she got her memory back, he'd want to know if she felt the same. But first, he had to keep her safe until they could figure out why someone wanted her dead.

As they went outside, he caught himself giving their surroundings a sharp inspection, just in case. MW noticed and nodded her approval. "Thank you," she murmured, leaning into him and bumping him with her hip.

Even that small gesture made him feel twelve feet tall.

When they reached the hospital, he pushed open the front door to let her enter ahead of him. Greeting the staff, he took MW to his office, pointing out the break room and gift store on the way.

Once she was situated in his office, he left her, striding down the hallway toward the elevators, needing to clear his mind. One day maybe he'd figure out the lure of MW, but right now he had surgery.

In the end, he did his job. Once the operation was finished—successfully, of course—he left the patient in Recovery and the capable hands of the nurses and headed off to find the chief of surgery and firm up his plans. He imagined old Cal would be pleased. Dr. Eric Colton would finally put in a request for some time off. Even though Eric would be giving short notice, there were plenty of other surgeons who could take over for two weeks.

As he'd suspected, his request for a vacation was immediately granted. Cal grinned and jumped up to pump Eric's hand. "Finally," he said. "You're the best surgeon in this place and I have been really worried you'd burn out."

Though Eric doubted such a thing would be likely— he loved his job—he smiled and nodded. "Since Dr. Patel is on call tomorrow, do you mind if I start my time off as soon as possible?"

"Of course not," Cal boomed immediately, making Eric suspect the other man felt afraid Eric would change his mind. "Leave early today, if you can."

Grinning back, Eric said he'd see what he could do. He knew the hospital management would frown on all of this, but what the suits didn't know wouldn't hurt them. Cal was the best and he took care of his staff. His reputation preceded him and there was a long list of capable surgeons willing to come work for him as soon as something opened up. Eric counted himself lucky.

Finishing up his shift, he knew he had a hundred small things to tidy up for whichever doctors took his place while he was gone. Though he only kept office hours twice a week, he'd called his staff and had them reschedule all his appointments, after first making sure there wasn't anyone with an urgent problem. Luckily for him there wasn't.

With that cleared up, he sat at the nurse's station and reviewed the charts of all his surgeries and consults. Briefly, he considered summoning a meeting of the on-duty surgical nurses, but decided against it, well aware doing so would only give them one more thing to grumble about. While he valued the nurses highly, he knew he was often short and impatient with them. More than once, he'd heard them use the word *arrogant*, though he considered this to be false. Due to the nature of his job, he often had to make snap life-and-death decisions. He didn't have time for idle chitchat or foolish gossip.

And until now, he hadn't had time to take a vacation.

Ignoring the faint tug of guilt mingling with his anticipation, he completed his tasks and went to collect MW.

As long as she didn't allow herself to reflect on the explosion, MW enjoyed her time in Eric's office. From inside the four small walls, she felt immersed in the hospital, listening to the pages, watching the nurses and doctors and aides rush past, always in a hurry. She'd snagged a magazine from the surgical waiting room and flipped through it, but truth be told she found the hospital's internal goings-on much more fascinating.

When Eric appeared in the doorway, she gave a surprised squeak and glanced at the clock on the wall. Almost noon.

"Wow," she mused, standing and moving out from behind his desk. "Time sure flies past around here."

For some reason her comment seemed to amuse him. He grinned. "All set. Are you ready?"

Confused, she peered up at him. "To go to lunch?"

His grin widened. "We can do that, too. But to get out of here. I've taken the rest of the day off."

Delighted, she hugged him. Just a quick embrace, since she liked touching him far more than she should. Until her memory returned, she needed to keep her hands to herself.

"How about we grab something on the way back to the town house," he said. "Do you like Chinese?"

Since she didn't know, she shrugged. "Sounds great. But is it safe?"

"It's right around the corner," he promised. "And from there, a straight shot home."

*Home.* She liked that word. Too bad right now his home felt fraught with danger.

The instant they stepped outside, her anxiety returned. Though not for long, as the all-you-can-eat buffet was right across the street from the hospital.

After their meal, they cut back through the hospital and hurried home. Though Eric kept his hand at the small of her back, she couldn't shake the feeling she was being pursued.

"Here we go." Using his electronic card, Eric unlocked the front door and ushered her inside. "Safe and sound."

Nodding, she breathed a sigh of relief and headed toward his kitchen, where she felt safe.

"We'll need to pack, but first I'm going to jump in the shower," he told her. "Will you be all right out here?"

"Of course." Her heart skipped a beat, though not because she felt threatened. Rather she immediately pictured him in the water, naked body gleaming. The instant rush of desire made her dizzy. Luckily, Eric didn't notice her heightened color.

While Eric showered, MW lost herself in recipes, trying to drown out the bone-numbing terror that grabbed her by the throat every time she realized how close she and Eric had come to dying.

He'd lost his car and nearly his life, due to her. By helping her, this kind and brilliant man risked everything. She didn't understand why, but someday if she was ever able, she'd do her best to repay him.

Though he'd said they were leaving town, she could make something to take with them. Like a dessert or something. Anything to keep her hands and mind busy.

She decided to make brownies, since she'd already made cookies. The simple movements of assembling ingredients and mixing them calmed her, and she lost track of time.

Once dessert was in the oven and cooking, she sighed. Now what? She began washing the mixing bowls and spoons, despite Eric's dishwasher. Humming under her breath, she jumped when the doorbell chimed. Heart pounding, feeling way beyond paranoid, especially since Eric was still in the shower, she looked out the peephole.

Greta. Jiggling her car keys impatiently while she waited for someone to open the door.

Should she let Eric's sister in? Or ignore her visitor and hide in her little cocoon of safety? Did Greta know about the explosion? She knew Eric would probably want to see her.

One had on the doorknob, she took a deep breath and opened the door. She liked Greta and knew she'd welcome the company.

"Honey, I just heard." As soon as MW opened the door, Greta rushed inside and enveloped her in a hug. After squeezing tightly, she pulled back and studied her.

"Are you all right?"

MW nodded. "Yes. And Eric is fine, too. He's in the shower."

Greta nodded. "Was Eric pissed about his Porsche?"

Swallowing, MW sighed. "I imagine he was."

"And relieved that you both made it out without being hurt, I imagine."

"I'm so sorry for endangering your brother. I'd hate for something to happen to him because of me."

"Honey, let me tell you something. My brother is the most hardheaded man I've ever met. If he felt threatened or worried about you being here, you'd already be gone. Now, tell me." Greta took a seat on the edge of the couch. "Have you remembered anything? I'm dying to know your story."

"I actually don't know." MW grimaced, embarrassed that she still couldn't remember. "I'm hoping at least some of my memory comes back soon."

"Nothing? Nothing at all?"

MW tried not to wince. "Sorry, no."

Greta gave an exasperated sigh and smiled. "And here I thought I'd be getting first dibs on hearing what happened to you. Besides Eric, that is."

"I'm sure when I do remember, it won't be that interesting," MW ventured, struck by the irony of her own words.

"Except for the someone-trying-to-kill-you part."

She had a point. MW moved into the kitchen and got them both bottled waters. After handing one to Greta, she shrugged. "I'm trying not to think about that."

"Sorry." Sounding anything but, Greta took a long drink of her water. "And you could regain your memory at any moment, right?"

For some reason, this comment depressed MW. "I suppose I could."

Greta sniffed. "What is that smell? Cake? Brownies? Whatever it is, if it tastes as good as it smells, it's to die for."

"Brownies." And they did smell pretty wonderful. "They still have a few more minutes to go before they're done."

Greta eyed her, her hazel eyes considering. "Do you like to cook?"

"Apparently." Again MW shrugged. "It's something that helps me occupy my time and soothe my frazzled nerves while Eric is at work."

"Speaking of Eric, how's that going? Are you two getting along?"

Oh, good grief. Briefly MW considered pretending not to understand. But there seemed to be no point to that, so she gave a straightforward answer. "He's a good man, your brother. I don't know how I'll ever repay him for how he's helped me."

And she prayed he'd finish his shower pretty soon and get out here so he could deflect some of his sister's curiosity.

Gesturing at the kitchen, Greta smiled. "It looks like you've gotten off to a good start. I imagine Eric hasn't eaten this well in ages."

"It's the least I can do for him considering all he's done for me."

The timer went off. MW took the brownies out of the oven, using a toothpick to check if they were done. "Perfect," she said.

Greta slanted her a look. "I'd like to try one, if that's okay. Unless you're making them for something special."

Special? MW shook her head. "I baked them because puttering around in the kitchen helps calm my nerves. Of course you're welcome to have one or two. I'm sure Eric would want one, too, even though we had dessert at lunch. Let's just let them cool a few minutes before we cut them."

"Lunch? Where'd you go?"

Something in Greta's tone told MW she shouldn't have mentioned going out with Eric. Of course. She flushed. Now Eric's sister would assume they'd been on a date. Flustered, she began cutting into the brownies, even though they were still too hot, which made a jagged line. "A Chinese buffet near the hospital. Really great food."

"I know it. I've been. It's one of Eric's favorites. Speaking of Eric, how well do you know him?" Greta asked, her tone casual as she helped herself to a still hot brownie. "Mmm," she moaned after her first bite. "This is unbelievably delicious."

Not sure what Eric's sister might be getting at, MW took her time replying. Was she actually matchmaking? She couldn't help but wonder if this was the real reason for Greta's impromptu visit.

"I don't," she finally said. "Quite honestly."

Narrow-eyed, Greta studied her while she took another bite of her brownie. "You didn't know him at all before all this happened?"

"No."

"So you're telling me he just happened to be there when you had your accident, showed up at your bedside at the hospital and asked you to move in with him?"

MW blinked. "When you put it that way, it does sound odd. Still, everything about this entire situation is strange."

"True." Greta still watched her closely. "It's so weird that you weren't seriously injured, yet you lost your memory."

Not sure what the other woman was trying to hint at, MW decided she might as well be blunt. "Are you saying you think I'm faking this?"

At MW's serious tone, Greta froze. "Not at all, though I guess I can see how you might have thought that. I just think it's strange, that's all."

Relaxing, MW nodded. "It is bizarre." She couldn't help but glance down the hall toward the still-closed bathroom door. Surely Eric would join them soon.

"Best brownie I've ever eaten." Grabbing a paper towel to wipe off her hands and her mouth, Greta leaned closer. "I'm sorry for the questions, but I'm very protective of my brothers. So, even though you didn't actually know him before your accident, how much do you know about him?"

"Just that he's a doctor and a very kindhearted man. He works a lot, and from what I could tell at the hospital, everyone respects him."

"What about his personal life? Does he ever talk about his family?" She eyed MW, her gaze intense.

Still not sure what Greta's purpose might be, MW continued to answer honestly. "He's mentioned you, of course. And his brother the police officer."

"Ryan." Greta nodded, still watching MW like a hawk. "Nothing about his parents, or the rest of his siblings, or where he grew up?"

Stomach beginning to churn, MW shook her head. "Not really. Why do you ask?"

Greta shrugged. "It's just that Eric never has time for anything. He won't attend family meetings, and I hear from the rest of the family that he rarely even goes home. Did you know our mother is in a coma?"

A coma? Blinking, MW realized how little she actually knew about Eric Colton. "Has she been ill long?"

"That's the thing. She wasn't ill. Someone attacked her. There's been a lot of weird stuff going on at home. Vandalism, fires and one of the family dogs was even attacked. Ryan's been running back and forth, investigating. The entire family has pulled together. Except Eric. Everyone wonders how he can be so…detached."

Detached might be putting it mildly. His mother had been attacked and was fighting for her life. Eric had mentioned none of this, almost as if he felt he needed to keep it from her.

This naturally made her wonder what other secrets the handsome doctor might be hiding.

# Chapter 7

Touchy situation. Aware she might be treading on dangerous ground, MW chose her words carefully. "No, I had no idea. Eric has never mentioned his mother. Since he's a doctor, I'd assume he was consulted on her care."

"Yes. Eric was monitoring her at the hospital, but our father hired around-the-clock nursing and had her moved home. I don't think Eric even visits her." Greta looked away, but not before MW saw the hurt in her eyes.

MW wasn't sure how to respond. "I'm sorry."

A curt nod of her head was Greta's only response.

"You're upset because Eric can't find the time to visit his own family, but can spend time with a stranger," MW guessed. "Again, I apologize, but I'm not at blame here. I'm completely unaware of the family dynamics."

"I know, I know." Finally, Greta smiled. "Nothing against you. I just don't understand my brother sometimes."

"Maybe you and he can discuss this after he gets out of the shower." If he *ever* reappeared. The shower had cut off several minutes ago.

"Maybe." Greta didn't sound too convinced. "But I don't have much time. I'm heading back to Oklahoma City tonight." She gave MW a look full of speculation. "You should know the entire family is buzzing over this."

"This?"

"You and Eric." Greta waved a hand. "I'm just giving you a friendly warning. Be prepared for the nosiness of a large family. If you stay around Eric long, sooner or later, I imagine every one of the Coltons is going to show up on Eric's doorstep so they can meet you."

Should she tell Greta she and Eric were about to go somewhere else? She decided to let him do that, if he ever emerged, which had begun to look less and less likely. For now, she judged it'd be far safer to keep the conversation on trivialities. "How many of you are there?"

Greta smiled, her hazel eyes a much muddier shade than Eric's bright green ones. "Jack's the oldest. He runs the family ranch. Eric's next, then there's Ryan—he's the Tulsa PD Detective. And the youngest of the boys is Brett. And me, of course. I'm the baby as well as the only girl. We also have a half brother named Daniel. All in all, there are five boys and me, the lone female."

"That must have been tough growing up," MW said, meaning it.

"It was, especially when I got boyfriends." Greta laughed. "It worked out, though. Now I'm engaged and living in Oklahoma City." Again, a shadow darkened her eyes. "My mother was very excited about planning my wedding, but since the attack, I've put everything on hold. I refuse to get married without her."

Saddened by this, along with the realization that she didn't even know if she had a mother to miss her, MW nodded. "I understand. When you start planning again, if you need any help, I'm willing. If you'd like, I could even make the cake."

The instant she spoke, she widened her eyes. Where on earth had *that* come from? A wedding cake was a big deal, not something one entrusted to an amateur.

Greta stared at her, clearly at a loss for words. "Actually, I'm planning on having a professional bakery handle that. Thanks for asking," she finally said, obviously trying to be polite.

"I'm sorry. I have no idea why I offered. I know better," MW apologized. "But if there's anything I can do, anything at all, let me know."

Luckily the bathroom door finally opened and Eric emerged, still toweling off his super short hair. He stopped when he caught sight of his sister. MW suddenly realized he wasn't wearing a shirt. His muscular chest attested to workouts with weights. MW struggled not to show her appreciation, though her mouth went dry just looking at him.

"Greta?" Eric looked from one woman to the other. "What are you doing here? What's up?"

Before answering, Greta gave MW a knowing look,

as if she knew about her reaction to Eric's bare, muscular chest. "I'm here because Ryan told me about the explosion. I wanted to make sure you were all right, so I came by on my way back to OKC."

"We're fine." Barefoot, he padded into the room. His low-slung jeans clung to his narrow hips, showcasing his washboard abs.

*Damn.*

MW swallowed and forced herself to look away. As she did, Greta caught her eye and she realized Eric's sister had noticed her reaction. Thankfully, Eric had not.

After exchanging a few more pleasantries, Greta left. Once she'd gone, MW felt unsettled and out of sorts. She needed her memory back immediately. Closing her eyes, she tried to concentrate, despite remembering Eric telling her not to push it.

Nothing. Of course.

"Are you okay?" Eric gave her a long look, his expression inscrutable. She managed to jerk her head in a nod and he turned to head back to his room. Halfway there, he glanced back over his shoulder, catching her eyeing his behind. Even though her cheeks flamed, he didn't appear to notice. "Go ahead and get packed. We'll leave in the morning."

He went into his room and closed the door before she could ask where they were going.

When Eric told his brother where he was taking MW, for once Ryan seemed at a loss for words. But then he sputtered what sounded like a curse and cleared his throat. "Okay, then. So if you truly want to act like a bodyguard for a woman you barely know, why on earth are you taking her to the Lucky C? I'm not sure it's safe there. You know I'm still investigating the attack on Mother."

Once not too long ago, Eric had refused to call Abra *Mother*. Years past, she'd let them all know she preferred her given name. Recently, due to her mellowing with age, she'd made an effort to grow closer to her children. Of them all, Eric had remained distant the longest. Mostly because he had difficulty forgiving, just like his father.

Now, with his mother in a coma from which he wasn't sure she'd wake, he regretted his stubborn pride.

He could forgive, but he knew he'd never forget.

When he'd been a senior in high school and expressed a desire to go into medicine, his father had been furious that his second-oldest son didn't plan to become a rancher like his older brother.

Crushed, Eric had looked to his mother for support. Abra had backed her husband, despite having made an earlier promise to Eric to help out in any way she could. When he'd stuck to his plan, she'd let him know he'd do so without the family's assistance, financially or otherwise. As a result, he was still paying off massive student debt.

But money he could deal with. The lack of support and pride at his accomplishments still rankled. Neither of his parents had attended his college or medical school graduations—both times Abra had conveniently been traveling in Europe. Eventually, she'd come to see the social value of having a physician for a son, but by then Eric's hurt already ran far too deep.

"Earth to Eric?" Ryan sounded amused. "I asked you if you knew there is still a bunch of weird stuff happening out at the ranch. And Mother is still in a coma, as I'm sure you're aware."

"Yes, I am. Though I haven't seen her since Dad moved her out of the hospital. He's assured me she has twenty-four-hour nursing care." That, too, had hurt. Eric hadn't been able to keep from feeling as if his father believed his son the surgeon wasn't competent enough to take care of his own mother.

"She does." Ryan sighed. "Sadly, she hasn't made any progress. And we're no closer to finding out who attacked her. I'm still on the case."

"I figured you were. No one's mentioned catching whoever did it, so…"

Ryan cleared his throat. "Again, in light of that, do you honestly think it's safe to bring MW there?"

"Like I said, the ranch is safer than here," Eric said. "I've already considered all the options. It's a done deal. I'm taking MW to the Lucky C."

Silence. When Ryan spoke again, he sounded dubious. "Have you talked to Dad about this?"

"No. I'm not sure I will, at least until I get there. Everyone's constantly telling me I need to go home more. Now they'll get their wish."

"True." Ryan cleared his throat, apparently waiting for Eric to say more. When he didn't, Ryan continued. "Fine, I understand. It's none of my business. That said, how long are you planning to stay?"

"I took two weeks' vacation."

"Two weeks? As in, fourteen days? Off work?" Ryan spoke as if Eric had just told him he'd quit medicine.

Biting back a laugh, Eric continued. "Yes, from

work. The chief of surgery has been trying to convince me to take time off for a while now. So I did."

"Wow. Just wow. This is one for the record books."

Warring between amusement and annoyance, Eric sighed. "First, everyone bugs me to take a vacation. Then, when I do, it's like I went crazy and jumped off a bridge."

His comment had Ryan chuckling. "Sorry. You just surprised me. Honestly, when you said you'd taken time off, I thought maybe a Friday and a Monday, to make a long weekend. But two whole weeks? That's just not like you. Why so long?"

Scratching his head, Eric decided he might as well admit the truth. "Because that's about the longest I can take away from the hospital." Something he'd never wanted to do before.

"I see." But his brother's tone made it clear he didn't. "Well, I for one am glad. Maybe with you being there, you can save me some trips home."

"What do you mean?"

"I'm always having to run out there for something. After Mother's attack, the drama has continued. It's one thing or another. Vandalism, fires, all kinds of annoying small stuff. Dad keeps threatening to shoot whoever is doing this. Jack's worried about Seth's safety." Their brother Jack's son, Seth, had recently turned five and all of his uncles adored him.

"I'll do whatever I can," Eric said. Privately he wasn't sure what he could do, other than try to keep people calm. "Do you think it might be a disgruntled ranch hand?"

"I've questioned them all. Every single one checks

out." Ryan sighed. "Maybe you can keep an eye open, assess the employees' attitudes."

"I guess I can try. But just so you know, I'm not planning on working the livestock with Dad and Jack." Their oldest brother, like their father, lived and breathed for the ranch. Ryan and Eric's lack of aptitude for ranch work had never sat well with either man.

"Why not?" Ryan teased. "You're taking a vacation, which is so unusual that I wouldn't be surprised if you told me you planned to try your hand at working cattle."

Both men laughed. Though they loved the Lucky C, neither Eric nor Ryan had been able to wait until they could get out of the rancher's lifestyle. Now Ryan worked as a detective in Tulsa and Eric as a surgeon in the same city.

"I guess this means you'll finally start making a few family meetings." Apparently, Ryan couldn't resist one final jab. Once a month, their father called a family meeting. He'd done this ever since they'd been little. Eric despised them and as a result hadn't been to one in years. Of course, he'd never wanted to be too far away from the hospital before either.

"If they have one while I'm staying there, I guess I won't have a choice." He kept his tone mild, ignoring Ryan's chuckle. "Meanwhile, would you mind swinging by here and picking me up and taking me to get a rental car? I need something to drive until I can buy a new vehicle."

"Another sports car?"

"Maybe. I haven't even thought that far ahead. This has been a shock. Right now I just need something to drive."

"Sure, I'll take you. I'm on my way," Ryan said.

After ending the call, Eric went to check on MW. Though she'd clearly packed, he found her sitting on the edge of her bed, so lost in her thoughts she didn't notice his approach.

"Hey." He kept his voice soft, not wanting to startle her. "Ryan's going to come by and take me to get a rental car. Will you be okay here or do you want to come with us?"

"Which do you think would be safer?" she asked, unable to hide the quick flash of fear from her expression.

He took an impulsive step toward her, barely stopping himself from touching her. "Come with. Ryan's a detective with the Tulsa PD. I'm sure you'll be safe if you go with us. Plus, you get to meet my brother."

Her gaze searched his face. Finally, she nodded. "That sounds good. Greta told me you have a large family, so meeting them one at a time might be easier."

He still hadn't told her where they were going. Since the ranch was the hub around which their entire family revolved, she'd be meeting a lot of people at once. To minimize stress, he figured he'd wait until they were on the way before he filled her in. "Are you all ready?" he asked. When she nodded, he told her he hadn't packed a single thing and hurried off to his room to get started.

When Ryan arrived, rather than ringing the bell, he rapped on the front door in a drum-like cadence. Grinning, Eric let him in, giving him a quick, one-armed guy hug. MW hung back, almost as if afraid.

Releasing his brother, Eric turned him to face MW. Noting her wide eyes and heightened color, he smiled, hoping to reassure her. As their gazes locked, a slow smile blossomed over her face, making Eric's chest tighten.

He cleared his throat. "Ryan, meet MW. MW, this is my brother Ryan."

"I'm pleased to meet you," she said, holding out her hand. "Since we don't know my name, Eric calls me MW for Mystery Woman. I'm pleased to meet you."

Instead of shaking hands, Ryan pulled her in for a hug. He met Eric's eyes, his own full of approval, as he released her.

She exhaled and stepped back. "You two look a lot alike," she said, glancing from one to the other. "I'm not sure who has the shortest hair."

"Ryan does," Eric put in. "He keeps his in a military cut. I keep mine short for convenience."

At his words, Ryan snorted. "Convenience. Right."

MW's uncertain expression told Eric she wasn't sure whether to be amused or worried. Clearly, she'd never had a brother or a sister.

She continued to eye Ryan, almost as if she was afraid he might bite her.

"What's wrong?" Eric asked.

Slowly, she shook her head. "I'm not sure. Ryan, were you there the night I got hit by that car?"

"No, ma'am. I was not. Why?"

"I don't know. You look…" She blew out her breath in exasperation. "So familiar."

As Ryan studied her, Eric couldn't miss the appreciative glint in his brother's gaze. The flash of jealousy tightening his gut stunned him.

He pushed away the thought and took her arm. From

the way Ryan narrowed his eyes, Eric knew his brother had noted the possessive gesture.

"Are you ready to go?" Eric asked, aware of his curt tone.

"Sure," Ryan drawled, giving him another long look. "Let's do this."

Once they'd all piled into Ryan's police cruiser—he made MW ride in the back, claiming it would be safer—they took off. On the drive, Ryan peppered her with a steady stream of questions. She didn't know the answers to most of them, of course. Hearing the growing frustration in her voice, Eric shot Ryan a warning look, but either his brother didn't see or chose to ignore it.

Finally, after hearing MW's husky voice apologize for what seemed like the twentieth time, Eric spoke up. "Stop. What are you doing?" he asked, glaring at his brother.

"What do you mean?" One corner of Ryan's mouth quirked up, as if he found Eric's aggravation amusing.

"Why are you interrogating her? She has spotty memory. It's coming back, but slowly. All the questions you're asking are making her feel worse."

Ryan glanced back over his shoulder at MW, who sat silently. "Is that true, sweetheart? Am I bothering you?"

*Sweetheart?* Pretending the endearment didn't rankle, Eric half turned in his seat to look at her. "It's okay. You can tell him the truth."

Her sigh expressed her frustration better than any words. "I figure he's doing what comes naturally to him. He's a cop. They question. I understand that. I'm more upset with myself since I can't remember anything."

"Not your fault." Again Eric shot Ryan a warning glare. "It'll come back in its own time."

Though Ryan shook his head, he didn't ask any more questions, much to Eric's relief.

Though Eric had originally requested a sports car, he changed his mind and decided he'd ask for a mid-size SUV. He wasn't sure why exactly, since he loved a fast car. But with MW and the ranch, he wanted something different.

When they pulled up at the car rental agency, the black Chevy Tahoe waiting for him fitted the bill perfectly.

Ryan hung around until Eric completed the paperwork, apparently to protect MW. Eric appreciated this, though part of him wanted to tell his brother he was perfectly capable of protecting her himself. The fierceness of his resolve didn't shock him—he'd always been determined and focused on something when he wanted it.

Or someone? Again, the odd thought. Since logic and facts had never failed him before, he applied them here while the rental clerk entered information in the computer.

MW was a very attractive woman. Her curves, her curly mop of light brown hair and the way her beautiful eyes sparked with life drew him to her. This was completely normal; as a healthy male, he'd expect no different from himself.

Just because he desired her didn't mean they'd become involved. He actually didn't have time for anything like that. He'd keep her safe until she figured out who she was, find out who was trying to kill her and why, and then he'd go back to his normal, busy and very fulfilling life.

Trying not to be nervous, MW waited in the lobby while Eric put their bags inside the SUV. If the counter clerk found it odd that her latest two customers had arrived in a police cruiser, she didn't comment. She didn't even raise a brow when a uniformed Ryan carried two duffel bags inside and set them on the floor. She'd packed her cookies and the brownies in a couple of plastic containers and Ryan brought them in, too.

Now Ryan had gone and Eric had finished the paperwork and had the keys in his hand. "Are you all right?" he asked, unsmiling.

She nodded.

"I'm sorry about all that." His gaze came up to study her face.

It took her a second to understand. "You mean about Ryan and his questions? That didn't bother me. I meant what I said. He was just doing what comes naturally. His job. He's your brother and wanted to look out for you."

He shook his head. "As long as you're okay…"

"I'm fine."

"Then let's get on the road." His green eyes glinted with either mischief or humor. "I'm glad you're so understanding. Just wait until you meet the rest of my family."

As she climbed up into the passenger seat, she found herself smiling at him. "If they're all as nice as Greta and Ryan, I can hardly wait."

"You won't be waiting for long," Eric said, smiling

back. His smile made her stomach turn somersaults, making her wonder what it must be like for his female patients. She'd bet most of them, no matter how old or how married, had a crush on their handsome doctor.

Eric gazed at her a moment longer before he started the engine. MW resisted the urge to squirm, glad he couldn't read her mind, even as her cheeks once again heated. And then they were off.

After they went through the rest of downtown, Eric picked up Route 75 and headed northeast.

"Are you ever going to tell me where we're going?" she finally asked. Now that they'd left the city and suburbs behind, the northeastern Oklahoma countryside looked surprisingly beautiful. Though much of her past remained a huge blank, MW felt it was safe to say she'd never visited this part of the country before.

He glanced over at her and then squeezed her shoulder. She wanted to lean into his side and take more of the comfort he offered, but glad of the seat belt, she didn't, aware nothing good could come of such a thing. She felt his touch through the lightweight material of her T-shirt, and swallowed hard, wondering how such a small thing could make her dizzy with desire.

"I wondered when you were going to ask," he said, leaving his hand for another second before returning it to the steering wheel. "I'm taking you to stay at my family's ranch."

She stared at him, not registering his words at first. When his meaning sank in, she couldn't conceal her shock. "Why? I mean, it's enough that you were kind and took me in so I wasn't out living on the streets. But someone wants to kill me. Bringing me around your family could also endanger them."

Eric only shook his head, his confident expression telling her he didn't put much stock in her fears. "The Lucky C is really remote. We have 4,250 acres. Believe me, no one will be able to find you there."

Instantly, tears welled in her eyes. "Are you sure you want to do that? Because of me, you almost died. And Greta could have been hurt as well. If you take me around the rest of your family, you'll be putting all of them at risk."

He smiled. "You don't know my family. Once I tell them what's going on, there's no way any strangers are getting anywhere near the Lucky C."

Still she persisted. "What if they do? Then what?"

"They won't. Don't worry. You'll be safe there."

Since he sounded so certain, she decided to believe him and dropped the subject.

Finally they left the interstate for a paved two-lane road. Ahead of them, the gently sloping plains seemed to stretch out for miles of warm gold and green.

"It's lovely," she said, wondering why the rolling hills and deep blue sky brought her such peace.

"We're almost there. The ranch is a beautiful place," Eric told her, smiling again. "It's a mix of flatlands and hills. We raise Hereford cattle. Ranching is something my family has always done. My father's father, him, and now my oldest brother, Jack."

The pride in his voice made her smile again. "You love it, don't you?"

He nodded, his eyes glowing. "I do. I can't live here, the lifestyle is not for me, but this is where I grew up. It's amazing."

After driving down a long, winding drive, they pulled up to black wrought iron gates flanked by a stone wall that seemed to stretch for miles. A large metal *C* decorated the middle of each gate.

"This is it." He rolled down his window and punched a code in to the metal control box. A moment later, the gates began to swing open.

"Wow." After they pulled through, she turned back to watch as the gates closed behind them. "Pretty nice."

"Just wait." His boyish smile softened the hard planes of his face. Again, she was struck dumb by the sheer masculine beauty of him. "You ain't seen nothin' yet."

Chest tight, she smiled back, hoping he couldn't tell how he affected her.

A huge building loomed in the distance. As they drew closer, she saw that it was a two-story house. A *huge* two-story house. All angles, with vaguely European architecture and tons of windows.

She couldn't believe what she was seeing. "This is a ranch house?" she asked, incredulous. "It looks more like something I'd see in the Hollywood Hills."

He laughed, but she wasn't kidding. The house had to be at least ten thousand square feet, probably more. She found herself wondering when she'd been to Hollywood.

"My father had this place built for my mother. The old house was the original homestead. It's located two miles south of this one."

"Gorgeous," she marveled. "I love the way it fits in with the landscape."

"That's because the outside is made of native Oklahoma stone."

Again she had to smile at the pride ringing in his voice. "How big is it?"

"It's roughly eleven thousand square feet, with seven bedrooms and 7.5 bathrooms."

She gasped. "You could fit ten of my apartments in there." It dawned on her that she'd remembered something.

Eric grinned, apparently realizing that as well. "So you lived in an apartment somewhere."

Frowning, she tried to remember. "In a city. A good-size one."

"Do you remember which city?"

Just like that, the wisp of memory dissipated. "No." She let her regret show in her voice. "I'm sorry, I don't."

"No worries. It'll come in time."

She'd started out believing him. But the longer she went without a solid memory, the more she began to wonder if she'd ever remember. "Tell me more about the house," she said, needing the distraction.

"Dad situated it on the highest point of our land, so we have unlimited views in all directions. He even put in a full basement, so we have a built-in tornado shelter."

"Tornado?" At the thought, she shivered. "I forgot Oklahoma is in Tornado Alley."

"No one here ever forgets that. Every spring and most falls, we are forcibly reminded."

"I'm glad you have a safe place to hide." Staring at the mansion, she shook her head. "I can't imagine growing up in a house like that."

"There are a lot of us, so we needed the room." He parked. "There's a pool out back, too. Let me tell you, we kids made use of that every summer growing up."

She tried to search her memory to see if she'd ever experienced anything like that, and realized with a degree of shock that she hadn't. "I grew up in the city," she said slowly. "Whatever city my apartment is located in. We didn't have a lot of room, but there was love."

Expression incredulous, he stared at her. "You remember?"

Stunned, she stared back. "I do." Bemused, she considered. "Not everything. But when you were talking about your childhood, that came to me in a flash. I don't remember where, or where my mom and dad are now. But that's something, right? More than I've been able to remember in days."

His encouraging smile struck her as unconsciously sexy. Damn. She felt warm all over and barely resisted fanning herself, aware he wouldn't understand or worse, if he did, he'd be appalled. Clearly, he had no idea of his appeal.

Parking the rental car, he turned to look at her. Something in his expression told her he might just be as nervous as she was.

"Are you ready to go in?" he asked. She caught herself swaying toward him, compelled by the most powerful urge to kiss him. And not a tentative movement of her lips on his either, but the slow and deep kiss of a confident woman who knew what she wanted.

*Him.* She wanted him.

Stunned, she turned away and reached sightlessly for the door handle. How could she, with no memory of her past, of her likes and dislikes, her passions or pleasures, find this man so utterly fascinating?

She barely knew him. Since she didn't understand the reasoning, she figured it had to be a physical thing only. After all, Dr. Eric Colton was a fine masculine specimen. Handsome and virile, confident and kind. Exactly the kind of man any woman would want. And the kind of man who didn't look twice at a women like her.

Which made her wonder why he'd decided to protect her himself.

MW considered herself a realist. She had access to mirrors and was well aware she wasn't a conventional beauty. Not the model sort at all, with her curves and the few extra pounds sampling her own cooking had clearly put on her frame.

As her memories seeped in, she knew she'd been both capable and confident, with an optimistic and outgoing personality.

What?

Another realization, another snippet of truth from her past life.

Now completely out of the car, she faced the house, still lost in thought. Had there been a man in her past, someone she'd cared for but who had let her down?

And was that man named Walter, the name Eric said she'd called out after the car had hit her?

# Chapter 8

Mildly apprehensive, Eric got out of the Tahoe and hurried around to help MW. Judging from the quick and nervous smile she flashed, she needed reassurance.

He figured she didn't need to know how long it had been since he'd set foot on Colton land.

"You'll be fine," he said. "I promise you, they don't bite."

At his teasing tone, some of the tension went out of her shoulders. "You're right. I'm being foolish." Though she managed a smile, uncertainty still lurked in her pale blue eyes.

Again, he fought the urge to reach for her and offer comfort. But then he realized there was no harm in offering reassurance, so he snagged her arm and pulled her up against him. Damn if he didn't like the way she felt.

Just as he'd begun considering taking it a step further with a kiss, the front door swung open.

"Eric!"

Edith. Keeping a casual arm draped around MW, he turned to face the family's long-term housekeeper and oftentimes mother figure.

"I can't believe it's you," Edith said, beaming as she hurried down the marble front steps. As usual, she wore her silver-gray hair in a tight bun.

He kept MW close as Edith reached them, letting the older woman pull them both in for a fierce hug.

"You're home," Edith's voice shook. Eric saw, to his shock, the tears glistening in her gray eyes. "It's been far too long."

Resisting the urge to hang his head, Eric nodded instead. "It has been. I'm sorry for that. But this time, I plan to stay awhile."

His words appeared to temporarily mollify her. Edith wiped at her eyes, and then fixed her attention on MW. "And who do we have here?"

Eric performed the introductions, keeping his tone casual. "MW, meet Edith Turner. She's been with our family since I was thirteen. Edith, this is MW."

If any of Eric's siblings had filled the housekeeper in on MW's story, Edith didn't reveal it. Instead, she hugged MW again, a full-fledged hug this time. "I'm so glad to finally meet any woman Eric has chosen to bring home," she said.

As MW's creamy skin flamed red, Eric understood what Edith apparently thought. He was about to correct her misconception, but one look at the panic in MW's gaze and he changed his mind. For right now, it'd be easier if people thought he and MW were together. At least until her memory returned.

Plus, he had to admit part of him really wanted Edith's assumption to become truth. Sort of. At least for a little while.

Then, because he knew MW would be horrified if she knew his thoughts, he focused his attention back on Edith.

"Your father will be so happy to see you," Edith said, still beaming. "Unfortunately, he and Jack are working in the north pastures today. Brett and Daniel are with him."

"Which means Seth…"

"Is helping the men." Edith checked her stylish watch. "He loves to help his daddy and Pa Pa."

"Did he finally graduate from Pooh Bear?" The little cream-and-tan pony had been Seth's first steed and was the perfect size for a five-year-old, even one with long legs.

"No. Seth's riding on Jack's horse with him. His daddy wanted him to spend an hour or so rounding up cattle. He should be bringing him back anytime now."

Scanning the horizon for a sign of his brother, Eric nodded. "A young boy with a short attention span won't be conducive to getting a lot of work done." Nonetheless, Eric remembered when his father, Big J, had done the same with him. And all the rest of the siblings. They'd learned to ride when they could barely walk. Even now, when he had been away from the saddle for years, Eric knew he remained a skilled horseman.

"Come on inside." Edith took MW's arm and led her up the front staircase, trusting Eric would follow. "Don't be intimidated by this fancy place. Though it looks all la-ti-da on the outside, the Coltons are just a bunch of regular people."

MW smiled shyly. "That's good to know."

Once inside, Eric saw the place hadn't changed one bit since he'd last visited. Same old two-story, open foyer with marble floors. The grand fireplace, the Venetian plaster walls. White and sparsely finished, the living room served one purpose only—to make a statement. No one ever used it. He'd often thought it would be better served if they'd take out the fancy furniture, put in a wet bar and pool table and turn it into a game room. But he knew his mother would never go for that.

"This way," Edith said, noticing MW's hesitation. "The faster you walk through the stuffiness, the better."

One corner of her mouth curling in amusement, MW shot Eric a look.

"She speaks the truth," he said, grinning. "My mother set up that front room as a showpiece. We all avoid it whenever possible."

"But it's such a lovely fireplace." MW cast a look over her shoulder. "I bet that's wonderful in the winter."

"We have another in the family room."

The kitchen and the family room were much warmer, the leather couches clearly lived-in.

"Upstairs are five bedrooms, each with their own baths," Eric told MW. "There are seven bedrooms total, and seven baths. All of us kids had our own rooms growing up. Now, Brett's the only one left still here."

"Not for long," Edith pointed out. "Once Hannah and Brett get married, they're planning to move into that new house they've started building."

"True. But the two of them are still the only ones living here in this gigantic house with Mom and Dad."

"And the on-call nurse," Edith pointed out, her voice matter-of-fact. "She's been given one of the guest rooms near your mother."

And just like that, the mood went somber. MW looked uncertain, shifting her weight from one leg to the other.

"Are we staying here?"

Though he was about to say yes, Eric reconsidered. "I'm thinking we might stay at the old house. I think it'll be a lot easier."

Edith pursed her lips, looking as if she'd tasted something sour. "I thought you said you were here to visit," she pointed out. "This is where the family comes together for meals, you know that. Your father will be terribly disappointed if you stay at the old house."

Privately, Eric doubted that. The old house—the original homestead—was located two miles south of the main house. It was a five-thousand-square-foot, ranch-style home built of wood and hand-carved stone. Eric had always loved the place. After the main house had been built, the old house had been used mainly for ranch meetings and the occasional guest. Eric thought longingly of the comfy furnishings and the way the numerous windows always let in a lot of light.

MW touched his arm, bringing him out of his thoughts. "We should stay here," she said softly. "I don't mind."

"I like her," Edith announced, before Eric had a chance to answer. "Now let me get you two some snacks and a drink." She headed toward the kitchen without waiting for a response.

Eric shook his head. "Well, I guess that's a done deal then."

"I'm sorry." Looking stricken, MW moved closer. "If staying here makes you uncomfortable, of course we'll stay at the other house. I shouldn't have said anything."

"I'm glad you did." This close, if he bent his head he could inhale the scent of her shampoo. He felt unable to resist the temptation.

"You are?" She raised her face to look at him, catching him in the act. He didn't care, though, because now all he could think about was how badly he wanted to kiss her perfect rosebud mouth.

Heat suffused him. But before he could give in to temptation, Edith bustled back into the room with a tray full of goodies and interrupted him.

"Here you go," she announced, setting the tray in the center of the coffee table. "I didn't know what you might be in the mood for, so I've got a little of everything. Cookies, fruits and vegetables, even chips and dip."

The whole family had always admired the way Edith could whip up a tray of snacks and make it look like they been delivered by a high-end caterer.

"Wow." MW's eyes were wide. "That looks absolutely fantastic."

Edith beamed, clearly pleased at the compliment. "Just a minute," she said. "I'll bring you something to drink. Would you like iced tea, lemonade or water?"

He noticed she didn't offer anything carbonated, which might mean she'd finally been successful in banishing all soda pop from the main house.

"Water, please," MW said.

"I'd love tea," Eric responded. "Unsweetened."

"I know that." Edith's frown made Eric want to laugh. It was the exact same, highly dramatic expression she'd used when he'd been an unruly teen and she'd chastised him for something. "I've been making your iced tea ever since you were thirteen," she reminded. "I didn't think you'd change the way you drink it just because you went to live in the city."

Before he could reply, she sailed out of the room, head held high.

"She's something else," Eric told MW, who'd watched the exchange with a slightly shocked expression. "I love her dearly."

"As she does you," MW replied softly. She couldn't seem to stop eyeing the food, making him realize she must be hungry. Of course she was. They hadn't eaten anything since that morning.

At the thought, his stomach growled.

Edith returned, bearing yet another smaller tray with their drinks and paper plates and napkins. She set this down next to the snack tray. "Here you go. Dig in. Enjoy."

And she perched on the edge of one of the armchairs, fixing Eric with a stern look. "Eat up."

MW evidently didn't need any prodding. She'd already gotten busy piling food on her paper plate, mostly fruit and vegetables. "I'm saving the cookies for last," she said, catching him watching her. Making a cute face, she popped a bit of apple into her mouth.

Smiling, Eric helped himself, too. He didn't know what it was about her, but simply being around MW made him feel good. Sure, lately just getting within a few feet of her got him aroused, but if he managed to put that aside, he realized he actually *liked* her. A lot. She was fun and sweet and sexy, not to mention a damn good cook.

While Eric and MW ate, Edith kept up a steady stream of chatter, mostly about everything that had been going on around the ranch. Content to listen, Eric did the same as MW, finishing up his healthy snack with a sinfully delicious oatmeal-raisin cookie. "Edith's specialty," he said when MW made sounds of pure pleasure after her first bite.

"This is delicious," MW said once she'd devoured her cookie. "I'd love the recipe, if you don't mind sharing."

Eric held his breath. Though she'd been asked many times over the years, Edith had never divulged the recipe for her famous cookies.

"Are you a cook?" Edith asked, smiling appreciatively when MW reached for a second cookie.

"I brought some cookies and some brownies," MW answered. "Once you try them, you can tell me what you think."

"Are you good at it or just learning?" Edith persisted.

"She's pretty good," Eric answered for MW, since she'd taken another bite and her mouth was full. "Almost as good as you."

Edith harrumphed, though she knew he was teasing. Plus, he'd said *almost*, which meant she couldn't get insulted.

The sound of the front door opening had them all turning.

Eric heard the pitter-patter of small feet running, and then his nephew, Seth, burst into the room.

"Uncle Eric!" Grinning, his green Colton eyes sparkling with excitement, the five-year-old launched himself at Eric.

Eric easily caught him. "How did you know I was here?" he asked, tousling the kid's already shaggy dark brown hair.

"Edith texted Daddy!"

Texted? Eric met the older woman's gaze over Seth's head. "When did you get so modern?"

"You'd know if you'd come home more," Edith gently chided him.

Before Eric could respond, his oldest brother, Jack, strode into the room, cowboy hat in hand. Since he'd met and married Tracy McCain, he appeared much more content and relaxed. When he caught sight of Eric, he stopped short and stared.

"You're really here," he drawled. "I almost thought Edith was joking."

Eric stood. "Edith wouldn't tease about something like that. How're you doing, big brother?"

They clasped each other close for a quick hug. Once they'd let go, Jack's sharp green gaze went to MW.

"Who do we have here?"

Eyeing him warily, she stood. "I'm MW."

"Eric's friend," Edith put in helpfully.

One brow rose as Jack studied her. She held out her hand and he shook it, then he again looked at Eric. "Your *friend*, huh? I'm glad you decided to bring her here to meet the family."

Though he knew what Jack thought, Eric didn't correct him. "Where's Dad?"

"He's still working." Jack dragged a hand through

his longish hair. "As a matter of fact, I need to get back out there to help. We're separating calves today."

"How about everyone meet here for dinner tonight?" Edith put in. "I'll cook us a feast, if you'll make sure everyone knows."

"Oh, that's not necessary," Eric tried, well aware he was fighting a losing battle. "No need to make a big deal out of anything."

Edith fixed him with her steely gaze. "You coming home for an extended visit *is* a big deal. I'm cooking, the family is coming to eat. Understood?"

Amused, Eric exchanged a look with his brother. "Yes, ma'am," he answered.

"Great. I'll make sure everyone is here." Jack crammed his cowboy hat back on his head and hurried out of the room.

Only then did Eric think to check on MW's reaction. He imagined the concept of a family get-together might intimidate her. Instead, she eyed Edith with a glint of respect in her eyes. When she caught Eric looking at her, she smiled. "Sounds like fun," she said, lifting her chin.

"If only you knew."

Tsking softly, Edith made a shooing motion. "Why don't you take MW and show her around? I've got to get busy if I'm going to have a feast for y'all ready to eat in a few hours."

Eric grinned and gave her a mock salute. Taking MW's hand, he pulled her toward the huge curving staircase. "Come on. I know you want to see the upstairs."

She shrugged and allowed him to tug her along. "I'd really like to see your old room."

The soft admission startled him. "Why?"

"I'm not sure." Her shy smile heated his blood. "Maybe because I can't remember my own past, I want to share yours."

Inexplicably, his throat felt tight. "Unfortunately, Mother had most of our rooms redone into guest rooms years ago. I could show you which one was mine, but there won't be anything of mine there."

"Oh. I guess that makes sense." She sounded so disappointed, he wanted to kiss her.

Because he needed to rein himself in, he showed her every bedroom on the second floor, except for Brett's and Greta's. Even though Greta had moved to Oklahoma City, she'd declared her room was to be untouched. Surprisingly, their mother had abided by her daughter's wishes.

"What about your parents?" MW asked. "Where are their rooms?"

He blanched, unable to hide his reaction. "They have separate suites downstairs. My mother's has been partitioned off, so the live-in nurse will have a place to sleep."

"I can wait in the family room if you'd like to go visit her."

Her not-too-subtle hint wasn't lost on him. "You don't have to wait. You can come with me if you want to."

He waited for her to decline. After all, why would anyone want to visit a woman in a coma whom she didn't know? He couldn't say why, but it suddenly seemed very important that MW accompany him.

Instead, MW squeezed his hand, making him realize he still held hers. "I'll go. Since you haven't seen her in a while, I figure you could probably use the support."

He didn't remind her of his occupation. As a physician, particularly as a surgeon, he'd grown used to seeing the human condition in all its frailties.

But then again, this was his own mother. He well remembered the last time he'd seen her, on the day Big J had announced he was having her moved out of the hospital.

Eric had argued and then, failing to convince his father, he'd pleaded. If she stayed at Tulsa General, Eric could monitor Abra's care, make sure she got the best treatment. He could look after her and would be there the instant she needed anything.

Big J had moved her anyway. Out here, to the remote and isolated ranch where medical help was a long drive away. Crushed and disappointed, Eric hadn't gone home since. Ryan kept him filled in on their mother's health status which always seemed to be unchanged.

"Are you all right?" MW's concerned voice broke through his thoughts. He glanced at her, finding her steady blue gaze calming.

"Yes." Inhaling deeply, he squared his shoulders and looked toward the stairs. "Let's go down and see my mother."

Side by side, they descended to the first floor. Glad of MW's small hand in his, Eric realized he felt slightly apprehensive. Not normal, not for him.

At the entrance to Abra's room, he hesitated. In a hospital, the closed door would have meant something, like a nurse was giving a sponge bath, or they were running tests. As a doctor, he'd always been able to enter. As a family member of a patient, he knew he should knock. Here, he didn't know the protocol.

Glancing at MW, who gave him a small nod, he raised his fist and knocked.

"Come in," a soft voice answered.

Eric pushed open the door and stepped inside the room.

Just like in a nursing home, the sharp odor of disinfectant mingled with the smell of various bodily fluids and permeated the room. Abra lay motionless on the hospital bed, reminding him of so many patients he'd treated over the years.

Coma patients were difficult. Often, their vital signs were good—heartbeat strong, lungs working—which made their lack of brain activity incomprehensible to grieving families.

He totally understood how they felt. Even knowing the medical science behind it, seeing his own mother lying so still, her normally animated face slack and lifeless, made him want to ram his fist through the wall.

She'd lost weight, her aristocratic face all hollows and shadows. Her hair, usually so beautifully styled, looked lank and lifeless. She looked like many of the seriously ill patients Eric saw on a regular basis at work.

A lump formed in his throat as he approached the bed. Behind him, he dimly realized MW had stopped in the doorway. He didn't blame her.

"Hey, Mom," he said softly, telling himself there was a 70 percent chance she could hear him. "Sorry I haven't been by to see you in a while."

He was a doctor, he knew better, but damned if he

didn't catch himself holding his breath waiting for a reaction. Expecting his mother to open her eyes and smile at him.

When of course she didn't, he had to swallow past the sudden lump in his throat.

"Anyway," he continued briskly. "I'm staying for a couple of weeks. I brought someone with me. A woman." If there was anything that could make Abra wake up, any of her boys bringing someone home would do it. "I'd love for you to meet her. She's got some memory problems and maybe you could help her."

He almost could have sworn he saw his mother's eyelids flutter. Almost. If he hadn't been a trained medical professional, he might have believed it. Even now, he watched intently, willing it to happen.

"Hi, Mrs. Colton." MW's husky voice felt more than welcome in the aching silence. As she moved to stand at Eric's side, she slipped her fingers into his and squeezed his hand.

To his absolute amazement, he felt tears pricking the backs of his eyes. He cleared his throat to cover his display of emotion, continuing to stare at his mother.

When he didn't speak again, MW did. "You have a very beautiful home," she said. "And tonight, I'm going to meet your entire family. I sure wish you could be there."

Still nothing. But then, he knew better than to hope for a miracle.

"Come on, MW." He gave her hand a little tug. "Let's go see where we're going to be sleeping."

MW looked at him, and then back at his mother. "Okay," she finally said, a hint of sadness in her voice. When they reached the doorway, still hand in hand, she glanced back over her shoulder. "It was nice to meet you, Mrs. Colton."

Not until they were several paces down the hall did Eric feel like a huge, invisible weight had been lifted from his chest and he could breathe again.

Edith waited for them near the staircase. "I've had two rooms prepared." Her tone dared them to argue.

Amused, Eric simply nodded. "Lead the way."

Stopping in front of a room near the top of the stairs, Edith smiled. "Dinner will be at 6:30. Since Abra can't be here, there's no need to dress up."

"Really?" For his entire life, Eric's mother had insisted everyone dress nice for dinner. Which meant dresses for the women, and slacks and a button-down shirt for the men.

"Yes, really." Edith fixed him with a stern look. "Jeans and T-shirts are what everyone wears these days. As long as they're clean, there's no problem."

"That's good," MW put in. "As I only have two dresses, and they're both sundresses."

Now it was Edith's turn to stare. "Two dresses?"

"Yes. Greta picked them out for me."

At the mention of Eric's sister's name, Edith's expression softened. "Ah, well, then. If Greta chose a dress, I'm sure it's nice." She opened a door and gestured inside. "Here's your room. You have your own connected bathroom. Your bag is already inside. I'll leave you here to rest and freshen up before dinner."

"And gather your strength," Eric put in, only half kidding.

MW simply nodded. "Thank you," she said, and went inside and closed the door.

Edith led Eric down the hall to his old bedroom.

Of course, it no longer bore even the slightest resemblance to the room he'd had as a child. His mother had redone each of the bedrooms with a different theme. If he remembered right, his had been done in patriotic colors of red, white and blue. Her bold designs made him wince, but he didn't have to live there, so he'd kept quiet.

When they reached his door, Edith turned and put her hand on his arm. "She seems like a nice girl."

"She is."

"Greta told me what happened to her and how you're helping her out."

"Greta did? When?"

At least Edith had the grace to appear sheepish. "Just now. I called her while you were visiting with your mother."

"Of course you did." He hadn't forgotten Edith's penchant for prying, so he wasn't surprised. "Then I'm sure you know I brought her here to keep her safe."

"Which may not have been the best idea. Ryan still hasn't caught whoever attacked your mother."

Eric nodded. "True, but I have a feeling that attack was personal. Someone who knows her."

"That's what Ryan thinks, too." Edith sighed. "I hope they catch whoever it is soon. And I pray every day your mother regains consciousness. Her illness is taking an awful toll on this family. I'm tired of worrying."

Eric hugged her, the same type of reassuring hug he sometimes gave to a patient's worried family. To his surprise, Edith sagged against him, briefly letting herself relax.

Since Edith's strong shoulders had, more than anyone else's, been what Eric and his brothers had relied on growing up, this gave him pause.

And then Edith straightened her shoulders and moved away. "Did you meet your mother's nurse?"

"No. I wondered about that. I didn't see hide nor hair of one."

"Well, she's here. After dinner, pop on back into your mother's room and introduce yourself."

The direct order made him smile. "I will."

"Good. Remember, dinner at 6:30." Her no-nonsense tone told him he'd better not dare to comment on her brief lapse. So he nodded and went into his room, closing the door behind him, remembering what Ryan had said about the never-ending volatility of life at the ranch. He couldn't keep from hoping he'd just experienced all of it that he would during his two-week stay, but he had a feeling the drama might just be beginning.

## Chapter 9

As MW had suspected it might be, the family get-together for dinner was sort of an organized chaos. Though Greta had gone home to Oklahoma City and wasn't in attendance, Ryan drove out for the meal. At MW's side, Eric had muttered that this was no doubt because his brother wanted a front-row seat to Eric's impending inquisition.

Despite her own nervousness, this statement made MW laugh.

Eric's father, Big J, had taken one look at him and pulled him in for a tight and quick hug, after which he'd headed toward the sideboard where he'd poured himself a three-fingered glass of scotch.

Eric shot her a quick look and mouthed, "Some things never change."

But when Big J offered to pour Eric a glass, judging from his surprised look, she guessed some things actually did.

As family members arrived, everyone talked at once, alternating between hugging MW and staring at her. She met Big J and Eric's half brother, Daniel, a handsome man who resembled Eric, but also appeared to be part Native American. "I'm a quarter Cherokee," he explained, almost as if he'd read her mind.

Though she knew she'd have trouble remembering the names, she met Eric's younger brother Brett, who was the spitting image of Eric and his other brother Jack.

Brett's fiancée, Hannah, a lovely woman with jet-black hair, smiled. Her curvy body showed off her pregnancy. MW tried not to stare, but when Hannah caught her looking, her smile only widened. "It's okay," she said, winking. "I seem to get larger by leaps and bounds."

MW nodded, not sure how to respond. One thing she could say for Eric's family, they were friendly. Each and every one of them, man or woman, pulled her close in a hug. Though she couldn't say for sure since her memory still hadn't returned, she thought she might not be used to this kind of greeting. Maybe not, but she found she liked it.

After the adults had finished, Seth ran right up to her and gave her yet another enthusiastic hug, which melted her heart.

Jack's wife, Tracy, a delicate, blond-haired woman with a calm sort of grace, introduced herself. "Don't worry," she said, correctly gauging MW's trepidation. "They're nice. You get used to them."

Again MW found herself laughing. "I'm trying to

relax. I just hope no one asks me any questions I can't answer."

For a moment confusion registered in Tracy's pale blue eyes. Then she nodded. "That's right. You have no memory of your past, do you?"

"I'm afraid not."

Seth tugged on his stepmother's arm. "I'm hungry," he announced, his clear and childish voice carrying to every corner of the room. "When are we going to eat?"

"I'm sure it will be soon," Tracy soothed, smoothing his hair with a loving gesture.

Just then, Edith rang the small dinner bell to indicate it was time. Relief flooding her, MW looked for Eric. To her relief, he crossed the room to her side and took her arm. "Are you okay?" he murmured.

She nodded yes.

As the family filed into the dining room, each and every person smiled reassuringly at MW, as if to empathize with her. Though she wondered if she'd be able to remember all their names, the small kindnesses warmed her heart and made her feel welcome.

Apparently everyone had assigned seats. As they all took them, Eric pulled out a chair for her. "Greta's usual place," he told her quietly. "Since she's in Oklahoma City these days, I don't think anyone will mind if you use it."

She nodded and sat. Across the table, Seth stared, his green Colton eyes wide.

"It's okay," she told him. "Greta told me I could sit here."

Relaxing, Seth nodded. He looked up at his father and tugged on his arm. When Jack leaned down, his son whispered in his ear. Jack nodded, then looked over at MW and winked.

Though she felt her face heat, she managed to smile back.

"You seem to be handling this pretty well," Eric commented in her ear, his warm breath sending a shiver up her spine. "I know this can be pretty overwhelming if you're not used to it."

"It's actually really nice."

Edith entered the room, carrying a platter with a perfectly sliced roast, the carrots and potatoes artfully arranged around it. She set this down in the center of the table, turned and went back for a huge basket of rolls.

"Normally, Edith doesn't cook," Eric told MW. He explained Maria Sanchez was the main cook for the Colton family, at least for lunch and dinner. "I don't get why she cooked tonight."

As Edith set the rolls on the table, she smiled at everyone, especially Eric.

"Where's Maria?" Eric asked.

"She took a day off," Edith answered. "Now dig in," she ordered, taking a seat to Big J's right. That was when MW noticed the chair directly opposite Big J's was conspicuously empty, which could only mean it belonged to his wife, Eric's mother.

Big J dominated the conversation. "Sweetheart," he drawled as soon as MW took a bite. "Tell me how you and my son came to know each other."

Immediately she blushed, trying to chew faster.

Noticing, Eric rushed in to tell the story.

"I asked her, not you," Big J groused, interrupting.

"She was chewing," Eric pointed out. "She couldn't answer you with her mouth full, now could she?"

"I can wait." The older man shot Eric a steely glare. "I'm trying to get to know your lady friend. Man has a right to learn about the future mother of his grand-children."

The future... Wait, what? MW's knew her blush darkened to a fiery red. She choked and, eyes watering, reached for her water. She took several slugs, trying to keep from making a spectacle of herself.

"Let's not rush things," Eric said, keeping his tone light. MW couldn't help but notice the way everyone openly watched him. All of his brother's green Colton eyes glinted with humor.

"It's okay," she put in earnestly. "We're just friends."

All of the men laughed. Perplexed, she glanced at Eric. A reluctant smile tugged at the corner of his well-shaped mouth.

"They're teasing you, darlin'," Big J said. "It just means they like you."

After the meal and dessert—two perfectly pre-pared apple pies—had been eaten, they all moved to the den. When Edith began gathering up the dishes, MW jumped up to help. She ignored Edith's attempt to wave her away and carried an armload into the kitchen. "I'll wash if you'll dry," she said, striving for a light-hearted tone.

Instead, Edith shook her head. "We have a dish-washer, honey. All they need is to be rinsed off and stacked in it."

Refusing to let her smile falter, MW nodded. "I can do that."

"Good." Edith got out another plate. "Abra's nurse should be stopping by to get her supper."

As if on cue, a short, round woman with a mop of curly dark hair the same color as her skin entered the kitchen. "Whew," she remarked to Edith, grabbing the plate and dishing up food. "I have to say, smelling this roast cooking the last couple of hours has made me mighty hungry."

Edith chuckled. "Help yourself. There's plenty left."

The other woman paused when she caught sight of MW. Her large brown eyes widened. "Who's this? Are you finally getting some help in the kitchen?"

Edith laughed. After a second, MW did, too.

"No, this is MW. Abra's son Eric brought her home for a visit. MW, please meet Latonia. She takes care of Abra."

MW moved forward and offered her hand. Latonia shook it, tilting her head as she studied MW. "Eric? Isn't he the doctor?"

"That's him," Edith said cheerfully. "That boy hasn't been home for a visit in forever. Now he's here, and he brought his lady friend."

Latonia looked MW up and down. "Must be serious."

"It's not." This time, MW managed to speak calmly. "We're just friends."

Though the two older women exchanged glances, neither one commented. MW went back to rinsing dishes and Latonia carried her plate over to the kitchen breakfast bar and began to eat.

MW finished and looked around to see if there was anything else she could do to help.

"You go on and join the others, honey." Edith

shooed her away from the sink. "I know they can be a bit much to take, but you can't hide in here the rest of the night."

At first, MW opened her mouth to protest, but closed it and nodded instead.

"Plus Latonia and I have a bunch to catch up on before she hurries back to watch over Abra."

Taking the hint, MW left the kitchen and headed toward the den. She took a seat by herself on the large couch, and sat back and watched everyone. The high-energy gathering was a bit overwhelming, but she also found the way everyone interacted fascinating. Due to the few flashbacks she'd had, she grew increasingly certain she hadn't come from a large family.

Everyone talked at once, except for Big J. When he spoke, all his children fell silent. But right now, he sat back and watched indulgently as conversation swirled around him.

Eric and his brother Ryan stood over by a huge grandfather clock, heads together while they conversed in low voices. Daniel, Brett and Jack made up another group, standing close to the massive fireplace and talking about cattle and pasture. Jack's wife, Tracy, had disappeared in the kitchen with Edith after she'd asked for a recipe for Italian stuffed shells.

To her bemused astonishment, MW had nearly jumped to her feet and offered to write down a recipe for her. Luckily, neither of the other women had noticed as they'd hurried off to the kitchen in search of Edith's favorite cookbook.

Seth appeared out of nowhere, just popping up at the end of the couch, grinning at her. "Hi," he said.

"Hello." She eyed him, hiding the tiniest bit of wariness. Though she couldn't remember most of her past, she felt pretty positive that she didn't have children. Whether or not she was good with them remained to be seen.

"Are you lonely?" The five-year-old scooted closer to her, only stopping when he was close enough for her to count the freckles on his face.

"Not really," she answered. "How about you?"

He shook his head. "Nope. Daddy says as long as we're around family, we're not alone."

This statement made her wonder if there were other little kids around for Seth to play with.

"Are you and my Uncle Eric gonna get married?" Seth asked. Unfortunately, due to the lull in the others' conversations, his clear, high voice carried to everyone in the room.

Everyone froze, turning to stare. And MW blushed, hating the way her face instantly got hot.

Jack hurried over. "Seth," he said calmly. "That was not polite. I'd like you to apologize to MW right now."

"I'm sorry," Seth immediately said, frowning as he looked from MW to his father and then back again. "But I really want to know, Daddy. It'd be really cool if Uncle Eric and MW got married and had a baby. When he grew up, I could teach him how to ride and rope and—"

"That's enough," Jack cut him off, clearly struggling to keep from laughing. "It's not nice to ask personal questions, especially to someone you just met. I'm really sorry, MW."

"It's all right," MW said softly, able to see the humor in the situation. As long as she didn't look at Eric, that is. "I'm guessing he just wants a playmate."

Jack exchanged a long look with his wife, who looked slightly flushed. "We just might have to work on that ourselves," he drawled, grinning as Tracy's color deepened. MW couldn't help but sympathize, since she blushed exactly the same way.

Eric came over and dropped down to sit beside her. "You know you're a guest here. You don't have to help Edith out in the kitchen."

At this, she lifted her chin. "I was raised that way. Guests always help the hostess." She froze as she realized what she'd just head. "Another fragment. More and more is coming back to me. I just wish it wasn't in so many tiny bits and pieces."

Eric reached over and squeezed her shoulder. "You never know. One morning you might wake up and find all your memory has been restored."

Hope filled her. "Is that the way it happens?"

"It can." His gentle smile told her not to feel too discouraged. "Since there's no medical reason for your amnesia, it's psychological. There's no way of knowing what might be the trigger to bring your memory back."

She nodded, trying not to let her disappointment show. "I met your mother's nurse in the kitchen. She seems really nice."

"I'm sure I'll meet her sooner or later." He made no move to get up. "I feel like I should apologize to you. I should have warned you about my family."

"You did, sort of." Peering up at him, she wasn't sure what he meant. "You told me there were a lot of them." She found herself wishing he would touch her again. But then, with his entire family probably watching them from the corners of their eyes, maybe it was better if he didn't.

As if to confirm this, Eric glanced casually around the room, still smiling. "I meant the way they'd automatically assume if I brought a woman home, then we must be in a serious relationship."

Again the familiar heat in her cheeks. Determined to ignore and vanquish it, MW shrugged. "You can't really blame them. From the sounds of things, you hardly ever visit. The fact that you are here now with me is bound to cause some talk."

Eric sighed. "I know. But I'm sorry you have to be put through this."

"Don't worry about it. They'll get used to me eventually. I do wish Greta was here. I like her." She glanced at the other two women. "Though Tracy and Hannah seem great, too. It'd be kind of nice to make a new friend or two.

Just as MW finished speaking, Tracy raised her head and smiled. Her porcelain skin gave her an ethereal sort of beauty. She spoke to her husband and the two of them headed toward MW and Eric.

"You must feel sort of overwhelmed by all this," Tracy said. "I remember the first time I met the family." Her delicate shudder made MW laugh. "I came because Jack used to be married to my cousin. Initially, I stayed here because I wanted to get to know Seth. He was the only family I had left."

"And then you fell in love and married Jack?" MW guessed. She loved happy endings.

"Yes." Tracy's expression turned earnest. "My ex-husband's parents had hired a hit man to kill me. Long story short, Jack kept me safe and the police killed the hit man."

"And then I married her," Jack added, putting his

arm around her shoulders and pulling her close. "Seth and I both adore her."

"As I do you." Beaming, she gazed up at him with obvious adoration before turning her attention back to MW. "My point is, I've heard someone is trying to kill you, too. And I'm sure you've probably been worried about putting anyone else in danger."

MW nodded. "I have been."

"Well, don't. If anyone can keep you safe, this family can." Voice fierce, she gave MW a quick hug. "I can personally attest to that."

"Drama, drama, drama," Ryan drawled, startling MW. He'd walked up behind them, along with Brett, Hannah and Daniel. Seth still played with his cars on the floor near the fireplace and Big J stood near the bar, talking quietly on his phone. "That's one thing you'll learn about this family. We're all about the drama."

"I can attest to that." Amusement rang in Hannah's soft voice. "I came here when my parents fired me from the family business and threw me out."

MW gasped. "Why?"

Brett placed his hand on her shoulder and kissed the top of her head. "They're superreligious and hated the idea of their daughter carrying a baby out of wedlock. Me, I'm happy as can be. I'm so glad she asked me to marry her."

"She asked you?" MW looked from one to the other, not sure if he might be teasing.

"Yep." Brett leaned in and kissed Hannah on the mouth. "But only once she realized how much I love her and our baby."

"And let's not forget about me," Daniel put in with

a grin. "The illegitimate one. My mom was the nanny. Talk about a cliché, right?"

"Wow. You all sure do lead exciting lives." MW felt a twinge of envy at the obvious affection the other two couples shared.

"That's not the half of it," Ryan put in. "As you know, someone attacked our mother. After that, more things have been happening around here. Someone set a fire. And the big barn was vandalized."

MW wasn't sure how to respond.

Edith hurried into the room and made a beeline to Big J. She tugged on his sleeve and once he ended his call, he leaned down. She whispered something in his ear. Immediately, his hard features shut down, as if he'd gone into shock. He followed Edith without a backward glance.

Everyone stared at everyone else in the now hushed room. Tracy and Hannah exchanged glances and each moved a little closer to their respective men.

"What do you suppose all that's about?" Ryan asked no one in particular. Though he kept his voice casual, he couldn't conceal a tinge of worry from his tone.

"Maybe something happened with some of the cattle," Tracy put in.

"Edith wouldn't be involved if it was ranch business," Jack responded, his frown attesting to his own concern.

"It's probably something to do with the house," Brett said. "Maybe she needs him to fix something. Who knows?"

But even MW could tell he didn't believe his own words.

"It has to be Mother." Eric frowned. "Maybe I should go check on her."

"Wait." MW placed her hand on his arm. She had a sudden hunch, but she didn't want to make a fool of herself by saying anything.

"I agree." Ryan gave them both a hard look. "Whatever has happened, if it concerns Mom, Dad needs to have his time with her alone."

The bleakness of his expression mirrored Eric's. MW's stomach lurched as she realized both men believed their mother might have passed away.

Jack and Tracy came over, Brett and Hannah right behind them. Daniel followed a moment later.

The men exchanged similarly worried looks.

"We need a distraction," Hannah said, her voice bright. "How about a game of charades?"

Ryan stared at her in clear disbelief. But the glare Brett shot his older brother said he'd better not say a single disparaging word.

"I think that's a great idea," Tracy chimed in. "It's better than standing around speculating on something we don't know."

Jack, Brett and Daniel agreed. Only Eric, the sole holdout, shook his head and crossed his arms. "I'm a doctor," he said. "If something has happened with Mother, I need to be there. I'm the only one in this house who can help."

And then, without waiting for anyone to reply, Eric turned on his heel and left the room.

"Is he going toward…" Hannah sounded dismayed.

Grimly, Ryan nodded. "He's right, you know. Even if our father doesn't like to admit it, Eric is the most

# Send For
# 2 FREE BOOKS
## Today!

## I accept your offer!

Please send me two
free novels and two mystery
gifts (gifts worth about $10).
I understand that these books
are completely free—even
the shipping and handling will
be paid—and I am under no
obligation to purchase anything,
ever, as explained on the back
of this card.

### 240/340 HDL GHTR

*Please Print*

FIRST NAME

LAST NAME

ADDRESS

APT.#                    CITY

STATE/PROV.          ZIP/POSTAL CODE

Visit us online at
www.ReaderService.com

# Send For
# 2 FREE BOOKS
## Today!

## I accept your offer!

Please send me two free novels and two mystery gifts (gifts worth about $10). I understand that these books are completely free—even the shipping and handling will be paid—and I am under no obligation to purchase anything, ever, as explained on the back of this card.

**240/340 HDL GHTR**

**Please Print**

FIRST NAME

LAST NAME

ADDRESS

APT.#                     CITY

STATE/PROV.              ZIP/POSTAL CODE

Visit us online at
www.ReaderService.com

RS-815-GF15

qualified to deal with any kind of setback. If I were a doctor, I'd have gone, too."

MW didn't really know any of these people, but she didn't understand why everyone immediately assumed the worst. She, on the other hand, figured maybe Abra had made progress, possibly even awakened from her coma. Since she wasn't a part of their family, she didn't voice her thoughts. No doubt they'd find her overly positive attitude a bit Pollyanna anyway. People certainly had told her that often enough in the past.

The past. Floored, she tried to expand on the memory, but the instant she focused, it was gone.

Still, she had something. Another tiny piece of the puzzle that had been her life. Since fragmented memories had been occurring with more and more frequency, she had to assume Eric was right. Before long, she'd be able to remember everything. Including her actual name, where she lived and also who Walter might be.

Edith came back into the room. A broad smile softened her austere features. "Everyone, I have good news. We've had our very own miracle. Abra is awake. Eric is tending to her right now."

# Chapter 10

Eric stood in the doorway of his mother's room, his stomach in knots. His father sat, hunched over her bed, his shoulders shaking as he unabashedly wept. The nurse, a plump woman with coffee-colored skin, noticed him and came over.

"It's a miracle," she whispered, her large brown eyes shining with tears.

Confused, Eric could only stare. As he realized the impact of her words, he straightened his shoulders and entered the room.

"Let me look at her," he said, glad he'd regained his professional detachment.

"I don't think—" the nurse began.

Big J raised his face, his florid cheeks wet with tears. "It's all right, Latonia. This is my son Eric. He's a doctor."

Both gratified and concerned, Eric approached his

mother's bed. Though she continued to lie completely still, her eyes were open. For the first time in months, her eyes were open. That didn't necessarily mean she was responsive.

"Mother?" Leaning close, he softly kissed her cheek. "It's Eric. Blink once if you can hear me."

Though no other part of her moved, she blinked. Elation filled him as he met his father's still-wet gaze. "Did you see that?"

Big J jerked his head in a nod. "I did." He lifted his hand, revealing he held Abra's. "She squeezed my fingers."

Eric's inhaled sharply. "Can you do that again, Mother? Just once, for me?"

As the seconds ticked by, Eric refused to let go of his hope. And then, slowly and painstakingly, Abra's hand moved. Just the tiniest bit. But that was enough.

"We need to get her to the hospital," Eric told his father. "Run some tests, get some images of her brain."

Big J stared back and then slowly shook his head. "No. When she comes all the way awake, I want her to be here at home surrounded by her family. That's what she'd want, too. She's staying here."

Somehow, Eric refrained from groaning out loud. "I understand and we can bring her back here as soon as the tests have been completed."

But the closed-off expression on his father's face said the elder Colton had already made up his mind. "No."

Eric glanced at the nurse, kind of hoping she'd back him up, but Latonia had busied herself cleaning up something on the back table. Clearly, she didn't want to get involved in family matters. Eric couldn't say he blamed her.

"Dad, please listen to me." Pitching his voice low so he wouldn't agitate his mother, Eric called on every ounce of his composure. Years of medical school, residency and practice had given him the skills to know exactly how to treat a patient in this kind of situation. His father couldn't take that away from him.

"We need to make sure she's meaningfully responded to external stimuli."

Big J snorted. "She is. You saw just the same as I. She blinked. She squeezed my hand. What is some big fancy machine going to tell us that we don't already know?"

"We need to know how much neurological damage exists."

The stubborn set of the older man's chin told Eric he wasn't buying it. Again, aware the worst thing he could do would be to agitate his mother, Eric gave up. For now.

"At least let me call her neurologist?"

To this olive branch, Big J nodded. "I'll give you his name in a minute."

Edith spoke from the doorway. "How is she?"

"Awake," Big J said, joy in his voice. "She still can't move much yet, but I'm sure that will come with time."

"I know the others would love to see her," Edith continued. "Would that be all right, Eric?"

Gratified that she'd asked him rather than his father, Eric nodded. "Maybe one at a time. We don't want to overwhelm Mother."

"I think she's done for today," Big J said, his soft

voice full of a mix of pride and sorrow. "Just that little bit wore her out."

A quick glance at Abra revealed she'd closed her eyes.

"He's right," Eric told Edith. "I'll let everyone know they need to hold off on visiting her for now. Maybe we can try again tomorrow."

And then he went to find his siblings, well aware they were going to want a complete rundown on what had just occurred.

The next morning, Eric woke with the strangest sense of anticipation. He sat up in bed and looked around the room, momentarily disoriented.

Home. He was back at the Lucky C. And his mother had appeared to wake from her coma, however briefly. More tests needed to be run to find out more, but since it didn't appear his father was going to allow them, Abra's healing would either happen or it wouldn't.

Eric hated to leave such a crucial and vital aspect of her recovery to fate. Especially when he knew how much modern medicine could help.

After showering, he dressed and made his way down to the kitchen. Since it was still relatively early, he didn't want to disturb MW. For all he knew, she might enjoy sleeping in.

But when he reached the kitchen, to his surprise he found MW sitting near his father at the kitchen bar, sipping from a mug of coffee. Edith stood at the stove with her back to them, cooking. She turned and smiled. "Good morning." Her cheery greeting sounded just the way it had for years.

"Good morning," Eric said back. MW echoed him.

"Mornin', sleepyhead," Big J said. "All that city life must have made you forget how early we get up on the ranch."

Oh, Eric hadn't forgotten. Not at all. Too many mornings of being dragged from bed at 4:00 a.m. to help work cattle had made sure of that.

Deciding it would be safer not to comment, he settled on a weary smile instead. "Good morning to you, too." After procuring a cup of coffee, he took a seat across from MW.

"Why don't you show your sweetheart the ranch?" Big J drawled, draping a heavy arm around MW's shoulders. Though Eric's jaw tightened, he didn't correct his father. Some things were more trouble than they were worth.

"Morning's the best time, darlin'," Big J told MW. "Otherwise it's too damn hot to do much of anything."

MW nodded. To Eric's surprise, she appeared relaxed, even with his father's arm around her. "Sounds good to me."

"Go on horseback," the older man ordered. "It's the greatest way to see the land."

Horseback. Eric wondered if MW could ride. When he glanced at her, she shrugged, apparently correctly reading the question in his eyes.

"That's a wonderful idea, Dad." It felt strangely gratifying to see the pleased expression on Big J's face.

"Yes, it is," MW agreed. "Although I'm not sure I know anything about horses and saddles or riding."

"It's easy, sugar," the older man reassured her. "And Eric can show you the finer points in case you forgot them."

Eric realized Big J didn't remember being told how

MW had amnesia. His brothers had mentioned several times before how worried they were about their father's faulty memory. He made a mental note to watch closely for any other signs that might indicate the beginnings of Alzheimer's or dementia.

"Well?" Big J demanded, holding up his coffee mug for a refill. Immediately, MW hopped up and fetched the coffeepot so she could carefully refresh his cup. "Are you going to take her or not?" the older man continued.

Though it sounded like a directive, Eric understood his father. Big J took pride in the Lucky C and this was his way of making sure Eric showed it off. Plus, the idea of showing MW the ranch from horseback sounded like a lot of fun.

"I think I will," he said. He glanced at MW. "How about we go right after breakfast?"

Gaze locked on his, she gave a slow nod.

"Edith's whipping up some scrambled eggs, sausage and toast," Big J said. "It ought to be ready any time now."

"It's done," Edith announced. She placed a large bowl full of eggs on the table, then a second one full of sausage patties. Finally she added a platter of toast.

"Anyone want juice? We have orange and tomato."

The delicious hot breakfast reminded Eric of his childhood. Since their cook, Maria, didn't come in until midmorning, Edith had always handled making breakfast. Funny how most of his favorite childhood memories of mornings centered around Edith and her home-cooked breakfasts. His mother had preferred to sleep in, so she'd rarely even been present.

Once they'd finished, Eric excused himself, motioning with his eyes at MW so she'd do the same. Getting the hint, she stood and followed him into the foyer. At the bottom of the staircase, he stopped. "You'll need to change," he said, glancing at the Bermuda shorts she wore. "Jeans and boots, if you have them."

"I don't." She grimaced. "I only have what Greta so kindly chose for me. Will sneakers do?"

"They'll have to, at least for now." The somehow sensual image of him helping her try on a pair of soft leather cowboy boots made him actually consider buying her a pair. Maybe he would, if it turned out she had an aptitude for riding.

"I'm going to pop in and check on my mother," he told her. "After, I'll meet you here."

She flashed him a smile that he felt all the way to his core. "Take all the time you need. It'll just take me a second."

He hoped her idea of a second wasn't the same as his sister's. He watched her hurry up the stairs, unable to keep from admiring her curvy figure. Greta would keep him waiting fifteen minutes minimum.

The nurse, Latonia, stood up when he entered his mother's room. "How is she?" he asked, keeping his voice low since Abra appeared to be sleeping.

"About the same." Latonia handed him a chart, just as a nurse would do if they were in the hospital. "Last night apparently plumb wore her out. She fell asleep and hasn't opened her eyes since."

Nodding, he studied the number on the chart.

"You don't think she's slipped back into a coma, do you?" Latonia sounded worried.

"That happens sometimes," he admitted, giving her back the chart. "Patients come in and out of consciousness for days. Right now, we need to let her get all the rest she can. It'll help her heal."

After checking his mother's pulse and her reflexes, he left the room and went back to the staircase, expecting he'd still have a few minutes to wait.

To his pleasant surprise, MW waited for him. She now wore a pair of faded jeans that fit her like a glove. His mouth went dry and he took her in.

"Are you ready?" he managed to ask. When she nodded, he took her arm and led her from the house. The sky had started to lighten, and the pinkish-orange tinge that heralded the coming sunrise also promised a scorching-hot day.

As soon as they were down the front steps, she pulled away and turned to face him. "Before we go any farther, I honestly don't know if I can ride a horse." The way she wrinkled her nose appealed to him. "I think I'm a city girl, through and through. I don't think riding lessons were part of my past."

"That's okay. I'll choose a gentle gelding for you. We won't be doing anything dangerous, I promise. It's just a matter of staying in the saddle and controlling the horse."

"Oh, I wasn't worried about that," she said, smiling slightly. "I'm pretty sure I can manage staying astride. I just don't want you to have unrealistic expectations about my abilities."

He hid a smile at her serious tone. "No worries. We'll take it easy, okay?"

"Okay." Then, to his surprise, she slipped her hand into his instead of taking his arm. "Lead the way."

A jolt went through him; one he took care not to

show as he took her to the barn where the ranch horses were stabled.

Big J must have called ahead, since two of the barn workers had already led out Smokey, a middle-aged and extremely docile quarter horse gelding, as well as Elvis, the gelding Eric had ridden the last time he'd been home.

"Wow. They're beautiful," MW breathed, stopping to stare.

"The gray one is for you. His name is Smokey." He noticed one of the workers emerging with a comfortable Western saddle. "You wait while they get him saddled up for you."

She nodded, clearly unable to tear her gaze away from the horse. Grinning, Eric hurried into the tack room, waving away the young ranch hand when he offered to take care of saddling up Elvis for him. "I'll do it," Eric said. "It's been a while, but I don't think I've forgotten."

"Just make sure and tighten the cinch," the kid advised. Eric nodded and hefted a saddle from its saddle tree.

As he'd figured, he hadn't forgotten the steps. He showed MW how to put the bit in her mount's mouth, and how to fit the bridle.

Once they were all done, he gave Elvis's reins to one of the hands and cupped his hands together to give MW a leg up in her saddle.

He waited until they got her stirrups adjusted before mounting Elvis, thanking their helpers. "Are you ready?" he asked MW.

She grinned, pure joy shining in her lovely eyes.

"I think so." And then she pressed her heels into Smokey's side, urging him forward.

"Looks like you know what you're doing," he observed, grinning back. As he'd expected, he still felt at home on horseback. Like he belonged. Eager to show MW the majesty of his family's ranch, he rode alongside her and slightly ahead, leading the way.

They rode from the barn to the gate that separated the closest twenty acres from the rest of the ranch. "We keep our ranch horses near," he explained, using his hand to sweep the landscape. "There are certain pastures we use at different times of the years."

"Do you raise horses, too? Or just cattle?"

"Mostly cattle." He reined in, so they could take in the sight of the sun rising over the flat horizon. "Look."

"Wow." The way she sucked in her breath made him look at her. With her face tilted up in wonder, and the yellow glow of sunlight bathing her skin and hair, he thought he'd never seen a more beautiful woman.

"Come on," he said, to cover his own confusion. "We have a few hours before it starts to heat up. I've got several places I want to show you."

If he kept busy, maybe he could banish the aching need that clawed at him every time he looked at her.

There were several gravel roads bisecting the Lucky C, all of them gated. Since he had a direction in mind, they cut across one of the unused pastures. At the gate, he dismounted, opened it and held it for MW to ride through. Once she had, he led his horse past and closed the gate after.

Astride again, he smiled at her. The morning breeze had tossed her hair into a mop of curls. She looked as disheveled as if she'd just risen from bed after making love. The thought made his body heat.

Quickly looking away, he took a moment to compose himself.

Luckily, she didn't appear to have noticed. Instead, she gazed ahead, where the road disappeared into the horizon. "This is absolutely beautiful," she breathed. "I can't imagine wanting to leave it."

Despite his fascination with her profile, her comment surprised him. "It is, I agree. But not everyone is cut out for wide-open skies."

Though she nodded, the expression of wonder remained on her pretty face, making him ache with the need to touch her. "True." She met his gaze briefly, just long enough to heat his blood. "But that doesn't mean it's any less lovely."

She had a point. He rode alongside her, trying to view the ranch with fresh eyes. The land undulated gently before them, with twisted trees permanently leaning in the direction the wind had blown them. The grass, acres and acres of gold-tinged green, provided nourishment for the family's herds of prime beef cattle.

It had always been beautiful. Though none of it could hold a candle to her.

His heart skipped a beat. He gave himself a mental shake, telling himself to get his libido under control.

Though it wasn't yet 7:00 a.m., the bright sun and pink sky blazed a promise of later heat. He suspected the temperature hovered around eighty-five; much less than the low hundreds that had been forecasted for later in the day.

August in Oklahoma was the time of grass fires. In the driest time of the year, these could race across the plains and take out hundreds of acres of pasture. All the ranchers had their own pumper trucks and each other's numbers on speed dial. The instant a fire was spotted, all able-bodied men dropped everything to go and help put it out.

When he told MW this, she appeared to find it fascinating. "I'm glad for sunshine today," she said. "But honestly, it feels like it's going to rain."

She was right. Something in the air felt different. Eric lifted his head, scenting a warning hint of moisture in the air. Out here in the plains, one could actually feel the barometric pressure change. Rain? He glanced up at the perfect blue sky, perplexed. As he turned in the saddle, his heart sank.

Instead of blue, dark gray clouds had begun to amass. Even as he watched, they blotted out the sun and were accompanied with a low rumble of thunder that sounded like a herd of cattle stampeding. Lightning flashed in the distance. Across the prairie, he could see the vertical slashes of deeper color telling him where the rain had begun to fall. The storm was moving their way, following the normal pattern of spring storms.

Except this was August, full-on summer. Late summer, everyone prayed for rain. Unfortunately, the sky rarely answered their prayers. Moisture was always considered a blessing and celebrated accordingly. Unless one was unlucky enough to be caught out in the open in one of the more violent storms.

This appeared to be one of those. Though he knew everyone would rejoice at the rain, it was a hell of a time for them to be caught out in the middle of a pasture, with no shelter for miles.

He eyed the rapidly gathering clouds with concern. "This is not good."

"Maybe it'll be a brief shower," she said, hopefully.

"Not with those clouds. We'd better head back," he told her, reluctant to end the morning. "We don't want to get caught out in the open, especially with lightning. We'll be sitting targets."

Her perfectly shaped brows knitted together. "True. But that storm is way in the distance. We should have plenty of time."

Which reminded him she had no idea of the capricious nature of weather on the Oklahoma prairie. "Do you notice how the wind's always blowing?"

"Yes. But that's just today, right?"

"Nope. It pretty much blows all the time here." He glanced back at the clouds, which had already grown much closer. "And it's fixin' to pick up."

As if he had magical control over the weather, a second after the words left his mouth, the wind began to howl. Eyes wide, MW twisted in her saddle to assess the approaching storm. This time, her mouth fell open in shock.

"We're not going to have time to make it back to the barn, are we?" She had to shout to be heard over the wind.

Scanning the landscape for anything they could use as shelter, he shook his head. "Follow me." And he dug his heels into his mount's side, checking to make sure she was right behind him.

They rode fast, heading toward an outcropping of boulders where, a long time ago when he'd been a kid, Big J had built them a wooden fort on the other side.

He wasn't sure it was still there or even standing, but it was the only chance at shelter they'd have.

He could feel the wet breath of the rain on the back of his neck. Still, the rocky ground ahead was too dangerous to bring the horses in at an all-out run.

Slowing to a walk, he hoped MW would hold on since he knew her horse would follow his gelding's lead. "Grip the horn," he called out her, inwardly wincing as her mount skidded to a stop.

Miraculously, she remained in the saddle.

"Good job," he began, just as the sky opened up and rain poured out, drenching them.

Reminding himself through clenched teeth that August rain on the prairie was a blessing, he didn't complain. He was more worried about the lightning anyway.

Thunder boomed. Out of habit he began to count until he saw the flash. "It's getting closer. Get down and follow me," he hollered, dismounting.

A second later, she did the same. And then, to his amazement, she laughed. "I love it," she said, tilting her face up to the downpour, lifting her arms as if she could channel the storm's energy.

What could he do then but haul her up against him and kiss her, long and deep and with all the hunger that had been building up inside him for so long?

She kissed him back, her eager response only stoking the fire in his veins. He lost track of how long they stood there, bodies locked together, mating with their mouths. His horse's sharp whinny brought him back to the present and he broke away.

Breathing in quick, shallow gasps, she stared at him, her eyes wide and her pupils huge.

"Come on," he rasped. "We've got to get out of this rain."

He led the horses around the boulders where, to his relief, the wooden fort still stood. Well aware his kids were always on horseback, his dad had made it large enough to accommodate two horses, including two covered stall areas with tie-ups.

"Here." He showed her how to secure the reins, praying she didn't notice how his hands shook. Once she'd copied his motions, she turned to face him.

Bracing himself, he waited for her to reproach him.

Instead, she stepped forward, putting her arms around him and burying her face in his throat. Though his body reacted immediately, he kept himself still, hardly daring to breathe.

And then she began to touch him, the movement of her soft, damp hands searing his skin. He tried not to move, though the effort nearly killed him. But once she slid her hands under his drenched shirt and splayed them over his stomach, his willpower went up in smoke.

A sound escaped him, a groan of need, and he lifted her wet T-shirt over her head. Removing her bra in a deft motion, he cupped her beautiful breasts before taking one nipple into his mouth. She gasped, delight plain on her lovely face.

She kicked off her sneakers and helped him remove her jeans and panties, her damp and glistening body more beautiful than he could ever have imagined.

"Your turn," she told him softly, her husky voice vibrating with a desire that matched his own.

Before he could even begin unbuttoning his shirt, she nearly tore it in her hurry to get it off him. When her fingers started on the button to his jeans, he thought he might explode.

"Wait," he rasped. Taking her hand, he guided it to himself, letting her feel the swollen outline of his arousal through his jeans.

"I want you," he told her.

The hitch in her breathing told him she wanted him, too.

But he had to be absolutely certain. If they made love, he didn't want there to be any uncertainty between them. He wanted to have all of her—body, mind and heart.

Inhaling deeply, he met her gaze. Her dilated pupils made his arousal swell against her fingers. "MW?"

Her way of answering the unspoken question was to slide her fingers over him and then pull him down for a deep, wet kiss.

Like a wildfire taking over the prairie, desire swept through him. Nearly out of control. Shaking, he forced himself to break away, once again needing to make certain she really wanted this as badly as he did. But she made a whimper of protest when he tried to pull away and held on with a fierceness that, under other circumstances, would have made him smile.

He kissed her once more, their tongues a dance of intimacy, of need, pure passion providing fuel to the fire.

Head spinning, for the third time he attempted to do the right thing. But MW was having none of it. She touched him, fierce and primal, her bold caress almost a command, and he went under, drowning in need.

Blood surging, his body throbbed under the sure stroke of her fingers. This time, when she unbuttoned his jeans and freed him, he let himself go, pressing against her, nearly mindless with desire.

When she'd gotten the rest of his clothes off, he stood naked while her gaze devoured him, lingered on his jutting arousal. Hands clenched into fists to keep himself from taking her right there on the dirt floor, he managed to speak.

"Are you sure?"

Passion blazing from her eyes, she nodded. "More sure than I've been of anything else in my life."

He should have asked about Walter, mentioned her memory loss, but she wrapped her hand around him and guided him to where her wet warmth waited.

Still standing, she backed him against the wall and took him inside her, sheathing him as if their bodies had been made for each other. He couldn't talk, couldn't even think. He could do nothing but move, passion and wonder filling him.

At some point, he slid to the ground while she rode him, her head thrown back and her eyes half closed. He struggled not to lose himself, refusing to let go until she found her own release.

And when her body clenched around his as she shattered in ecstasy, the last remaining shred of his control vanished. Helpless, he followed her, the pleasure pure and explosive and completely, utterly mind-blowing.

# Chapter 11

Panting, MW fell against Eric, exhausted and spent. And happy. Deliriously, amazingly happy. She adored the way he continued to hold her, as if she was precious to him, their sweat-slick bodies fitting together like two long lost puzzle pieces.

"I refuse to regret this," she announced, as soon as she could speak again.

He chuckled, the movement making her wince. "Are you all right?"

"A bit sore," she admitted, smiling as she, too, found the humor in the situation. Outside, the rain appeared to have moved on, judging from the complete lack of sound. "I'm not sure how I'm going to ride that horse back to the main house."

His chuckle turned into a laugh, making her rise up off him. Once she had, he shifted and eased himself out from under her. "That might be a bit of a problem," he admitted. "But I think you'll survive."

"I imagine I will." Turning away, she began trying to gather up her clothes. Weirdly, her amusement from before had vanished, leaving her on the verge of tears.

"Now what?" he asked quietly, handing over her bra and T-shirt.

She tried for a shrug. "I don't know."

"Are you limping?" he asked.

Surprised, she realized she had been. "My leg's a little sore. I'm not sure why."

He made short work of getting dressed, studying her while she tugged on her T-shirt. When she went to step into her jeans, he stopped her. "Wait just a second. Is that a scar?"

"Where?" Looking down, she tried to see what he saw.

"On your right femur."

She supposed she should know where a femur was located, but she had no idea. "Show me."

His gentle touch made her shiver. "The femur is the only bone in your thigh. See this, right here?"

To her shock, she saw the slightly puckered, silvery line on her skin. "It does look like a scar."

"You had some sort of surgery."

Slowly she nodded. "A metal plate to fuse my femur. I broke it when I was in France."

His stunned stare mirrored her own shock. "You remember? Was that a memory?"

"Yes. It was." She waited to see if anything else came, but that was it.

He shook his head. "What I want to know is how did they miss this when you were brought in after your accident?" He sounded furious. "Surely Dr. Patel ordered an X-ray."

He yanked his jeans on and pulled his cell phone from his pocket. A second later, he muttered a curse. "No signal. I forgot how it is out here in the boonies."

Fully dressed now, she faced him. "I had X-rays or something. I remember because they told me I had no broken bones."

"Which means that metal plate you say you have must have shown up." Now he sounded distracted. "Let's get back to the house. I need to talk to Dr. Patel or whoever is on call."

She nodded, glancing around them. "Before we go, I do have one question. Why is there a barn way out here?"

"It was a play fort my brothers and I used when we were kids."

"Not Greta? What, were no girls allowed?"

Her teasing coaxed a reluctant smile from him. "Sorry. Yes, of course Greta played here. She was a tomboy to the core. If we'd tried to tell her she wasn't allowed, I think she might have beaten us all up."

That image was so in keeping with what she knew of his sister that she laughed.

"Come on," he told her, his smile fading. "I really need to make that call."

Once they were mounted, she turned to look at him. "I don't understand. Why is finding out about my X-ray so important?"

"Because if you do have a metal plate inside you, there might be a serial number. It'll be registered to you—the real you." The intensity of his voice matched his expression. "Don't you see, MW? We should be able to find out who you actually are."

With that pronouncement, he rode away, urging his horse into a jog, and once they'd cleared the rocky area, a lope.

Stunned, she sat for a moment before following. For an instant, just a flash actually, she didn't want to know. She liked being MW, liked the new life she'd started. Of course, a second later, she realized how foolish such a notion was. Of course she needed to find out her real name, where she came from and what she did for a living. And, maybe most important of all, who Walter might be.

She rode as fast as she dared behind him, and when he stopped his horse and waited for her to catch up, her relief was palpable. "Thank you," she said, breathless. "I'm still not entirely confident on horseback."

The ride appeared to have calmed him somewhat. "I apologize." His formal tone chipped at her heart. "None of this is your fault."

"True." She wanted to ask if learning her name would change this thing—whatever it was—that had started between them, but stopped herself just in time. Of course it would. Or might. For all she knew, she might have just cheated on a husband.

Stomach roiling, she looked past Eric toward the direction she thought they needed to go. "I'm ready to ride," she told him.

The grin he flashed devastated her, though she took care not to show it. "Follow me."

And they were off.

Once they went through the gate and rode across the final pasture, she could see the barn and the main house in the distance. Eric slowed his gelding to a trot and her mount immediately did the same. When they arrived at the barn, two grooms were waiting to take their horses.

Eric dismounted with ease and hurried over to her side. "Do you need some help?"

Instantly, she shook her head. If he touched her again, her fragile composure would shatter. "I can do it, thanks."

Imitating the movements she'd seen him make, she swung her right leg over the saddle and dropped to the ground. While not as graceful as his dismount, she thought she'd done pretty well. "Easy peasy," she said, waiting for his approval.

But he'd already turned away, intent on getting back to the house.

Once they reached the impressive foyer, Eric excused himself and hurried away, his phone already against his ear. She stood at the bottom of the massive, curving staircase and debated between going to her room and heading into the kitchen to see if she could help with anything.

But since right now she needed a hot shower, a change of clothes and time alone to think, she climbed the stairs and headed to her room.

Thirty minutes later, showered, dressed in a clean T-shirt and shorts, she finished blow drying her hair and tried to decide how she felt about what had happened today.

She didn't know what kind of person she might actually be, but the fact that she'd given in to the sexy temptation Dr. Eric Colton presented gave her pause. Especially since she had no idea about her past. For all she knew, she could be a wife and mother, though she thought if that was the case, by now someone would have raised a fuss about her disappearance.

All she could do now was wait—and pray that when she did learn the truth, no one else was hurt by her impetuous actions.

Still, the uncertainty didn't erase the beauty of the sensual time she and Eric had spent together. Nothing could take that away from her—the images and emotions would forever be seared into her soul. Right now, though, she didn't dare examine them too closely, afraid she might be the one who ended up getting hurt.

A quiet tap at her door made her jump. She peeked out, biting her lip at the sight of Eric, who clearly had come directly from the shower. He hadn't even taken the time to towel dry his hair.

"Come in," she said, stepping aside for him to pass. Once he had, she left the door open a crack, just in case anyone passing by might get the wrong idea.

"Dr. Patel said the radiologist made a notation about your metal plate, but it was overlooked." Fury underscored his low-pitched voice. "True, it's highly unlikely that it could have a serial number, but she didn't even check."

MW nodded, even though she had no idea what made him so angry.

"If it does have a serial number, it will be registered to you," he continued. "All this time, we could have had answers rather than speculation. We could have *known*."

She eyed him, intrigued by his fervor but feeling strangely distant, as they were discussing someone else. "And if there is no serial number?"

"Then I can have Ryan run a check on women

who've had this type of surgery in the last few years. Your scar is fairly recent. There can't be that many."

This time, she nodded, unsure what he wanted her to say or do.

"I've already called Ryan so he can get a head start." He cleared his throat. "I'm also making a trip back to Tulsa," he said. "I want you to stay here, where I know you're safe."

The thought of him leaving made her feel more bereft than she should. To cover, she shrugged and tried to appear as if being left alone on his family's ranch didn't bother her. Before today, Eric might have noticed her odd behavior and called her on it. Or at least made a comment asking if she was all right. Now, he appeared too distracted to even notice. He'd gone to her window and stood with his back to her, staring outside.

"When are you leaving?" she finally asked.

"In a few minutes," he answered without turning. "I'm hoping to be back by nightfall, but if not, it'll be tomorrow."

"Drive safely."

Now he looked at her. "I will." His expression softened. "About today—" he began.

"Don't." She cut him off, not wanting him to ruin what had been a perfect afternoon. "We'll talk about that later. Some other time."

Slowly he nodded. Crossing to her, he cupped her chin and kissed her softly on the lips. Then, as she stood absolutely still, almost afraid to breathe, he strode toward the door and left.

Eric kicked himself mentally at least a dozen times before he even reached the main road. He'd seen the hurt in MW's beautiful blue eyes and knew what she thought. Still, he didn't know a way to fix things. At least not until he knew who she really was.

What had happened between them never should have, and yet damned if he could make himself regret it. He'd had his fair share of lovers over the years, but what he and MW had shared…

Lost in thought, he stared as his cell phone rang. Again, caller ID showed the hospital. "Dr. Colton?" Dr. Patel's voice, sounding tired.

His heartbeat sped up. "What have you learned?"

"Nothing yet."

"I see." As his pulse went back to normal, he exhaled. "Then what's up?"

"I just wanted to let you know that your brother has been here. He's input the information we have into some sort of national law-enforcement database. I'm sure he'll be in touch with you soon."

Thanking her, he ended the call. Next up, he punched in the command to call his brother.

Ryan answered immediately, sounding cheerful. "Well, hello there, my impatient brother. I'm working as fast as I can."

"Thank you. Dr. Patel told me you'd been in to pay her a visit."

"I have, I have. Figured I could fast-track this thing."

"Thank you." Eric gripped the wheel, wondering why he felt so apprehensive. Instinct? Or the fear he might lose MW forever?

"Once we know who she is, maybe we can figure out why someone is trying to harm her," Ryan continued. "That's amazing luck that she had a metal plate."

"Yes, it is. I just wish Dr. Patel had seen fit to mention it earlier."

"How'd you find out about it anyway?" Ryan asked.

Silence. Eric didn't want to out-and-out lie, but his brother didn't need to know about what had been a private moment. He finally settled on a partial truth. "She noticed a scar on her leg and showed it to me."

"And you being a doctor, you knew immediately what it was from," Ryan finished.

"Something like that."

"They're running the number now. Once they get a hit, they'll let me know and I'll call you. I imagine finding out her story will be a relief for you."

"Yes, it will." Eric took a deep breath. "As a matter of fact, I'm on my way to Tulsa now."

"You're bringing MW back?" Ryan sounded shocked. "I'm not sure that's wise," he continued, without waiting for Eric to answer. "She's safer at the ranch."

"Which is why I left her there."

"Oh. I see." For some reason, this seemed to amuse his brother. "Anyway, I'll get in touch with Forensics tomorrow and make sure they put a rush on running that number."

"I appreciate that. Any word on the bomb that blew up my car?"

"Nothing yet. Though your insurance company has been here harassing my people." Ryan sighed. "I had no idea that little sports car of yours was so expensive."

"It was. I really liked that Porsche."

Ryan chuckled. "Good thing you had remote start. Who knew such a thing could save your life?"

"True." And he'd never have a vehicle without it after this. "I'm glad to be alive."

"I'm kinda glad you're alive myself," Ryan teased. "And I'm pretty sure once we find out what's going on with your MW, we'll know more about why someone blew up your car."

Eric debated correcting his brother for referring to MW as his, but decided against it. "Probably."

"So, where are you heading?" Ryan asked. "Do you want to grab dinner later?"

"To the hospital. I want to see the X-rays for myself. After that, I'm free, so sure."

"Great.

He drove to the hospital and headed to his office, where he used the computer system to log in and view MW's X-ray report, which had been filed under *Jane Doe*. Sure enough, the radiologist had noted the presence of a metal plate in her femur. Beyond that, nothing else had been written.

He checked all the other records in the hospital database, but everything looked routine.

Sitting back in his chair, he dragged his hand across his chin and tried to figure out what to do next. Coming back to town had been an impulsive reaction to the closeness he'd felt making love to MW. When he'd caught himself entertaining the idea of a future together, he'd known it was time to get out of Dodge. He needed to put some distance between them and try to think rationally.

Had he lost his mind? He knew nothing about this woman, nothing beside the fact he found her beautiful and sexy and fun. Nothing except the way she made him feel.

His analytical brain couldn't process such an illogical idea. Therefore, the sooner he learned the truth about MW, the better off they'd all be.

His cell rang as he was walking to his car.

"You're not going to believe this," Ryan said, sounding grim. "When I ran the search in the national database for MW, it must have set off some kind of alarm. The US Marshals office just contacted me. They want to meet at the police station now. Maybe you'd better join me, especially since they specifically requested you."

Stunned, Eric climbed into the rental SUV. "Did they say why?"

"No. Just that it concerned the person I was searching for."

"MW."

"Exactly."

Taking a deep breath, Eric started the engine. "I'm on my way. I'll be there in ten minutes."

After finding a good book and a comfy chair in the den, MW nearly jumped out of her skin when Eric stepped into the foyer and called her name. She'd dimly heard the sound of the front door opening, but since someone always seemed to be coming or going in the monstrous house, she hadn't paid too much attention.

"In here," she responded, checking her watch. It was barely after seven and the sun hadn't even set. She hadn't expected Eric back this early.

She got to her feet and waited, trying to hide her happiness at his return. Still, she felt her face color at her foolishness.

"There you are." His intense gaze made her entire body feel warm.

"You're back early," she said brightly, aware her cheeks probably looked like ripe tomatoes.

"Yes." Unsmiling, he regarded her. "Are you all right? You look a bit flushed."

Thoroughly embarrassed, she nodded. "I didn't expect you, so I was taken by surprise, that's all."

He nodded. "Why don't you sit down?"

At his words, she froze. Her stomach churned. Though she had to admit to being curious, she was also afraid. Panic fluttered in her chest and she had to remind herself to breathe. Part of her wanted to run. Instead, she went with that little spark of defiance and lifted her chin. Time to face the truth, whatever it might be.

"Thank you, but I'd rather stand." She exhaled, then inhaled. "You've learned my identity, haven't you? Please, tell me what you've found out."

"Sit first. Please. It's a lot to take in at once."

Reluctantly, she complied. "Well?"

"When Ryan ran a check on your metal implant, he got an almost immediate response. From the US Marshals office."

"What?" Bewildered, she waited. "Why?"

"I'm getting to that. There's only so much they'd tell us. I do know this. Your real name is Kara Sheppard. You're thirty-one years old and from Manhattan, New York." He scratched the back of his neck, his green gaze direct. "And you're in the Federal Witness Security Program."

The Federal Witness Security Program. Since that didn't make sense, she focused on what she'd been longing to know ever since she'd woken up in that hospital: her real name. "Kara. Kara Sheppard."

"Yes."

"The name doesn't ring a bell," she said, her voice faint. "Kara Sheppard. From New York City." She might as well have been talking about a total stranger. "I'm sorry, but are you absolutely certain?"

Slowly, he nodded, his sharp green gaze never leaving her face.

Though she knew she needed to address the rest of it, she wasn't sure she could. "That is a lot to take in," she admitted.

His nod let her know he understood.

Since she didn't want to be a coward, she forced herself to continue. "And Kara Sheppard—me—is in the Witness Security Program." Her stomach, already upset, twisted. "Do you know why?"

"Ryan's working on it. They refused to tell either of us too many details. He's going up the chain of command, trying to set up a meeting with someone who has authority. Dealing with the US Marshals office apparently takes time."

Now glad she'd done as he'd asked and taken a seat, she attempted to focus. Her life had gone from strange to downright unbelievable. "What else? I'm sure there's more."

"That's about it, so far. Hopefully, we'll know more once Ryan gets it cleared."

"Wow. Just wow." She shook her head, as if doing so might help her make sense of things. "I don't know which is worse, losing my memory or finding this out. Because this means that the guy who tried to run me down, the abduction and the car bomb really were attempts to kill me."

His silence made her realize he'd understood that all along.

"I guess I was trying to live in a fairy-tale world." She couldn't quite keep the bitterness from her voice.

Deep breath. Bracing herself, she asked the other question she really needed an answer to. "And Walter? Who is he?"

"That's another thing I don't know." The intensity glittering in his eyes told her he wanted that answer as much as she did. "I'm sure we'll find out once we talk again to the US Marshals."

The US Marshals. Witness Security Program. And the fact that someone really *was* trying to kill her. Suddenly, all she wanted to do was run.

She covered her face with her hands. Once she had a grip on her emotions, she raised her head and looked at him. "What do I do? Where do I go? I can't stay here, because by default, my presence means you and your family are in danger, too. Do the Marshals come and get me? Move me to a safer place? Or what?"

"Hey." His smile, though clearly meant to reassure her, couldn't take the place of his touch. And the one thing he didn't do was put his hand on her. "Try to remain calm. Nothing's going to happen to you, I promise."

She stared, hating that things were already changing between them. "How can you know that?"

"Because I'll keep you safe." The conviction in his voice left no room for uncertainty, despite the fact that both of them now stood on shaky ground. "I give you my word. And I promise you, Kara Sheppard, I always keep my word."

The instant he heard himself promise MW—no, her name was *Kara* now—that he'd keep her safe, Eric mentally winced. What the hell had he just done? He didn't yet know her full situation, or what kind of authority the Federal Witness Security Program had over her. For all he knew, they could show up and whisk her away without even a word or a question.

And even if they didn't, even if they let her stay here with him, what did he plan to do once his vacation was over? How would he keep her safe in Tulsa, when the people who wanted her dead knew she lived in the general vicinity of the hospital?

Short answer—he couldn't. Even if that wasn't the case, with the kind of hours he worked and the way his life was dedicated to his job, why make a promise he wasn't entirely sure he could keep?

Except he would. Because, just as he'd told her, Dr. Eric Colton, whenever possible, always kept his promises.

# Chapter 12

The next morning, Eric rose before dawn and prepared to head back to Tulsa. The higher-ups had finally agreed to send a couple marshals with more authority to meet with Ryan around eight and had specifically requested that Eric be there. They'd also asked for Kara, but Eric had refused to bring her.

Until he got a damn good explanation for how they'd managed to lose someone they were supposed to be protecting, Kara wasn't going anywhere.

He parked when he reached the downtown police station and went inside. Ryan led the way back to a conference room, where the US Marshals already waited.

Whatever Eric had expected, it wasn't two men in cowboy hats who looked like they worked at a cattle ranch similar to the one he'd just left.

"US Marshals Tom Field and Gus Thomasson," Ryan said. "This is my brother, Dr. Eric Colton."

After the obligatory handshakes, Ryan closed the door, gesturing that everyone could take a seat. Tom Field remained standing. Tall and lanky, he towered over the other marshal, even after he removed his hat.

His cool brown gaze zeroed in on Eric. "I'll begin. This woman, Kara Sheppard, is a key witness in a very important case. The DEA and ATF have been working jointly with the FBI to bring mobster Paul Samboliono down. Every time we think we have him, he slips out from under our fingers."

"Paul Samboliono?" Eric asked. "Never heard of him."

"He's head of the Samboliono family," Tom continued, as if that explained everything. At both Coltons' blank looks, he elaborated. "New York mobsters. Dealing in weapons and drugs and prostitution. Allegedly."

Both Eric and Ryan nodded, waiting to hear the rest.

"We need her back. She has to testify."

Eric debated whether or not to tell the other man that Kara had lost her memory, but then decided against it for now. Why cause a panic? Plus, he wanted to hear what else these two had to say.

"If Kara is so important to your case, how'd you lose her?" Eric crossed his arms. He figured he might as well cut to the chase.

Both marshals exchanged a glance. "We had a man taking care of her," Tom admitted. "Walter Randolph. He was supposed to protect her. He was murdered."

Walter. Though Eric felt terrible for the guy, it was as if a thirty-pound weight had just been lifted from his shoulders. "That explains why she asked for Walter after she got hit by that car."

"What?" Tom sounded shocked. "Hit by a car?"

He and his partner exchanged glances. "Could you please explain?"

Once Eric had finished outlining everything that had happened since the night he'd witnessed MW—er, Kara—getting run down, both marshals wore identical grim expressions.

"This is not good," Gus finally spoke, his thick New York accent sounding exotic. "Really, really not good. This means the mob has somehow learned where we took her."

"Like maybe you've got a mole?" Ryan asked.

His mouth thinning with displeasure, Gus nodded.

Eric looked at Ryan, debating if he should tell them the rest of it. Ryan gave him a nearly imperceptible nod, indicating he should.

"There's more," Eric said. When he told them Kara had no memory of her life before the accident, Tom looked as if he might get sick.

"You're a doctor. What's the probability of her regaining her memory before the trial?"

"The brain is a curious instrument," Eric said. He elected not to tell them there was no clear medical reason for Kara's amnesia. "There's no way for us to know a timeline. When it happens—if it happens—it will be on its own."

"But there is a chance, right?" Tom persisted. "Is there anything you can do to help her along?"

Ryan made a sound and turned to look out the window. Eric knew his brother well enough to realize right now Ryan was struggling to hide the urge to laugh.

"If only you knew," Ryan finally said, his back to them, his shoulders shaking. "He's been trying exactly that."

Tom nodded. "And you became involved because you were her doctor?"

"No. Actually, I was never her doctor. I just happened to be there when the Lincoln ran her down. I was leaving work. And when the hospital released her, she had no memory of who she was and therefore, no place to go. Of course I let her stay with me."

"Of course," Ryan echoed. "And the fact that she's gorgeous didn't weigh on that decision in the slightest."

Glaring at his brother, Eric sighed before returning his gaze to the marshals. "Gentlemen, you should know Kara means a lot to me. I'll do anything I have to in order to keep her safe, to protect her."

"You're not exactly qualified," Tom began.

"Maybe not," Eric cut him off. "But since protecting her was your job and you failed miserably, why don't you outline what plans you have to do exactly that?"

Tom opened and closed his mouth. This time, Ryan didn't bother to try to hide his amusement. Eric eyed the other marshal, Gus, who appeared about to come out of his seat and take both brothers on.

Ryan cleared his throat. "Just remember, we are all professionals here."

Unable to resist, Eric had to chime in. "If they're professionals at protecting witnesses, they're going to have to prove to me they can do better."

As he'd suspected it might, the meeting went downhill from there.

This time, since Eric had promised to drive back to the ranch as soon as the meeting ended, Kara couldn't relax. She paced, irritating Big J, who sent her to the kitchen to see if Edith could use any help.

This turned out to be exactly what Kara needed. Edith put her to work doing prep to help Maria make that night's dinner. "I help her whenever I can," Edith confided. "She's a really good cook and we don't want to lose her."

Kara nodded. Head down, she tackled the task of washing and cutting celery. The rhythmic motion of dicing felt like a balm upon her nerves.

"When you get done with that, you can chop onion," Edith said cheerfully. "I've always hated that job. The smell of those dang things make me weep."

Happily distracted, Kara did as told. When she'd finished that task, she turned to ask Edith what she should do next.

Instead, she found Eric standing in the doorway, silently watching her. "How long have you been there?" she asked.

"Not too long," he said. "When you have a minute, we need to talk."

Eyes watering, Kara knew better than to touch her fingers to her face. "Let me wash my hands," she managed, wondering if he could see her heart pounding through her chest. "I just need a second to try and get some of this onion smell off me."

Edith studied them both silently, saying nothing. She did, however, hand Kara lemon juice to help destroy the pungent odor.

"I'll wait for you in the living room," Eric said.

Once Kara had cleaned up, she turned to the other woman. "I can come back and help after, if you'd like."

Edith shook her head, her gaze sympathetic. "Go talk to Eric. All I have left to do in here is clean up. Maria will take over once she gets back from the store."

Taking several deep breaths to calm herself, Kara went. Looking devilishly handsome, Eric waited for her where he'd said he would, in the entrance to the living room. Since she knew he'd met with the US Marshals, she immediately zeroed in on the manila folder he held in his hands.

"Well?" she demanded, sounding much braver than she felt. "What'd you find out?"

"Let's sit." Clearing his throat, he moved into the living room. "They brought me the rest of the information on your background."

As she eyed the folder, curiosity warred with the strangest compulsion to run away. Briefly, she wondered if she really wanted to know. Of course she did. This was her life, even if she didn't remember it. She needed to learn the truth. Especially since her memory had shown very few signs of returning. Who knew, maybe this information would help jar her mind into remembering.

"Let me see." Though her voice sounded steady, her hand shook slightly as she reached for the paperwork.

Once she had it, she carried it over to the couch and sat down to read.

So much more than she'd expected. Inside she found a dossier, complete with photos.

Kara Sheppard, age 31. She'd been a professional chef. No, she corrected herself. She *was* a professional executive chef. She had her own kitchen at an upscale surf-and-turf restaurant called Keogas in Lower Manhattan, no less. Which meant she was a very good cook indeed.

Something clicked in her brain. A chef. In fact, she'd graduated at the head of her class from the Institute of

Culinary Education in New York City. After that, she'd spent some time in Paris learning more. She was good. Damn good. Her talent stemmed from more than just skill—it was also because she *loved* to cook. Even as a teenager, she'd turned to cooking as comfort when the drama of life seemed about to overwhelm her.

Suddenly, the dry facts on paper became real. Until she'd witnessed the murder, cooking had been her entire life. She'd devoted every waking second toward work and saving up so one day she could open her own restaurant.

Wait, what? Witnessed a… She'd witnessed a murder. Scanning the papers, she found the reason she'd been taken into the Witness Security Program. Even as she started to read, the memories came flooding back.

Paul Samboliono had been a regular in the restaurant. As a VIP, he even had his own table despite, or maybe because of, his rumored mob connections. Kara had made it her business not to know too much about the customers or their lives. She cooked, they ate and this was her cycle of life. She'd been content, even happy.

Until she'd walked out of the kitchen into the dining room in time to see Paul shoot and kill two men. Later she'd learned they'd been undercover DEA agents.

He'd spotted her, but she'd run away as fast as she could, aware she was running for her life. She'd bypassed the NYPD, going to the FBI building at 26 Federal Plaza. Once she'd reached the twenty-third floor, she'd asked to speak to an agent and told the man everything she'd seen.

After that, her life had completely changed. She hadn't even been allowed to go back to her apartment.

She inhaled sharply, not daring to look at Eric. Her memory had returned. All of it, and she had no more gaps in her recollection of her life prior to being hit by a car.

Just to be absolutely certain, she continued reading. There, she saw photographs of her apartment, there on East 20th Street in Midtown. It was a nice place, and she'd been lucky to find it. She could afford something that nice because she made a very good living as an executive chef.

As she read, she found herself nodding. True, she was single, with no pets or significant others. Absolutely correct. The US Marshals Service had done their homework.

There was more, and she continued to read even though she already knew the rest. Her parents were deceased, killed in a helicopter crash while on their dream vacation in Hawaii. She had no siblings, though she had a lot of friends, some so close she considered them her sisters.

Tears stung her eyes as she realized how much she'd given up. They'd sent her to Tulsa, Oklahoma, where she'd taken a job as a prep cook in a chain restaurant. How far she'd fallen. Her only consolation had been the fact that she was alive, and that once she testified against Paul Samboliono her life could return to normal.

Or so she'd been promised. Now, she wasn't so certain. Putting the papers down, she closed her eyes and rubbed her temples, hoping to stave off the beginning of what felt like a monster headache.

"Does anything seem familiar?" Eric asked, his voice hopeful.

"Yes." Opening her eyes, she met and held his gaze. "I remember everything. Everything." Her voice caught.

At her words, he dropped down on the couch alongside her and wrapped his arms around her. "Are you okay?" he whispered, his breath hot against her ear. She nodded, leaning into his strength as he held on tight.

His masculine scent comforted her. She found herself relaxing against him, relieved to be rid of the distance he'd briefly put between them.

She closed the folder. "I don't need to read the rest of it, except to check their facts."

Glad he kept his arms around her, she told him everything, finishing up with the name she'd called out the night she'd been hit by a car. "Walter was the marshal assigned to protect me. I overheard him talking on the phone, telling someone he would hand me over in exchange for money. When I ran, he came after me."

Eric leaned forward, touching his forehead to hers. "Is he the one who tried to run you down?"

"I think so, but I don't know for sure."

"The marshals mentioned him. I've been told he was killed. Shot dead, execution style in the back."

Wincing, she closed her eyes. "Probably because he tried to associate with the wrong people. They probably blamed him for my escape."

"It's possible."

She breathed deeply, loving the masculine scent of him. "And that's how they know where I am."

"Probably so." Though he tightened his hold on her, he didn't sound concerned. "I left the meeting before they were done talking. I wanted to give everyone a little time to cool off."

Perplexed, she tilted her head back to look up at him. "What do you mean?"

His smile made her curl her toes. "Let's just say we disagreed on the best way to keep you safe."

She wanted him to kiss her. Right there, in the middle of his family's living room, where anyone could walk in on them. Not a good idea, and she tried to suppress the dizzying desire racing through her veins.

Gaze darkening, he leaned in. Her breath caught as she let her eyes drift closed. She wanted another soul-searing, heart-melting, deep and sensuous kiss like the others they'd shared. Instead, Eric delivered a chaste peck on the lips, patting her shoulder as if that was all he could think to do to comfort her.

Her protest died on her lips as he released her.

"Let me go get cleaned up," he said, looking past her as he pushed up off the couch. "And then we'll talk more. I'm waiting for a phone call, either from Ryan or one of the men who attended the meeting today. Once that happens, I'll have a few things I need to run by you."

Somehow, she managed to nod.

"Feel free to use that laptop," he pointed. "It's the one you used in my town house. I've already connected to the Wi-Fi. You can look up anything you want to, in case you want something to do while I'm gone."

Instantly, she thought of Facebook. "Thanks, I will."

Eric cut his eyes left. When she looked that way, she noticed Big J standing near the foyer, silently watching them. When his gaze met hers, confusion flickered across his face, making her wonder if he even recognized her. Which didn't make sense.

"Hi there, Dad," Eric said, starting to move past him.

"Wait." Big J grabbed his son's arm. "I need to talk to you about your mother."

Eric froze. "Is she all right?"

"Yes, she's getting stronger every day. But I'm worried about something. I think she might know who attacked her."

"Why do you say that?"

"Because every time I ask her about it, she gets scared. I've known that woman for half my life, and I recognize fear in her eyes when I see it. She knows, but she doesn't want to tell me."

His frustration evident in his tone, Big J stalked over to the liquor cabinet and poured himself a drink.

"I'll be talking to Ryan in a little bit," Eric said. "I'll pass that information on to him. Maybe she'll tell him, since he's a cop."

"Maybe so," Big J allowed. "Maybe so."

"I'll be right back," Eric told him, glancing at Kara and flashing a half smile. She watched as he took the stairs two at a time.

When she looked back in the direction of his father, she realized Big J had left the room.

Immediately, she headed for the laptop. She sat down and turned it on. Once she had it going, she went online, visiting her own Facebook page. Now that she was back to normal, she even managed to remember the password—no small feat. It felt oddly discomforting, reading all the concerned messages posted after her abrupt disappearance by her friends and coworkers, even customers.

She studied the photographs of her—laughing with friends on a night out, cooking some fancy, unpronounceable dish. There were also a lot of pictures of the expensive restaurant where she worked. Keogas appeared to be a popular place.

As she studied all this, her throat ached. After all she'd been through, she felt like the woman she'd once been was a complete stranger. Her life had completely changed.

Worse, she couldn't help but wonder if she'd ever see Eric again once the US Marshals came for her to take her to some other safe place. Heck, the way things had been going, she'd begun to doubt she'd even live long enough to be able to testify.

Suddenly, she couldn't bear to see any more. She shut the computer down and headed up the stairs to her room. Once there, she studied herself in the mirror, trying to find some resemblance between the woman staring back at her and the laughing, confident woman she'd seen on the Facebook page.

A light tapping on her door roused her from her reverie.

"May I come in?" Eric asked.

She couldn't help but give herself one final quick check in the mirror before answering. "Of course."

When he entered, his rough good looks made her catch her breath. He'd changed into a pair of well-worn jeans and a button-down Western shirt. A rush of desire heated her blood. Right now, he looked more like a cowboy than a surgeon. A sexy-as-hell cowboy. She wanted to jump his bones. Apparently, she would always have this reaction to him, no matter the circumstances or her mood. Her mouth went dry at the realization.

"I have good news," he said, clearly oblivious. "The US Marshals just called. They've agreed to my plan."

Confused, she frowned. "What plan?"

"I figured out what to do with you."

His words instantly turned her insides to ice. Steeling herself, she waited for him to continue.

"Yesterday when they learned about all the attempts on your life—the guy running you down, the failed abduction and finally the car bomb—they realized the immediate need to get you someplace safe. That's what I disagreed with them on. So I came up with my own plan. Today, they called to say they'd considered it and my idea would be a go."

His idea. What to do with her. She felt as if she had no say, no control, in her own destiny.

And now she felt pretty darn sure Eric was about to wash his hands of her for good. She nodded and braced herself. Would he miss her?

"Don't look like that." He cupped her chin. "I promise, it's not bad news."

Heaven help her, her knees went weak. "It's not?"

"No. At least, not as far as I'm concerned. It's been decided that for now, you can continue to stay with me here at the ranch. The trial is in less than two weeks, so we're going to keep you safe until you can testify and put the mobster guy behind bars."

Mobster guy. She winced. "No one has ever successfully testified against Paul Samboliono. Usually, anyone who's tried in the past has met an accident before the trial."

"Well, you'll be the first then. Because I personally am going to make sure you make it to the courthouse alive."

Hope warred with trepidation. "Why are the Marshals agreeing to this? I would think their first priority would be to keep me safe themselves. That's what they do, supposedly."

"They haven't done a very good job of it so far, now have they?"

She couldn't argue with that. Best of all, she got to stay with Eric a little longer. "I need to find out if I have access to funds. I'd like to repay you for all the clothing you had Greta purchase for me."

Smiling, he shook his head. "Don't sweat the small stuff. We can deal with that in good time."

"I don't know how much time I'm going to have left," she confessed. "Who knows if the bad guys will succeed the next time?"

"They won't. I told you that I'd protect you," he reminded her.

"Thank you," she told him, blinking furiously to keep from crying.

Evidently her effort didn't fool him. "It's all right," he said, and brought her into the circle of his arms.

She moved without thought, stepping right into his embrace. She told herself that all she'd wanted was comfort and reassurance. Instead, wrapped in those muscular arms, pressed against his broad chest, desire once again slammed into her. He smelled like soap and man, an arousing scent. She inhaled, her heart pounding in her chest, afraid to move, afraid to raise her head to look at him in case he read the strength of the need in her eyes.

They stood together, holding on to each other, neither speaking.

"Are you two at it again?" a deep voice boomed, making her jump. Big J.

Eric released her and stepped back. "I'm just comforting her, Dad."

The older man harrumphed. "Right. I've *comforted* a few women in my younger days, too. Just remember, you're in our house. And your mother is awake again. Have you been to see her today?"

"Not yet." Eric's polite tone came out both grim and cheerful. "I'll make sure and do that soon."

Despite the pointed hint to leave, his father stayed put, his gaze flickering back and forth from Eric to Kara.

Eric sighed. "Kara, are you all right now?"

Trying to avoid meeting his gaze, she nodded. "Yes. Go and visit your mother," she said. "I'll see if Maria needs any help with anything in the kitchen." She brushed past both men, forcing herself to walk when all she wanted to do was run out of the room.

Unable to tear his eyes away, Eric watched Kara go, admiring the gentle sway of her curvy hips, but inwardly wincing. Clearly, her apparent haste was due to the violent physical reaction he'd had when he held her in his arms. He shook his head, wondering why his self-control had deserted him.

Even now, after she'd left the room, he burned hot for her. Sure, he found her attractive—what red-blooded man wouldn't? Despite that, he hadn't expected this. In his personal life, just like in his profession, he preferred things neat and orderly. Wanting

Kara would only unnecessarily complicate things for both of them. And she had enough on her plate.

"That girl's a looker," Big J drawled, reminding Eric of his presence. "Are you going to make an honest woman out of her?"

At a complete loss for words, Eric met his father's gaze. "You never know," he answered. "You just never know."

With that, he headed into his mother's room.

Latonia had propped Abra into a sitting position by using several pillows. Her unfocused gaze worried him, making his fingers itch for a pin light to check her pupils.

Instead, he reminded himself that as far as his father was concerned, Eric was not his mother's physician.

"Go ahead," Latonia prompted. "Visit with her. I know she looks like she's far away, but she's been in and out all day. She hears everything you say to her."

He nodded, curbing the impulse to tell her he already knew that.

"Hey, Mom," he said softly, approaching the bed. "How are you feeling today?"

Her gaze never wavered, though the beginning of a smile curved her mouth.

"See!" Latonia clapped her hands. "She heard you."

"Of course I heard him," Abra snapped, startling them both. This time, her eyes were wide-open and focused on her son.

Eric grinned. "Well, look who's back."

Her quick frown told him what she thought of that. "Come over here and give your mother a hug," she ordered.

So he did exactly that. Though her embrace was

weak and she felt like skin and bones, anything was better than the state she'd been in before.

Pulling up a chair next to her bed, he sat. "Mom, do you remember what happened?"

Instantly she looked away, but not before he'd seen the stark terror flash into her eyes. "No," she said, in the high-pitched, querulous voice that told him she was lying. "Why?"

"Because you were attacked. Ryan has been trying to find out who did this to you."

Suddenly, all her energy seemed to leach out of her. "I'm too tired to talk about this now," she said, closing her eyes. "Please leave me alone and let me sleep."

Exchanging a quick look with Latonia, who shrugged, he sighed. "All right, Mother. Sleep well." After kissing her forehead, he left.

On the way to find Kara, his cell phone rang. Since the caller ID showed *US Marshals Office*, he answered immediately. His heart sank as he listened, unable to get a word in and aware it wouldn't make any difference even if he did.

## Chapter 13

When Kara heard the light tap on her bedroom door, her heart skipped a beat. "Eric?"

"Yes."

Yanking open the door, she resisted the urge to fling herself into his arms. And then she got a good look at him.

His flat expression and clamped mouth warned her that something had happened. Whatever it was, it hadn't been good. He met her gaze and she couldn't help but notice the muscle flicking angrily in his jaw.

Her first thought was his mother. "Is your mother all right?"

"Oh, sure." He dismissed her concern with a wave of his hand. "She's awake and talking. It's not her. The US Marshals office just called."

"Bad news?" she asked, keeping her tone light, as if

she thought she could change whatever had just happened.

"Yes." Dragging his hand through his short hair, he stalked to the edge of the room and back. "They've changed their mind about letting you stay here. They're coming to get you. They'll be here by nightfall."

At first, she wasn't sure she'd heard correctly. Her stomach dropped as she peered up at him, trying to make sense of his words. "What? I thought you said they'd given their okay for me to hide out here at the ranch."

"They did. Turned out the two men I met didn't have the authority to do that. Someone from higher up pitched a fit. There's been a direct order. You have to go."

Terror turned her blood to ice. "What if I refuse?"

"You can try." But his expression said he didn't hold out much hope.

She wished he'd touch her, take her in his arms and comfort her. Instead, he stood several feet away, as if he'd already let her go.

Enough. This was too important. She couldn't afford to make a mistake. "I'd rather stay here."

"I told them that." For the first time she noticed his hands were clenched into fists. "I even called our family attorney. He advised me to stay out of their way. And..." He hesitated.

"What?" Bracing herself, she waited.

"He pointed out something I don't think either of us has considered. If Samboliono is acquitted or escapes, you'll have to stay in witness protection the rest of your life.

His words felt like a slap in the face. "I hadn't

thought of that," she admitted. "I never really looked beyond the trial. This isn't fair. It's not like I asked to witness a double homicide."

Listening to her own words, she winced. Police lingo. A few days ago she wouldn't have even known the term.

"I agree. It's not fair at all."

She grabbed his arm. "There must be something we can do."

His gaze softened. "I swear to you, we'll try." He covered her hand with his and squeezed. "We'll do whatever we have to do."

While she wished he'd pull her into his arms and kiss her senseless, she'd take what she could get.

The two marshals who'd been sent to collect her looked more like football players or bouncers for a nightclub. Goons, she thought to herself, eyeing them. They stood with their massive legs spread and muscular arms crossed, waiting for her to pack a bag. After requesting and reviewing their ID, Eric handed back their badges with a grimace.

"Where's Tom Field and Gus Thomasson?" Eric asked.

"They have other assignments. Our job is to pick Ms. Sheppard up and take her to safety."

"And your names?" Eric persisted.

The two men exchanged glances.

"I'm Gray," the shorter, stockier one said. "And he's Shelton. Are you ready, ma'am?"

"What if I refuse to go?" she asked, trying not to sound too desperate.

Shelton shook his head. "Not an option, ma'am.

Please pack or we'll have to take you without your things."

The other man, Gray, apparently taking pity on her dejected expression, moved toward her. "You know this is for the best. You'll have a guard 24/7. We won't let anything happen to you."

"Forgive me if I say I've lost all faith in your ability to do that," she said. "The last person you assigned to watch me tried to sell me out to the highest bidder."

"I'm sorry about that. I promise it won't happen again."

As she debated how to respond, Eric moved to stand beside her. Putting his arm around her shoulders, he drew her close. "She'll go. Give her a few minutes to get everything packed."

Stunned and hurt at his betrayal, she let him lead her up the stairs toward her room. Once there, she pushed him away. "How could you do that? You don't know if these men are competent or as inept as the last guy."

"I'm not worried."

That declaration hurt twice as bad. "I don't believe you," she managed, her voice hoarse, tears stinging her eyes.

"Wait." He grabbed her hand. "There's a reason I can say such a thing."

Unconvinced, she waited, trying not to tremble.

"I'm not worried about their ability to protect you, because we aren't going to rely on them alone. I'm going with you, Kara Sheppard. No way am I letting you out of my sight."

At first, she wasn't sure how to react. Relief, disbelief and joy filled her. "Are you sure you want to do that?" she asked.

"Positive."

Now came the question she knew she shouldn't ask, but also knew she had to. "Why? Why would you do such a thing?"

"Because I just found you. No way am I letting you go. Not now. Not until we've explored this thing between us."

Her heart jolted as she gazed up at him, wondering if he could read the raw emotion shining from her eyes. As declarations went, this might be a bit on the vague side, but again, it was more than she'd expected. "Thank you," she said quietly. "And Eric, I agree."

If she expected him to say more, now was not the time.

"Come on, get packed," he told her, giving her a gentle shove. "I'll do the same and meet you at the top of the stairs."

Eric didn't want to analyze his feelings or even discuss them. He just knew he couldn't let Kara leave his life. Not now, not just yet. Not until he knew exactly what these feelings she roused in him might be. He had a hunch, but he'd never been the impractical sort. He believed in science and logic and that side of him figured this might just be an extreme case of sexual attraction coupled with infatuation.

His heart kept insisting it might be more.

Either way, there was no chance he planned to let the US Marshals Service take over keeping Kara safe. As far as he was concerned, they'd already proven themselves inept at the task. He figured if he stepped back and let them do their job, as they put it, the next call he'd get would be informing him Kara had been killed. And there wasn't a chance in hell he'd let that happen.

Once he'd thrown some clothes into a duffel, he grabbed a brand-new cell phone he'd purchased to give Seth as a surprise. Aware it would have to charge, he took it anyway and left his room. Kara waited at the top of the staircase. She'd loaded everything into the same small suitcase she'd used before.

"Here," he told her, handing her the phone. "Hopefully they'll let you charge it in the car. I've jotted down the number so I can call you. And here's mine on this sticky note. Once the phone's charged, we'll program it in."

"Thanks." Accepting it, she dropped it in her pocket, her expression worried. "Are you thinking we'll get separated or something?"

"You never know." He kept his tone light. "Best to be prepared, just in case. You know they're not going to be too happy about me insisting on going." He gave her arm a light touch and they went downstairs where their escorts waited. Big J stood a slight distance from them, his arms crossed. From the thunderous expression he wore, the marshals had evidently filled him in.

"Come here, son." Big J beckoned Eric into another room. Steeling himself, Eric followed. He felt pretty sure he knew what his father would have to say.

Instead, Big J surprised him. "You take care of your sweetheart, you hear me?" His green gaze, the same one he'd passed down to all his children, was intense. "Don't let those yahoos mess up again."

"I won't." Giving in to impulse, Eric hugged his father, something he hadn't done in years. "Thank you," he managed, difficult since his throat had gone tight.

"You bet." The older Colton gave Eric a tiny shove. "Call if you need any help."

"I will." Eric turned. "Let me stop in and tell Mother goodbye."

"Wait." Big J grabbed his arm. "Hold off on that for now. I don't want to upset her. She's been doing so well, I don't want to do anything that might cause a setback. Understand?"

Slowly, Eric nodded. Though he felt disappointed that he couldn't see his mother, what his father said made sense. "What are you going to tell her?"

"Just that you're busy," Big J drawled. "She'll understand. She's used to that."

Eric refused to take his father's bait. Jerking his chin in a nod, he took Kara's arm and they followed the marshals out the door and into the car. Once inside, he captured Kara's hand with his own, glad that she let him. They sat that way the entire time the vehicle jolted up and down on the dirt road.

Once they reach the blacktop of the main road, Eric glanced at Kara. Her full lips twitched as if she was trying not to laugh. He shook his head, his own mouth curving in response. The absolute silence in the car could be either intimidating or funny. Both he and Kara found it the latter. Somehow he didn't think the two US Marshals would find their amusement humorous.

They continued down the road in silence. Finally, Eric's cell phone rang, earning him a hard look from Marshal Shelton, who sat in the passenger seat.

Ignoring him, Eric answered. It was Ryan.

"Where are you?" his brother asked, not bothering to mask the urgent tone in his voice.

"En route," Eric answered, which garnished him another quelling look, this time from the driver.

"To where?" Ryan persisted.

"Ah, I don't actually know."

Shocked silence from his brother. "Okay," Ryan finally responded. "I'll let that one go for now. I've got some bad news. Eventually, I'll have to relay this to the US Marshals office, but I wanted you to know first."

Gratified, Eric kept his face expressionless. "Hit me."

"When we were doing the search to find out about the orthopedic insert in MW's leg—"

"Kara," Eric interrupted, correcting automatically. "Go on."

"I'll cut to the chase. Bottom line, when everything matched up, before we knew who she was, her picture and name went out over the wire."

"What's that mean?"

Ryan sighed. "Every police station and law-enforcement office was notified. That's how the US Marshals found out. Unfortunately, I got a report from a NYPD buddy that the info was leaked to the mob. Not just any mob. Samboliono's group, to be exact. Even though he's in prison awaiting trial, his men are working off his orders."

Almost afraid to ask, Eric did anyway. "What's that mean for us?"

"They not only know where she is, but I have no doubt they're sending men to get her."

Eric cursed. "Which means it's a damn good thing that I don't have any idea where they're taking us." Now he had both marshals' attention. The driver—Gray—kept an eye on Eric in the rearview mirror while Shelton had turned to face the backseat. The questioning look on both their faces demanded answers. Eric ignored them, at least for now.

"Maybe," Ryan allowed. "But you need to know. I'd suggest you find out as soon as you can. And Eric, stay alert. Watch and be ready for anything."

"Thanks, I will." Keeping his tone light, Eric knew Ryan wouldn't have given him such a warning if he wasn't worried. Heck, with the way the US Marshals had performed so far, Eric couldn't blame him.

After ending the call, Eric smiled at his front-seat pals. "Well?" Shelton asked, not bothering to hide his impatience. "What was that all about?"

Eric gave Kara's hand a quick squeeze. "That was my brother Ryan. He's a detective for the Tulsa PD. Y'all should know he's learned there's been a leak somewhere in the NYPD. Samboliono and his men know where Kara is—at least the general vicinity."

"How?" The marshal barked. "How do you know this?"

"My brother has a buddy in the NYPD. When Kara's picture went out over the wire, he heard some scuttlebutt. Samboliono's guys know. Word has it they're heading for Tulsa right now, so I hope you're not taking us anywhere near there."

"We're not," Gray spoke up. "Actually, we're heading south, to Texas. She should be safe there."

"Texas isn't that far from Tulsa," Kara worried. "Shouldn't you take me farther?"

Neither of the marshals answered. Kara swallowed, glanced at Eric and shrugged.

Slightly annoyed, Eric leaned forward. "I believe the lady asked you a question."

"Sorry." Glaring at Eric, Gray sounded anything but. "Ma'am, I promise you we have everything under control. Please, let us do our job."

She nodded and opened her mouth. Eric shot her a look telling her she'd better not apologize. "You've done nothing wrong," he whispered in her ear. "Don't let them intimidate you."

Exhaling, she leaned into him. "Thank you," she murmured. "Especially thank you for coming with me. I feel a lot safer with you here."

A warm glow filled his heart at her words. To keep from revealing his emotions to anyone else in the car, he turned and focused his attention out the window. Ryan had said to stay on his toes. So he couldn't afford to let anything or anyone distract him, especially not his beautiful charge.

While Kara wasn't 100 percent sure why Eric had decided to accompany her, the fact that he had made her heart sing with joy. She knew he cared about her, even though he hadn't said all that much. Sometimes, actions definitely spoke louder than words. Still, she longed to tell him her own growing feelings, and maybe show him how she felt with her body. Not now, certainly. But she hoped soon.

Though patience had never been one of her strengths, she knew the time would come when they'd talk and share their feelings. She believed Eric cared for her as strongly as she did for him. Though her immediate future might be in jeopardy until the trial and conviction of the mobster, she refused to let go of the shining hope for her life beyond all this. She'd always envisioned her future, and the possible life she could see ahead of her now beckoned like a bright light on the dark horizon.

Her life. A life that hopefully would include Eric. She'd wanted to open a restaurant; her pretty hefty savings account could testify to that. What better place to do that than Tulsa? With Eric by her side, anything seemed possible.

Once she made it past all this, that is.

Her stomach flip-flopped. Despite her mental admonishment not to be anxious, she couldn't seem to calm herself. It didn't help that the two US Marshals entrusted with her care were clearly on edge. Both the driver and his shotgun passenger kept checking the side mirrors as well as the rearview mirror, as if they expected to be followed. Or shot at. Or something.

Twice she opened her mouth to ask about this and thought better of it. She wasn't sure she really wanted to know.

Still, their edginess increased her nervousness, and she fidgeted in her seat. Eric finally reached for her and pulled her close against his broad chest.

Relieved, she gave up all her tension and relaxed against him. "Thank you," she murmured, knowing he'd understand.

"It's okay." The deep rumble of his voice under her ear made her smile. "We have to trust that these guys know what they're doing."

"Do we?" she murmured back. "Look how edgy they are."

He nodded and tightened his arms around her. "After what's happened so far, do you blame them? I'd rather them be watchful than complacent."

The words had no sooner left his mouth when something exploded outside the window. The car swerved, tires squealing.

"Blowout," the driver shouted, his grip white-knuckled on the wheel as he fought to maintain control.

Eric tightened his grip on her. "Hold on," he ordered. "We'll be all right."

But as the vehicle spun and hit the guardrail, metal screeching and sparks flying, she knew they wouldn't. They'd been going at least seventy when the tire had blown. They'd be lucky not to roll over.

Dimly she heard a scream and as she realized it was her own voice, the car spun again, slamming into the concrete median with a sickening crunch of metal.

Someone shouted, and then the car shuddered before coming to a halt—upside down, she thought, the seat belt cutting into her so tightly she couldn't turn.

"Eric?" As she tried to speak, she coughed, horrified to see the bright red specks of blood on her hand. "Eric?" she tried again, louder this time. Still no response.

Blinking, she tried to see, but couldn't—the thick smoke made it impossible. Smoke? Even as she registered that, she felt heat and heard the awful crackle of fire. Gasoline and flames meant danger. There'd be an explosion if the flames weren't put out.

Crud. Heart pounding, she struggled to free herself. If she didn't get Eric and herself out of here, they'd die.

Twisting again, she tried to take stock of the situation. Beyond the smoke, something else was wrong with her vision; she managed to bring her hand up to wipe at her eyes. When her fingers came away covered in blood, she suddenly felt pain. She'd been injured. A head wound, and more.

Tough. Gritting her teeth, she fought to unclip the seat belt. When she succeeded, she fell forward. Turning to her left, she found the door handle and pulled. Locked. She tried again, using all her strength. Still nothing.

The hiss and roar of fire grew louder. Horrified, she saw that the entire engine was ablaze. Both men in the front seat had either fallen over out of sight or had already gotten out.

She'd help them if she could. Right now, she needed to try to get Eric out. He slumped against the opposite door, covered with blood, unconscious and way too still.

Crawling over him, she yanked at his door handle, grunting as her first attempt succeeded and she pushed the door open.

She tumbled to the pavement, the pain on top of her other injuries bringing tears to her eyes. Ignoring this—ignoring everything but Eric—she managed to undo his seat belt. She used strength she had never possessed to pull him from the car, wincing as he hit the concrete, but still half pulling, half dragging him away from the now fully engulfed car. Tears stung her eyes as she said a quick prayer for anyone who hadn't escaped.

Another vehicle approached, the headlights blinding her. "Help!" She attempted a scream, though the sound coming from her raw throat sounded more like a croak. "Help!" She tried again, letting Eric go once she had him safe—far enough away and out of the roadway. The instant she did, she staggered and nearly went to her knees.

Footsteps sounding behind her made her turn. Too slowly. She saw the blur too late right before something smashed into the back of her head and everything went black.

When she came to, her first thought was that everything hurt. Throbbed. So painful she could barely even breathe. She ached from the top of her head down to her toes. Confused, she tried to process what had happened.

A blown tire. A car wreck. Eric. With a strangled gasp, she attempted to jump to her feet to look for him. That's when she realized her arms and legs were tied.

"There you are," a vaguely familiar voice drawled. Squinting, she stared as a man came into view, trying to make out his features.

Shocked, she realized she knew him. Gray. "You're the US marshal who was driving the car," she said, her voice wobbly and too high, even as she tried not to reveal her terror.

"You got one thing right," he responded, coming close enough that she could smell the sourness of his breath. "I did drive the car, but I'm not a US marshal."

Her heart skipped a beat as she realized what he meant. "Obviously."

Though every muscle in her body had tightened, she forced herself to try to appear calm. "What are you going to do with me?"

His casual shrug scared her more than a simple declaration would have. "Depends," he said. "I'll do whatever I'm told to do."

"What about Eric? And the other marshal?"

Again the deliberately nonchalant shrug. "What about them? You got your guy out of the vehicle, so assuming someone eventually showed up to help him, I'd guess he's okay."

"And your partner?"

"The real US marshal?" His stare hardened. "Shelton wasn't my partner. I didn't get him out of the car. Since it probably exploded, I'm going to take a guess and suggest he didn't make it."

Her breath caught, though she looked down to hide it. Tears pricked her eyes and the back of her throat ached. And then, inexplicably, fury filled her. None of this would have happened if she'd just stayed on the ranch with Eric.

"We would have found you anyway," her captor said, speaking as if he knew what she'd been thinking. "Just think of how many casualties there might have been if we'd figured out where you'd been hiding earlier. That old guy at the ranch might have been the first to go." He mimicked shooting a gun, the amusement flickering in his eyes turning her blood to ice.

Though any movement felt excruciating, she slowly turned her head, trying to figure out where they were. The floor and three walls were unbroken concrete, the fourth, though also cement, had a single window halfway up.

She'd been tied to a ladder-back wooden chair. Hands behind her back, feet to the bottom. Her captor sat in a similar chair, about ten feet way, next to a folding card table with a laptop on it.

Smirking at her, he took out his cell and checked it. "No missed calls," Gray said. "I'm waiting to be told to kill you. They usually leave the method up to me. I can be pretty creative, you know. The more you scream, the more I enjoy it."

And then, as if he hadn't said something so horrific that the words made bile rise in her throat, he began to play a noisy game on his phone, humming along as he did.

## Chapter 14

Eric coughed, eyes watering as he attempted to breathe through the thick smoke. Smoke! He gasped, choking on the foul air. *What the...?* He grimaced, struggling to push to his feet. "MW?" he called. The pain pounded in his skull. Wrong name. "Kara?"

*Bam.* The explosion sent him back to the ground, arm up to protect his face. A wave of heat singed his skin. Fire roared, the blaze reaching hungry flame fingers up to the sky. The car. The car was burning.

"Kara!" Screaming her name, he crawled to the guardrail and managed to pull himself up. He took a step forward, staggering, trying to find the strength to push on.

"Hey, man. Are you all right?" One of the US marshals, looking almost a bad as Eric felt, appeared in the smoke. Shelton's dark blue pants were sooty and torn, a large hole near his bloody knee. The white shirt had been shredded and also appeared to be dotted with dirt, soot and blood. His cowboy hat was gone.

"I'm okay." Lurching forward, Eric met him half-way. "What the hell happened? Where's Kara?"

"Gray, the guy who was driving, took her." Attempting to drag his hand through his short hair, the other man winced as he connected with a cut. He held up bloody fingers and muttered a curse.

"The driver took her?" At least she wasn't still in the burning car. Then, as the words registered, Eric stared. "That doesn't make sense. A tire blew," he prompted. "Gray lost control and we wrecked. Tell me what exactly happened after we came to a stop?"

"That wasn't a blowout. Best as I can tell, some-one shot out one of the front tires. Gray apparently expected it. Clearly, it was a setup." Shelton doubled over, coughing and wheezing, blood pouring from a gash on his shoulder.

"Are you all right?" Eric asked. "Let me take a look at that wound."

"I'm fine." Shelton waved him off. After a second, he continued. "Once we stopped, Gray—if that was really his name—got out. He didn't bother to help me, so I did it myself. Kara did the same, despite being pretty banged up. She's a strong lady. Somehow she managed to haul your unconscious ass from the car. She saved your life, man."

Since Eric remembered none of this, he nodded, gri-macing as pain shot through his skull. "That sounds like her. Then what?"

"I blacked out for a little bit. When I came to, the

last thing I saw was Gray carrying Kara and loading her into a white van."

Kidnapped? Or taking her to a hospital? If the latter, why wouldn't he have taken Eric and his partner, too? Unless… Eric's blood turned to ice. Unless Gray worked for Samboliono and had taken her to kill her.

Which meant they needed to find her now.

"What's your full name, Shelton?" Eric asked.

"Smith. US Marshal Shelton Smith."

"Okay. Marshal Smith, have you called it in?"

When the other man just stared at him in confusion, Eric repeated the question. "Have you called your office to see if they sent backup? Maybe checked on the possibility that Marshal Gray rushed Kara to a hospital."

Still Shelton didn't move. "I doubt very much he was actually a marshal."

"I do, too, but you don't know." Eric barked the words. "And since I'm pretty sure you were trained not to go on supposition, for now we need to proceed as if he is." Ryan's words, put to good use.

The other man stared, his eyes narrowing. "If he's a marshal, why would he take Kara and leave us? I mean, if that white van was our guys, why would—"

"Call," Eric ordered, cutting him off. "Right now."

Fumbling in his pocket, Shelton located his cell phone. After punching in a number, he spoke a few words and then listened before he began answering questions. From what little Eric could make out, this accident had not been an accident.

"They think it was a planned attack," Shelton said once he'd finished the call. "They're reviewing nearby highway cameras now. And they're sending someone to retrieve us and take us to the closest hospital to be checked out."

"Screw that." Though he could barely stand up straight, Eric itched to take action. "As soon as they locate that white van, I want to go after them."

The marshal stared in disbelief. "You're in no shape to—"

Eric held up his hand, effectively silencing anything else. "Let me see your phone," he demanded.

Shelton stared at him for a second. "Don't you have your own?"

"Of course I do." Eric held out his hand. "But I want to use yours."

Shelton finally shrugged and handed it over.

First, Eric used his own phone and dialed the number on the phone he'd given Kara. As he'd expected, it went directly to a recording saying the mailbox hadn't been set up yet. The next call he wanted to make would have to be without an audience, so he dropped Shelton's phone in his pocket. "You'll get it back soon," he said.

Though the marshal glared at him, he didn't protest.

When the ambulance showed up a few minutes later, Eric allowed himself to be loaded on board, along with his equally battered companion. Lights flashing, siren wailing, they raced toward a hospital.

As soon as they pulled into the ER bay, Eric brushed off the EMT's attempts to assist him. His strength had begun returning, no doubt fueled by adrenaline. He walked inside under his own power, making a quick turn as he spotted a restroom a few doors down from a supply closet and an employee lounge.

Thankful that things didn't vary much from hospital

to hospital, he slipped into the supply closet and located some bandages and antiseptic, along with some antibiotic salve. He snagged a pair of scrubs off a hook in the doctor's lounge and headed toward the restroom. There, he cleaned up as best he could, finally changing out of his torn and bloody clothes into the scrubs. Though the pants were a little short, they fit.

Stepping into the hall, he made his way to front door. As soon as he reached the outside, he stopped and hit redial on Shelton's phone. The last call the marshal had made had been to his office.

When a woman answered, "US Marshals Office," Eric identified himself. Then he asked for the status on locating Kara. The woman on the other end hesitated before stating she'd need to check with someone before she could release that information.

Barely keeping his frustrated impatience in check, he told her he'd wait.

A moment later, she returned. "Good news," she said. "I've been cleared to brief you. The white van has been spotted heading south on 75. We've got a chopper in the sky en route, plus people on the ground. As of right now, they're just past Sherman, Texas."

Thanking her, he ended the call. Eyeing the ambulance still parked in the ER bay, he strode over to see if they'd left the keys in the ignition. They had.

He ignored the pain and heaved himself up into the driver's seat. He started the engine and, lights still flashing, tore out of there and headed for the highway.

Tied to a chair, hurting and bleeding and not even being allowed to clean up, Kara couldn't help but feel her luck had finally run out.

Luck? She snorted, lowering her gaze as her captor stared at her. Who did she think she was fooling? She believed in a lot of things—dedication, hard work, loyalty, for starters—but luck wasn't one of them. In fact, if she believed in luck at all, it was with the knowledge that she made her own luck. She always had, except for recently.

Ever since she'd lost her memory, she'd drifted along, a victim of circumstance and, yes, fickle fate. Maybe even, if she really reached, luck. No longer. Now that she had herself back, Kara knew if she wanted to live, she'd have to make her own good fortune.

And the first order of business would be to figure out a way to escape before Paul Samboliono ordered her killed. There had been two men—the driver of the white van, and the man who'd been impersonating a US marshal—Gray. Right now, she saw only one.

Since she had no really great ideas, she figured she'd start simple. "Excuse me." She cleared her throat. "I need to use the bathroom."

Her captor gave her a brief dismissive glance. "No."

Biting down hard inside her lip, she began to cry. Loud, crocodile tears that she hoped were at least the slight bit convincing.

"Stop that," Gray ordered, his voice sharp. "Don't make me hit you and give you a reason to cry."

Of course this made her amp it up. Weeping and wailing, she somehow managed to make real tears stream down her face.

"Stop it, I said." Was that a note of panic she heard in his voice? "Why in the hell are you crying? I haven't touched you."

"I have to use the bathroom," she wailed. "And you…you said no!"

"Maybe once my partner gets back with lunch," he told her. "No way am I taking a chance on letting you loose without backup, just in case."

"I can't wait that long." She began weeping in earnest, great big gulping sobs of anguish, hoping she at least sounded believable. "I swear to you, I can't."

Staring at her, he finally shook his head. "All right, all right." He put his phone back in his pocket, stood and strolled over to stand in front of her. Apparently, judging by his crisp white shirt and pressed khakis, he'd had time to clean up after the accident.

She wiped at her streaming eyes and gulped back a sob. "I'm so, so sorry." She hoped she hadn't gone too far, done too much overacting.

"If I let you use the toilet, do you promise not to cause trouble?"

Sniffling, she wiped her hand across her face, registering the smears of grime and blood. "What kind of trouble could I cause? I can barely walk."

Grimacing, he looked her up and down. "You are pretty banged up. Actually, you look like crap." Why he seemed to find this amusing, she didn't know.

Praying he didn't notice she hadn't actually answered the question, she waited. Finally, he untied her feet.

"I wonder…" Stepping back he eyed her. "I think you can just take the chair with you into the bathroom."

"If I was a guy, maybe." Sniffling again she made sure he saw her eyes filling with tears. "But I need to be able to use the toilet…"

"Okay, okay." He held up a hand. "No more crying. Just let me warn you, I am armed."

She nodded, noticing he'd left his pistol on the table. Now she had two options. She could meekly go to the restroom and try to escape from there or...

She could be bold and brave and daring, and go for his gun.

As she flexed her legs, she winced. She wasn't entirely sure she hadn't broken a bone or two. Hurting this bad would definitely slow her down. She didn't know if she could get to the pistol before her captor.

Which led to a third, and even riskier option. She could try to knock Gray out, then get the weapon and flee. Try? No. She had to succeed. There wasn't an alternative.

She trembled as she waited for him to untie her. Instead, he eyed her once again, his suspicious gaze sliding up her body and lingering on her breasts. Yuck. A cold chill snaked up her spine.

"Please," she squeaked, willing the tears to return. "I have to go soooo badly."

That last bit worked. Evidently, he believed the helpless airhead woman routine. Finally, he untied her hands.

As soon as she was free, she flexed her fingers, trying to get some blood flow back.

"Go," he ordered, his tone full of irritation.

To buy herself time, she gave him a confused look. "Where? Out that doorway?"

He laughed, a harsh sound. "I'm not that big of an idiot. You're not leaving this room. There's a big cooking pot over there in the corner. Use that."

Gross. She didn't have to fake her shudder. "While you watch?"

Leering, he chuckled again. "Maybe if you're nice to me, I'll turn away."

Which meant he wouldn't. Since the last thing she planned to do was play nice, she supposed it was lucky she didn't really need to use the bathroom.

Slowly, she stood, testing her legs to see if they'd hold her weight. When they did without buckling, she pretended to stumble, reaching for the chair to steady herself.

"Sorry," she said. "Just trying to get up enough strength to walk." And then she grabbed hold of the chair and swung it with all of her might, aiming for the middle of his body, specifically his groin.

Driving as fast as he could—which turned out to be pretty darn fast due to the way every other vehicle on the road pulled over at his approach—Eric kept the lights and sirens on. He had no doubt that the local police would soon be made aware of the theft of an ambulance, so he figured he'd make full use of the vehicle as long as he had it.

Speeding south on Route 75, as he approached the exits for Sherman he kept his eyes out for a white van. The pain in his side had grown worse and he found himself gripping the wheel and perspiring heavily. Still, he kept his focus on the road and tried to ignore the persistent ache in his side. He figured he might have broken a couple ribs—most likely nothing serious, but damn, it hurt.

Again he fiddled with the knob on the radio. Most ambulances had the ability to listen in on police broadcasts and he hoped this one had that capability. If the US Marshals were trailing the white van with a chopper, once they broadcast the location, he hoped he could get there before them.

One thing was for damn sure—if he succeeded in getting Kara out, no way did he intend on letting the marshals have her back. Not now, not ever. He'd transport her to the trial himself if he had to.

"White van spotted on service road near Howe," the radio crackled. "Units responding."

The next exit sign loomed ahead. His heart sank as he realized it wasn't the right one. Stomping on the accelerator, he barreled forward, slowing as he finally approached the correct exit, a quarter mile away.

Ahead, on the service road, two police cruisers, lights and sirens on, had pulled over a white van in a restaurant parking lot.

Eric took the exit and pulled in behind the police cars. Since ambulances were common at accident scenes, no one paid him any attention. The uniformed officers were approaching the van with their weapons drawn. When the driver's-side door opened, Eric watched in disbelief as a short and chubby white-haired woman got out with her hands up and her expression confused and frightened.

Wrong white van. Not waiting, aware he couldn't afford to waste another second, Eric swung the ambulance around and headed back toward the freeway.

Now what? Though the local police hadn't paid any attention to the ambulance, he figured it would only be a matter of time.

His cell phone rang. Now what? Fishing it from his pocket—next to Shelton Smith's phone—he answered.

"Eric?" Kara's voice, hoarse and pitched low. "I stole Gray's cell, since the one you gave me is dead."

Alive. And with Gray. Heart pounding, he took a deep breath. "Where are you?"

"I'm in a Walmart parking lot. Beyond that, I don't know." She sounded worried, yet exhilarated. "I hit Gray—he captured me—with a chair. Hard. First in the groin, then when he was doubled over, I hit him again. In the head. I knocked him out and took his gun."

"What?" So relieved a wave of dizziness made him blink, he gripped the phone. "You are amazing, you know that?"

"I did what I had to do." She took a deep breath, and continued. "Before I left, I called 911. Then I took the keys to his van, and drove it down the street to this store. I'm parked, but worried. I'm thinking I need a different vehicle. Also, he has an accomplice out there in a different car or truck. I don't know what kind. He was gone when I escaped."

Astounded, he gripped his cell phone. The other US marshal—Shelton—had been right. Kara was an extremely strong and resourceful woman. His heart swelled with both love and pride.

"Stay right there," he told her. "I stole an ambulance. I'm driving down the service road right now. I'll find the nearest Walmart and come get you."

"You stole what?" To his shock, he realized her voice hovered on the edge of laughter. God, how he loved this woman.

Loved.

This realization so stunned him, he couldn't speak for a second.

"Never mind," she said, clearly taking his silence for reticence to explain. "You can tell me all about it later."

Either the stars were in alignment that afternoon, or he'd simply lucked out, but ahead he saw the familiar Walmart sign.

Once he'd pulled into the parking lot, he called Kara back. "Do you see the ambulance? I've got the lights flashing and I can hit the siren if need be."

"Yes." Voice relieved, she laughed. "I do see you. Park that thing and let's use the van. It'll be much less conspicuous."

He did exactly that, killing the lights before he parked. He pulled Shelton's cell from his pocket and dropped it on the passenger seat. Ahead, he saw her standing behind a battered white panel van, waving frantically.

Pulling into a spot a row away, he threw the ambulance into Park, pushed open the door and tried to sprint. One step and the pain nixed that idea, so instead he hobbled over to her as fast as he could.

"Eric." Launching herself at him, she wrapped her arms around him. The pain nearly made him pass out.

"Hey, hey," he told her, gently extricating himself. "Easy now. I'm guessing I might have a couple of bruised ribs."

She apologized profusely. "What now?"

"I think we need to call Ryan and let him handle this for now. I want to make sure I'm not facing charges for stealing that ambulance."

After having a good laugh at Eric's expense, Ryan promised to send someone from the local police to collect them. Though Eric made it clear he had absolutely no intention of letting Kara go back into the Witness Security Program, Ryan informed him he might not have a choice. He ordered them to wait there in the Walmart parking lot until a marked police cruiser showed up to collect them.

"He wants us to wait? To hell with that," Kara said, once Eric told her. "I don't feel safe with them. And we can't go back to your family's ranch. The guy that captured me knew about that."

She was right. In fact, she'd echoed his own gut reaction. Just like that, he reached an instant decision. "I have five hundred in cash," he told her. "That won't last long, but at least it will be enough to buy us some time. If I hit the ATM before we leave town, I can get a few hundred more."

"What are you thinking?" She leaned close, excitement lighting up her eyes. "Going on the run?"

The rational, logical part of him thought he ought to tell her not to be so dramatic. But in a way, if they disregarded Ryan's instructions, that would be exactly what they were doing. And if the fight—or flight— exhilarated her, so much the better. She needed to be sharp and on her toes in order to stay alive.

"Yes." He finally gave the simplest answer. "Though we can't use the ambulance or the white van—they're looking for them. We're probably going to have to steal a car."

"No. Let's find out how far the bus station is from here. Maybe we can walk."

Checking on his cell phone, he learned the Greyhound station was 4.3 miles south on 75.

"Yikes." She winced. "That's too far to walk."

"Yes, it is. We'll *borrow* a car to get closer, how about that? Not all the way there, or maybe a little past it. If we leave the car parked in a safe, public place, it's sure to be found and returned to its owner."

Finally, she nodded. "Fine. Just pick one that's sure to have insurance. I want to cause as little inconvenience as possible."

In the end, they decided on a nondescript Chrysler 300. While big, the eight-cylinder engine would provide enough power, and that type of car usually wouldn't garner a second glance. He made sure it wasn't a newer model, since he wasn't sure he could get past the electronic keys.

He managed to hot-wire the thing in under thirty seconds. "This proves there are some things you never forget," he told Kara, motioning for her to get in.

"When did you learn how to do that?" she asked as she buckled her seat belt.

He waited until he'd pulled out of the parking lot before answering. "Dad taught me. He showed all of us boys, just in case keys got lost or someone needed to start one of the ranch trucks in an emergency. I swear that's a skill I haven't used since I left the ranch."

"Well, it sure came in handy today."

They picked up the service road again, still heading south. He stopped at a red light, resisting the urge to glance around and see if anyone was watching them. No one appeared to be. Once they found the Greyhound station, they'd need to make a quick decision. Eric didn't have any idea where they were going to go, other than far away from here, but he felt confident he'd eventually figure something out.

His cell phone chimed, indicating a text message from Ryan. He glanced at it quickly. It said simply, Call me as soon as you can.

Eric exhaled and dropped the phone into the drink holder in the console. He had a pretty good idea what his brother would have to say. The light changed to green and they began to go. Ahead, he spied the Shell gas station with the small blue-and-white Greyhound sign.

"What is it?" Kara asked, her tone worried, glancing sideways at the phone.

"Ryan's texting me, asking me to call him."

"Why didn't he just call you?"

"I'm not sure. But I'm sure he's not happy with me right now since I told him I'd wait for his guys to collect me. I'm guessing he thinks we're in hiding or something." He shrugged. "Or maybe he's worried I'm speeding around in another stolen vehicle. He knows I won't usually check a text if I'm driving, though I would try and answer the phone."

"Oh, I see." Her light blue gaze touched on his. "Are you going to call him back?"

"Eventually," he said. "Though I'm not really in the mood for a tongue-lashing."

The amusement in her expression made him smile. "I think you should just go ahead and get it over with. Who knows, he might have learned something important."

Because he knew she was right, he sighed. "Here," he said, handing her the phone while he drove. "If you touch the phone icon at the top of the text message, it'll call him."

Once she'd done that, she handed the cell back to him.

When Ryan answered, the exhaustion coming through in his voice worried Eric. "Are you all right?"

Ryan snorted. "Shouldn't I be asking you that?"

"Don't start. I did what I had to do to save Kara. I made a choice. I couldn't wait. Right now, neither of us trusts anyone."

Silence while Ryan digested Eric's words.

"Other than you, that is," Eric elaborated. "What's up? I assume you have news?"

"Yeah. That's actually why I'm calling. Not to chew you out for vehicular theft or failing to do something you said you would." Sarcasm rang in his voice. "Anyway, we got the guy who impersonated a US marshal, Gray. The one Kara apparently knocked out. She must have called 911 from his house before she escaped."

"She did." Eric smiled at Kara. "She's not only smart, but resourceful, too."

"I agree." Ryan paused. "I'd say she's a keeper, brother. You need to hang on to her."

"I intend to. Oh, and she said there's another one out there. An accomplice. He's the one who drove the van and picked Gray and Kara up after the accident."

"We figured that. Here's the thing, though. This guy refuses to say much, except for one thing. This is actually why I'm calling. He wanted me to pass a message along for Kara. It's important."

Eric's blood went cold. "And that would be?"

"Are you going to tell her?"

"That depends on what the message is."

Ryan swore. "While I do agree, he is really adamant that she hear this. And I feel it's something she needs to know. Let me talk to her."

"No."

Ryan went silent. "You can't protect her by keeping the truth from her. She has the right to know what he said."

"I don't know about that." But Eric's initial determination had begun to fade, especially at the questioning look on Kara's beautiful face.

"You should," Ryan argued. "Kara is a fighter. She's fierce. She deserves to hear what he has to say, no matter how much it might initially frighten her."

Eric cursed under his breath. "You know I hate it when you're right. Here, you tell her." Eric handed Kara the phone. "That guy who captured you gave the authorities a message for you."

Taking the phone, she nodded. "Thank you," she said. "Hi, Ryan."

Eric watched while she listened to whatever his brother had to say. Her expression changed, became determined, though she wasn't able to hide the flash of fear that came and went from her gaze. Finally, without saying another word, she handed the phone back to him.

"Ryan?" Eric asked. "What did you say to her?"

But no one was there. Ryan had already ended the call.

Concerned, he tried to touch Kara's arm, but she moved away so fast she might have been dodging him. She scrunched herself into a little ball next to the door frame, her expression remote as she stared out the window.

Fierce protectiveness welled in him. Ryan's words had hurt her, and Eric knew he'd do anything to make her feel better, to make her feel safe.

But first, he needed to find out what the heck Ryan had told her. Whatever Gray had said, Eric couldn't fix it if he didn't know.

# Chapter 15

The so-called Greyhound station was actually a tiny office built into the side of a gas station, which was next door to a pawn shop.

Both she and Eric immediately headed for the restroom, aware they needed to clean up as much as possible before purchasing their tickets.

When she caught sight of herself in the cloudy bathroom mirror, she gasped. Luckily, the women's room had no other occupants, so she grabbed a handful of paper towels and tried to wash as much of the dirt and dried blood out of her shirt as she could.

It rapidly became apparent that she was making things worse.

Slipping into the hall to meet for Eric, she shook her head. "It's a lost cause," she muttered.

"They sell souvenir T-shirts," he told her. "Let me buy a couple and we can change."

"But what will the clerk think when he sees you?" If anything, he looked worse than her.

Eric shrugged. "I don't care. It's not like we have a choice."

After he selected a couple of T-shirts, she listened as he stood at the counter and purchased them. As she'd expected, the clerk asked about his appearance. To her surprise, Eric made a joke claiming they'd gone "mudding," whatever that was. Apparently, it was a good answer since the clerk laughed and rang up the shirts.

Back in the ladies' room, Kara used wet paper towels and hand soap to clean as much of the grime and blood as she could off her skin. After blotting herself dry, she put on the new T-shirt and eyed herself critically in the mirror. Better. But still...

She wished she had a brush but since she didn't, she combed her fingers through her tangled hair, trying to restore it to something resembling normal. When she'd finished, she still looked a bit disheveled but less so than before.

When she finally emerged, Eric waved two bus tickets at her. "We're going to Shreveport," he said, smiling.

The name of the city didn't ring a bell. "Where?"

He gave her a quick kiss. "Louisiana. I'm thinking no one will look for us there. It was only fifty dollars each, though the trip is kind of long."

"How long?"

"About eight and a half hours."

Even though sitting on a bus for that long didn't sound enjoyable, as long as she and Eric were together, she knew it would be all right. Still, as she caught herself constantly watching every person who entered the bus station, she wondered if she'd ever feel safe again.

Eric had cleaned up better than she had, Kara thought. His new black T-shirt accentuated his broad and muscular chest and in some circles, the ripped jeans might have even been a fashion statement. If she'd just met him, she'd never have guessed he was a surgeon. Instead, she might have said country music star or sexy rodeo cowboy.

He put his arm around her shoulders, the possessive gesture sending a thrill through her. "It's going to be all right," he promised. For just that instant, she let herself believe him.

When the large bus finally pulled in thirty minutes later, they climbed on board and chose their seats. Once every passenger had gotten on, the inside wasn't packed, but there were quite a few more people than Kara had expected. She had no idea so many chose to ride the bus as their form of transportation to travel long distances.

She and Eric chose seats near the back. After they'd settled in, he took her hand in his. "We're going to be fine," he repeated. His steady gaze and calm voice were designed to help soothe her, she knew.

"I know," she lied, sighing and resting her head on his biceps and shoulder. She stayed that way until the bus started moving.

Though she'd never say anything to Eric, the cold hard knot in the center of her stomach refused to go away, no matter how many miles they traveled. His concern, rather than soothing her, only made her feel worse.

Because of her, everyone he loved was in danger.

Because of her, innocent people would be hurt. The time had come for her to end her involvement with them. Only by doing so could she insure they'd stay safe.

Tears stung the back of her eyes.

Finally, she slept.

When she woke up again, the bus had stopped. "Rest stop," Eric said, brushing her hair away from her face with his fingers. "Might as well get out and stretch your legs."

Yawning, she pushed to her feet. Holding Eric's hand, she exited the bus and headed for the giant convenience store/gas station. After freshening up in the ladies' room, she browsed the store, amazed at the variety of junk and junk food.

"Are you hungry?" Eric spoke from behind her. She turned and once again let her gaze drink her fill of him. Devilishly handsome, he carried himself with an air of self-confidence that made him even more attractive. He was everything she could want in a man, would ever want.

He bought them coffee and submarine sandwiches. They sat at one of the little tables in the restaurant area and ate.

When they'd finished, Eric reached across the table and took her hand. "Are you ever going to tell me what message Ryan passed on from Gray?"

She shrugged, aware she wasn't fooling him. "Threats," she said. "You'll discount them as empty threats."

His gaze searched her face. "Do you?"

"I might have, except for one thing. I know I won't be able to live with myself if anything happens to your family." The family of the man who'd been kind enough to help out a stranger. The man she'd come to love more than life itself.

He could never know how she felt. Though she might long to tell him how much he meant to her, she knew she couldn't. The inevitable break would have to be clean and devoid of sentiment.

She'd need every bit of her inner strength to do this right. But when? This tormented her. How would she know the right time? The only thing she knew for certain was that it needed to be soon.

"My family will be fine," he said. "We Coltons can protect ourselves. Tell me what threats he made."

Taking a deep breath, she nodded. Just the thought of the threats made her feel queasy. "Gray was at your ranch, remember? He knows how to get there and he passed the info on to whoever he works for in the mob. That means Samboliono's thugs know where the Lucky C is located. Even worse, according to Gray, somehow they know where Greta lives in Oklahoma City."

Eric swore under his breath.

"That's not all," she told him. "They want me to turn myself in to them, or Samboliono will give the order to have your family killed, one by one. Execution style."

She could barely make herself look at him now, aware if she did, he'd read the emotion in her eyes. "The last thing he said was when he got to Dr. Eric Colton—you—Samboliono sends word from prison. He swears he'll have you killed slowly, and order his men to make sure you suffer."

Finishing, Kara felt as if she might become ill. She

swallowed hard, taking shallow breaths, staring outside at the scenery through the window.

"Ryan told you this?" Eric swore, hitting the top of the table with the palm of his hand, sending their trash scattering. "What purpose did he think that would serve?"

Not understanding, she eyed him.

"We can protect the ranch, no problem," Eric continued. "But what exactly is Ryan going to do to keep Greta safe?"

He got up from his seat and picked up their trash, carrying it to the waste receptacle. When he returned, the anger simmering in his eyes spoke louder than his otherwise calm demeanor. "Did my brother happen to tell you how he planned to safeguard Greta?"

"No, he didn't." Taking a deep breath, Kara stood, too, touched his too-tense arm, unable to keep from noticing the way her hand trembled. "It doesn't matter. I'm going to do as Samboliono asks and turn myself in."

"No." The word exploded from Eric, garnering curious looks from a few of the other customers. "Walk outside with me."

Once they'd left the gas-station restaurant, he stopped. He reached for her and took her in his arms. "You are not going to turn yourself in. Absolutely not. That would not only be suicide, but you'd be allowing a killer to go free."

"I know." Smiling sadly, she held on to him, too, breathing in his beloved scent. "But it would be a good trade. My life for the lives of many. Everyone who's important to you."

"You're important to me," he told her, his fierce

voice matching his expression. "So get that thought right out of your head. It's all a bluff, a last-ditch attempt to get you out of the picture. His guys won't get near the Lucky C. Ryan will make sure of that."

She wanted to believe him. Oh, how much she wanted to believe him. But she had to make him see how real the danger was. "What about Greta?"

Eric kissed the top of her head. "I'm sure Ryan will have her go home. He can protect everyone better if they're all in one place."

"You don't know Samboliono." She let her resignation and determination show in her voice.

"To be honest, I've never heard of him. I told the US Marshals that, too."

"That's because you're not from New York. He's well known in the Tri-State area. Anyone who gets in his way, Samboliono has killed. He's even taken out the chief of police and a district attorney. Plus probably hundreds of less prominent people, whose deaths went unreported. It's rumored he even has a United States senator or two on his payroll. He is one evil guy."

"I don't care." Eric sounded equally resolute. "He'll have to get through me to get to you."

Which was exactly what worried her.

Something in her face must have told him her thoughts.

"Kara, you can't turn yourself in. Not for me or my family or anyone else. We Coltons take care of our own. And you're one of us now. An honorary Colton."

Emotion clogged her throat at his words. "I'm honored," she said, managing to force the words out. "But don't you see? If I'm an honorary Colton, then I have an obligation to make sure no one else gets hurt."

She could tell her logic, no matter how faulty, frustrated him. "All right, what about your duty to law enforcement? To the family of the man who was killed? If you don't testify, then Samboliono will go free. Think about that, if nothing else. The prosecution needs you to be there in court for the trial. It's a little over one week away. You have to show up. If you don't, he can simply continue killing innocent people."

Humbled by his words, Kara realized Eric was right. She couldn't bail on her promise to appear in court. What she could do was stay hidden somewhere else. Somewhere that didn't involve the Coltons—or anyone else. She couldn't take the chance that any of Eric's family could be endangered because of her. Surely she could keep herself alive for one more week and a couple of days.

"You're right," she said, letting him think he'd convinced her of everything. "I've got to appear in court. Let's get back on the bus. I don't want to be left behind."

If he noticed she didn't agree to anything else, he didn't comment.

When they finally reached Dallas proper, the bus driver took I-20 east, heading toward Louisiana. "I think you'll like Shreveport and Bossier City," Eric said, his tender gaze making her chest hurt. "We'll have a nice dinner, maybe even gamble a bit on the boats. I'm pretty good at blackjack and I think I can increase our stash of cash."

Normally, his self-confidence would have made her smile. Now it did nothing but reinforce how much she loved him.

Her nod might have been perfunctory, but the smile

he gave her in return made her soul ache. Again she tried to reason with herself. While she had no intention of turning herself in to the Samboliono goons, if she disappeared from Eric's life, he and the rest of the Coltons should be safe. The mob would have nothing to gain by hurting them once she was gone.

Though leaving Eric would feel like ripping out her heart, she knew she had no choice. Her lids were so heavy she could barely keep them open.

Eric noticed. "Go ahead and take a nap," he told her, kissing the top of her head. "I'll stay awake and watch after you."

So she did.

When she woke again, they were still driving. The sun had set, and though it wasn't yet full dark, most of the other vehicles had their headlights on.

"How much farther?" she asked Eric.

He shrugged. "No idea. Now, if you don't mind, let me take a quick nap, too. I'm going to need all my energy for tonight."

What could have been a loaded statement was ruined when he closed his eyes and almost instantly dropped into sleep.

She gazed at him, her heart both full and breaking, until she could take no more. Then, she watched the flash of traffic going in the opposite direction.

Finally, after what seemed an eternity, the bus pulled up to the Greyhound bus station on Fannin Street.

"We're there," she whispered, gently shaking Eric's shoulder. "Wake up."

Just as quickly as he'd fallen asleep, Eric snapped into wakefulness. "It's a skill I learned in residency," he said, correctly guessing her thoughts. He consulted his phone. "At least we don't have to walk too far. The Horseshoe Casino is about four blocks that way."

Luck must have been smiling on them. Despite having no reservations, they were able to get a room.

"The last one available," the smiling desk clerk said, handing over the keys.

Kara took one look at the single queen-size bed and knew how she wanted to spend the rest of her time with Eric. If she was going to have to give him up, she planned to spend every last minute she could scrape together loving him. And allowing herself to be loved in return.

"I'm starving," Eric declared, apparently oblivious.

"Me, too," she replied, drifting into his arms and gazing up at him. "I want you."

At her words, his amazing green eyes widened. A split second later, his mouth covered hers hungrily, passion flaring instantly between them.

How could she bear to leave this man?

Tugging at his shirt, she helped him out of it, feasting her gaze on the bare expanse of his muscular chest. Slowly, she got rid of her own shirt and jeans, standing in front of him clad only in her lacy bra and matching panties. Mentally, she sent a thank-you to Greta for talking her into buying them. Her own taste usually ran to less frilly underwear.

His swift intake of breath told her he liked what she saw. "Come here," he rasped, holding out his hand.

Gladly she went, gasping as he pulled her up against his hard body, letting her feel the strength of his arousal. She couldn't hide her body's reaction, nor did she want to. Every molecule, every cell, became electrified at the contact. With him, she felt more alive than she ever had in all her thirty-one years.

He slipped his fingers around her back and divested her of her bra. Her breasts tingled as he caressed them, and she fumbled with his belt, wanting no cloth between them. He helped her, his manhood pushing against the edge of his underwear, thrilling her.

"Wait," he rasped, hauling her up against him for a long, deep kiss. The heat emanating from his body set her on fire.

Impatient, she moved against him, the thin material of her panties making her realize she had one more article of clothing to remove. Somehow, she managed to tug them off without breaking the passionate kiss. She tried to touch him, to urge him to move faster, but he captured her wrists with his hands and held her still. Even this she found erotic, and shudders of delight inside her made her realize she stood very close to the edge.

When she thought she could take no more of the sweet torture, she moaned in protest. "Now," she urged against his lips. "Take me now."

Raising his mouth from hers, he looked deeply into her eyes. "Kara, I… You're very special to me, you know that, right?"

Talk about stabbing her in the heart and twisting the knife. Mutely, she nodded, the contrast between her fiery arousal and her sorrow a sweet and sad agony. The emotion filling her made it impossible to speak. Which was for the best anyway, she thought. Though she longed to tell him her own feelings, she saw no reason to cause him any more pain.

Nonetheless, she saw her silence had hurt him. To

make up for it, she curled into the curve of his body and pressed her open mouth to his corded stomach. His swift intake of breath made her smile.

"I want you," she whispered, meaning every word. Heart bursting with anguish and love, she grazed her lips down lower, close to where his engorged body jutted proudly, ready for her.

"No." He stopped her, leading her to the bed and pulling back the bedspread. "I want to go slow. We have all the time in the world to explore each other."

Though she wanted fast, hard and furious, she sensed this was important to him, so she nodded. Slow, sensual lovemaking might be a better way to hold him forever in her memories.

Because no matter what happened, she knew she'd never forget him.

Easing her back onto the bed, he smiled. "Let me go first," he said, gliding his hands up the curve of her hip. "I want to feel every inch of your skin."

A shudder of desire shook her, though she tried to hold herself still. His touch, confident and sure, sent a jolt of pure lust coursing through her veins. He caressed her, stoking the fire of need into an inferno, until she couldn't take any more.

"Enough," she cried, her movements frantic. Arching her back, she writhed beneath him, needing him inside her, right that instant.

Pupils dark and engorged, he finally complied, slipping deep into her, filling her until she thought she would explode.

And then he moved, taking her with him, over the edge, into the abyss, where nothing else existed but the two of them.

Afterward, he held her as if he found her infinitely precious. She let herself hold him back, aware there might never be a forever, no matter how this felt. Maybe after the trial, if Eric could forgive her for what she was about to do. But for now, she had to believe their romance was over, or else she'd never find the strength to slip away later.

Later, after they'd showered and dressed, he took her to dinner. "I want something romantic," he said, grinning. "We've gone about this all backwards. You need to be properly courted."

Her stomach tied in knots, she managed to smile back.

"There." He pointed. "Jack Binion's Steakhouse. Right here inside the casino."

Again, despite not having reservations, they were seated. "I'm thinking today might be our lucky day," he told her, grinning.

The restaurant was elegant and intimate.

She let him order for her, not sure how she'd manage to choke anything down, but aware she'd need to eat to keep up her strength. When the food arrived— a petite sirloin for her, a rib-eye steak for him—she managed to perform a reasonable facsimile of enjoying her meal, even though in her current emotional state everything tasted like sawdust.

"You're quiet tonight," he remarked, after the waiter had cleared their plates and gone to fetch the dessert menu. "I know everything that happened has to be a bit of a shock."

"It was." She hoped her sleepy smile looked convincing. "Just a bit tired," she said. "Even though I slept on the bus, it's been a long, rough day. I'm still trying to process the fact that both of us are lucky to be alive."

Immediately, he nodded. "Then we'll skip dessert. I'm planning to make a quick stop at one of the casinos. Would you rather I walk you back to our room so you can rest?"

Straightening her shoulders, she shook her head. "I want to go with you." Every second they could spend together would soon be only a precious memory. She wasn't about to waste even one by sleeping.

His pleased grin told her he wanted her to come, too.

Once he'd settled the check, he took her hand and together they walked out into the large gaming area. The sounds of slot machines and chatter, plus the constant smell of cigarette smoke, made a headache start behind her eyes.

"All the casinos here are on boats," he told her. "Though you can barely tell."

He held her hand as they walked deep into the casino, and she let herself enjoy the warm fuzzy feeling his touch caused. When he found a blackjack table, she stood behind him to watch.

In less than an hour, he'd tripled their stash of money.

"Fifteen hundred dollars?" she said, unable to believe it as he cashed in his chips.

"Yeah." His confident grin made her toes curl. "I always try to stop playing while I'm ahead."

On the way back to the room, they stopped at one of the bars for a drink. Sitting in the small booth next to him, she allowed herself the luxury of pretending they were really a couple. Together and in love.

If only things were different, if she didn't have a ruthless mob kingpin out to eliminate her...

But then, she'd still be in New York and would never have met Dr. Eric Colton.

"We need to buy some more clothes," she told him. But the gift shop had already closed, so Eric said they'd take care of that in the morning.

By the time they got back to the room, Kara realized she could no longer fight her exhaustion.

"You're right, it's been a long, rough day," Eric said, yawning. "Car crash, capture by a bad guy, you escape, I find you— By the way, did I ever tell you how amazing it is that you managed to take that guy out all by yourself?"

"Yes, you did." She smiled and stood on tiptoe to press a kiss to his mouth. "And if you're not too tired, maybe you can show me."

He wasn't. This time their lovemaking was fast and furious, exactly what they both needed. After, she fell into an exhausted sleep, still cradled in his arms.

When she woke again, the nightstand clock showed 3:22 a.m. Next to her, Eric slept deeply, even occasionally letting out a light snore. She slipped out from his arms, watching with her heart in her throat to make sure she hadn't awakened him. When the even cadence of his breath told her she hadn't, she scooped up her clothes from the floor and carried them to the bathroom.

There, she cleaned up and dressed, blinking back tears. Inhaling deeply, she went back to the main room, located Eric's jeans and removed his wallet.

She felt like a thief, but ruthlessly she silenced the pangs of conscience as she emptied the money he'd won. Counting out nearly fourteen hundred dollars, she left him one crisp hundred dollar bill. Hopefully, he wouldn't need more than that. After all, once everyone knew she'd gone, he wouldn't have to worry about keeping his location hidden.

Taking one last lingering look at him, aware she might never see him again, she slipped out the door and into the darkness of the early morning.

Eric woke feeling happier than he had in years. Maybe even his entire life. Suddenly, the future shone unbelievably bright. While he loved his job, his calling, since meeting Kara he'd suddenly come to realize there was more to life than work. Much more.

Rolling over with a smile on his lips, he frowned as he realized her side of the bed was empty. He sat up, padding over to the open bathroom door. Though clearly no one occupied it, he checked anyway. Empty.

Heart pounding, even though deep down he already knew, he searched every corner of the motel room.

Kara was gone.

And since there was no sign of forced entry—he would have heard if someone had tried to break in to the room anyway—he could only face the truth. Kara had left of her own free will. A flash of wild grief made him stagger. How? Why? And then he remembered his winnings at the blackjack table.

With a sinking heart, he checked his wallet and realized almost all the money he'd won playing poker last night was gone, and the last shred of doubt he'd had regarding Kara's disappearance had vanished.

In place of the thick wad of bills, she'd left a note.

"Eric, I'm sorry," it began. Her loopy handwriting,

all flourishes and curves, reminded him so much of her it made his chest hurt.

> I considered the risks, and what we both had to lose. You're correct, I do have to testify, but I have no right to drag you or your family into my troubles. I appreciate everything you've ever done for me and when this is all over, if I survive, I promise to pay you back every cent. Both from today and from before, when you cared enough to spend your own money on a woman who was a total stranger to you.
>
> Don't look for me, please. I'll find you after the trial. Until then, stay safe.

And then, three little words that broke his heart.
"I love you. Kara."

Stunned, he read it again.

She loved him? His first impulse was to wad the note up and throw it at the wall. How could she say such a thing and then do something like this? If she truly loved him, she'd have stayed and let him help her fight this battle. She'd have a much better chance of staying alive.

Kara. Beautiful, brave, resourceful Kara. His mystery woman.

So many emotions. Fury, disappointment, shock. And most of all, hurt.

Swallowing past the lump in his throat, he knew what he had to do. Damned if he was going to give up and walk away. Not now. Especially not now, when he'd come to understand he loved her, too. Enough to want to spend the rest of his life with her. He had to find her, talk to her and make her understand that they were in this together. They always had been, ever since he'd seen her get hit by that car on that fateful day when his life had changed forever.

# Chapter 16

He had to find her. She couldn't have gone far. The first thing Eric needed to do was check at the bus station. He had no doubt she'd headed there and purchased a ticket to somewhere.

Skipping a shower, he hurriedly brushed his teeth and pulled on his clothes. Then, fueled by determination, he jogged and walked the four or five blocks over to the Greyhound place.

First he checked the restaurant attached to the station. While the brick building seemed full of people having breakfast, he didn't see Kara anywhere. When he asked the hostess if anyone matching her description had been in, the woman shrugged. "I just started my shift," she said. "The girl who worked before me has already gone home."

Just in case, he walked from booth to booth, checking. He also looked at the breakfast bar, his heart sinking when he found no sign of her.

Of course, depending on what time she'd left the hotel, she'd probably already eaten, gotten on some bus and headed on her way.

After that dead end, he went into the terminal proper, determined to find out where she'd gone. Even though there were only three ticket counters open, none of the workers claimed to remember a woman like her. Two of them were so flat-out disinterested they'd barely speak to him, while the other eyed him sideways as if he was a criminal.

When Eric asked to speak to the manager, a balding, middle-aged man with a huge paunch wobbled out from a back room somewhere and asked how he could help him.

Eric explained his girlfriend had gone missing.

"That sounds like a domestic dispute to me," the man drawled. "I can't get involved with your personal issues."

Gritting his teeth, Eric ignored that. "I'd like to view the security camera footage taken at your ticket counters since midnight," he said, managing to keep his tone pleasant.

At the request, the manager frowned and scratched his oversize belly. "No can do. You'll need to get a warrant for that. I'm really sorry," he said, sounding anything but. "Come back and see me once you have one."

A warrant. Great. After thanking the man, Eric went outside and called his brother. "Ryan, I need your help," he began.

"Where are you?" Ryan practically shouted, cutting him off.

"Trying to find Kara," Eric answered. "I'm at a bus station in Louisiana. Though it's not that big of a place, no one here seems to remember her. They refuse to let me view the security video without a warrant."

Silence. Then Ryan gave a loud, beleaguered sigh.

"And so you called me." Ryan's tone, layered with sarcasm, didn't sound sympathetic at all. "You do realize it's impossible to get a warrant in another jurisdiction without proper cause, don't you? Never mind working through the legalities in another state." He paused, took a deep breath, clearly just now processing what Eric had said. "Kara's missing? How the hell did you manage to lose her?"

"That's just it. I didn't. Not in the way you're suggesting anyway. She took off from our hotel room while I slept. Cleaned out my wallet and everything."

Silence while Ryan digested this. "Why?" he finally asked. "Why would she do such a thing?"

"Her note says she wanted to protect me and our family. I'm guessing she figures if she's gone, that mobster won't make good on his threats."

"What the hell could she be thinking?" Ryan swore. "There's no way she'll stand a chance on her own. How much cash does she have?"

"Around fourteen hundred," Eric said grimly. "I had a good night at the blackjack table."

Again stunned silence. "You're *gambling*?" Ryan's tone echoed with disbelief. "Yesterday the two of you were in a car crash, she was captured and escaped from an imposter law-enforcement guy, you stole an ambulance and ditched it, and the two of you went on the run. Then, to cap it all off, you went *gambling*?"

"It's a long story. And we got some rest on the

bus. But believe me, I gambled for a good reason. We needed to increase our cash." Idly, he watched as a bus pulled in and parked. When the doors opened and passengers began disembarking, he watched them head into the restaurant, one by one.

Except for a curvy, auburn-haired woman. Once she got off the bus, she turned and headed in the opposite direction from the station. Toward the hotel, her stride confident and sure.

His heart stuttered.

Kara.

"I think I just found her," Eric said, fumbling and almost dropping the phone. "Sorry, I've got to go." Ending the call, he shoved the phone in his pocket and sprinted after her, his heart pounding nearly as loud as his footsteps.

As he approached, Kara didn't even turn, either lost in her own thoughts or completely focused on her destination. Not street-smart, or safe.

Finally, he caught up to her, grabbing her elbow and spinning her around to face him. "Kara."

Jerking away, she met his gaze, her own face so expressionless he might have been a stranger. "What do you want? Who are you? I don't know you."

For one swift second, he thought her amnesia had somehow returned. But he knew such a thing wasn't even remotely possible.

"What?" Almost too late, he saw the way she cut her eyes to the left, letting him know she believed she'd been followed.

"Leave me alone," she ordered, backing away from him. "I'm armed and if you keep bothering me, I will defend myself."

"My mistake." Turning away, he caught the palpable relief in her eyes. Even though he knew she didn't have a weapon, her claiming to be armed was a smart move.

Despite every primal instinct screaming at him not to, he let her move away and searched for the threat.

There. He saw the man, looking every bit the movie-type gangster, sitting on a bench pretending to read a newspaper, his left knee jiggling up and down. Every few seconds, he'd look up from the paper and study Kara, who continued to walk away.

Though he wanted to go after her, Eric couldn't take a chance, not if somehow one of the mob goons had found her. He noted the man kept moving his right hand into his jacket pocket, indicating he probably had a weapon.

To Eric's shock, Kara turned around and came back. "I couldn't leave you," she murmured. "I don't know how I'd live if you were shot."

Stunned and horrified, he couldn't find any words. Sweet, beautiful Kara, who surely must be absolutely terrified, even now thought only about saving him.

"Get behind me," he ordered, finding his voice. Stepping in front of her, he looked around and quickly led them to a battered telephone pole, keeping his body in front of her like a shield. It wasn't much protection, but it would have to do.

The guy on the bench glanced at his watch, almost as if he was waiting for a signal.

Then, while Eric tried to figure out how to get Kara safely out of the area, the man got up, folded his paper and headed toward the bus station.

"Wow," Kara said, sagging against the telephone pole. "Once again my imagination got the better of me. I really thought that guy was one of Samboliono's goons."

As his heartbeat slowed and he caught his breath, he stared at her. He couldn't believe she was acting as if the night before hadn't happened. As if she hadn't emptied his wallet and sneaked out of their hotel room in the middle of the night, and left him.

"What are you doing, Kara?" He kept his voice gentle, struggling to contain his frustration and anger. "I woke up and you were gone."

"And now I'm back." Swallowing hard, she looked away. "I'm sorry."

"Sorry?" He didn't even try to hide the bitterness in his tone. "Sorry isn't going to cut it. I need more."

There were a thousand other things he wanted say, but couldn't. Not yet. Not until he knew exactly why she'd run away. "I have a right to know why. Explain."

When she dropped her head and held on to her silence, he took a deep breath. "Look, Kara. I know you're scared. That's understandable. But help me understand. I went to sleep with you wrapped in my arms. I woke up and you were gone. I'd like to know the reason why."

The tortured expression in her eyes when she met his gaze quelled his hurt anger and made his heart turn over.

"Here?" She gestured around them, reminding him they were exposed, out in the open, and in a very public place. "Can we go back to the room?"

Part of him, the primal, primitive side that wanted to claim her right then and there, and tell her in no uncertain terms that she was his, wanted to have this out here, now.

Fortunately, the more rational, reasonable side of him prevailed.

Resisting the urge to take her arm, he gave a curt nod. "Sure."

Neither spoke the entire walk back to the Horseshoe. They traveled in silence through the lobby, the noisy and already crowded and smoky casino, and rode the elevator to the third floor. He couldn't help but wonder if she felt as battered inside as he did.

He let out a breath he hadn't even realized he was holding once they were inside their room and the door had swung closed behind them. He secured the dead bolt and the chain, for good measure. When he saw the bed, still rumpled from their lovemaking the night before, the memory of how he'd felt when he'd found her gone stabbed him.

The note, still in his pocket, mocked his tumultuous emotions. He couldn't help but wonder if she'd truly meant her words, or if she'd written them as some kind of balm on what she might have viewed as a wounded male ego.

And then he faced her. The pain and sorrow still flickering in her eyes wounded him.

"I'm sorry," she whispered. "I'm really, really sorry." Biting her lip, she looked past him at nothing. "I thought I was doing what would be best, but after I left I realized I was only running away."

Clenching his jaw, he kept his arms crossed so he wouldn't touch her. Though he wanted to. With every fiber of his being.

"I came back." Her voice broke. She reached into her pocket and pulled out a neatly rolled wad of bills.

"Here's your money. It's all here, except for what I spent on the bus ticket."

When he made no move to take it, she gave a muffled cry and threw it on the floor at his feet. "You act like you wish I hadn't returned."

"Not that," he told her, his low voice vibrating with intensity. "Never that. And I don't care about the money. I'm still trying to understand why you thought you should go in the first place."

"I made a mistake." Drawing herself up, she faced him, tears filling her eyes and muffling her voice. "The instant I realized my error, I corrected it. Eric, I've told you I'm sorry. I came back to try and fix what I did. If you can't accept that…"

"Did you mean this?" Slowly, Eric withdrew the note she'd left him. "What you wrote in here? Did you mean it or were you just trying to say something you thought I wanted to hear?"

Wiping at her eyes, she sighed. "I would never do that. I meant every word. I love you, Eric. That's partly why I came back."

"Partly?" He saw the hurt flash across her face when he didn't immediately reciprocate.

"Yes, partly. Even if you don't return the feeling, the other reason I came back is because we've always been a damn good team. I didn't want to lose that."

His heart squeezed at the fact that she seemed unaware of the tears snaking silver streams down her face.

"I guess I'm too late," she said, her voice breaking. "Apparently, I've managed to lose it after all."

When she went to turn away, he caught her and hauled her up against him, swallowing tightly. This woman. His. For now and forever. "My beautiful mystery woman. Kara, I love you. I'm not about to lose you, no matter what the cost. I know you're worried about my family. I'll stay away from them—we can even have Ryan tell everyone we've separated. We need to keep hidden, at least until this trial is over, as long as we're together. I want to be with you, no matter what, wherever you need to go, whatever you need to do."

Her stunned gaze searched his face. "Are you sure?" He couldn't help but see the way her hand trembled as she reached up and laid it alongside his cheek. "Because I need you to be very, very sure."

"Positive." He placed his own hand over hers. "We'll face this side by side, the way we have since we met."

And then he kissed her. Neither of them spoke again for a very long time.

After they'd made passionate love, Kara watched Eric doze. She was still trembling inside. She'd come so close to losing him, yet her conscience continued to prick at her. Samboliono always did what he said. Even if Eric didn't understand what kind of danger his family was now in, she did.

He woke a few minutes later, smiling to find her watching him. "Come here," he said, his low voice seductive as he stroked her arm.

Instead, she got off the bed and stood. Out of reach, since she couldn't think straight when he touched her. "Would you mind calling Ryan first? I'm sure Samboliono has already put out the word to his men. We need to act fast if we're going to put your plan into action."

"Of course." Pushing back the sheets, he padded

over to the hotel dresser and retrieved his pants. Digging into one of the pockets, he frowned. After searching the other, his frown deepened. "My cell isn't here. Help me look for it."

Despite both of them searching the room and the bathroom, neither found any sign of the missing phone.

"It must have fallen from my pocket when I went running after you."

At her crestfallen expression, he squeezed her shoulder. "It's okay. Let me use your phone."

Crud. Staring at him, she sighed. "I tossed it in the trash can at the bus station, right before I got on the bus."

He appeared dumbfounded. "Why?"

"Because I remembered reading somewhere that cell phones have tracking devices. And I figured with Ryan's police connections, you two could find me, so I got rid of the phone."

"Maybe it's still there." Grabbing his clothes off the floor, he began getting dressed. A split second later, she did, too.

"Come on." Grabbing her hand, he pulled her out of the room and down the hallway toward the elevator.

They were the only two people in the elevator, which was good since that meant they wouldn't have to stop at any other floors. If time hadn't been of the essence, Kara thought she would have liked to steal a few kisses, but for now she tabled that thought.

Once the elevator reached the first floor, they hustled through the casino, heading for the exit. As soon as they stepped outside, they started running.

When she reached the trash can where she'd tossed the phone, she saw immediately that it had been emptied. "It's only about a third full," she said, trying to catch her breath. "It was overflowing earlier." She pointed to a foot-long stick lying on the ground. "I had to use that stick to push the phone down deep."

Eric didn't seem nearly as winded. "Okay, that's fine. We needed to buy some more clothing anyway. We'll pick up a phone, too."

Her stomach growled and she eyed the bus-station restaurant. "Do you think we could get something to eat while we're here? I haven't eaten since yesterday."

"Sure." He took her arm. "I'm kind of hungry myself."

After filling up on scrambled eggs, bacon, sausage, and biscuits and gravy, not to mention several cups of strong coffee, Kara felt ready to face the rest of the day.

They headed back to the hotel and rode the elevator back to their room.

She stood back and waited while he went to open the door. But when he inserted the key, the light didn't turn green.

"The key won't work." Eric tried once more. "Come on, let's go check with the front desk."

"Okay." When he grabbed her hand and tugged her down the hall, she beamed. Sappy as it might be, she loved being part of a couple with him. She'd been a fool to think she could give this up. Eric knew how to defend himself. Together, they'd keep safe until she could testify.

And then? Thinking of a future once Samboliono had been put away for good made her giddy. She pushed the thought from her mind, not wanting to jinx anything. For now, she and Eric needed to concentrate on staying alive long enough for her to get to the trial.

She waited while Eric went to talk to one of the desk clerks. After a moment, he returned, frowning.

"We missed checkout time, and they assumed we'd left," he told her. "But that's not the biggest issue. Someone tried to leave a message for us while we were gone. Since they believed we'd checked out, they didn't get the name or the message, just that whoever called said it was urgent."

Trying not to worry, she glanced around. "Maybe it was Ryan?"

"That's possible, but he has my cell number. Even if I didn't answer, he'd just leave a message or text me. Also, I didn't tell him where we're staying. There are several hotels with casinos here. I doubt he called each and every one and left a message for me."

Resisting the urge to immediately scope out their surroundings, she kept her gaze locked on his. "If you think we're in danger, let's get out of here. We can buy a bus ticket and start making our way east, since I have to be in New York in less than a week anyway."

But he shook his head. "No bus. If they know we're here, they'll be checking the bus station, too. I'm going to call a cab and we'll find a used car lot and purchase the cheapest car we can find."

"We only have about thirteen hundred left," she pointed out. "Unless you use plastic or something."

He considered. "That's a thought, too, especially if they've already figured out we are here. Let's see what we can find. I'm hoping someone will have an old beater we can get for less than a thousand dollars."

"We have to make sure it's good enough to get us to New York. That's quite a drive."

"I know." Smiling, he gave her a quick kiss. "Let's

get out of here and see what we can find. On the way there, I'll have him stop at a store so I can buy a cell phone, and I'll check in with Ryan."

Though she had her doubts, his enthusiasm was contagious. "I'd like a change of clothes, too," she said.

They hailed a cab in front of the hotel and asked the driver to take them to the nearest store where they could buy a cell phone. He agreed and they were off.

A few minutes later he pulled up in front of a shabby-looking convenience store in what could only be called a disreputable neighborhood.

"Here you go," the cab driver said, smiling. "My cousin owns this place. He'll give you a good deal."

Kara and Eric exchanged a glance. Finally, Eric shrugged. "Be right back," he told her.

This idea made her nervous. For all they knew, the cab driver could be working for Samboliono. Paranoid? Maybe. But why take a chance?

"I want to go with you." She slid out of the backseat after him. He grabbed her hand, which made her ridiculously happy, and they went inside. Twenty dollars later and they were the proud owners of an untraceable cell phone. The shop owner had been adamant about that last fact.

Once back in the cab, Eric asked the driver if he had any friends or relatives who sold used cars.

Though Kara wouldn't have thought it possible, the man's grin grew even wider. "Yes! I will take you there now!"

While they drove, Eric punched Ryan's number into his phone. She listened while Eric greeted his brother, and then hardly got a word in after that.

Finally, Ryan apparently wound down. Eric asked

a few questions, thanked his brother and told him he'd check back in later.

When he turned to face Kara, his green eyes gleamed with excitement. "You're not going to believe what Ryan told me," he began.

"Here we are," the cab driver announced, interrupting. As they coasted to a stop, he jumped out and opened the back door. "Come on, you two. Let me introduce you to my friend Tyrone. He owns this lot and I'm sure he can fix you up with something."

Eric nodded. "Let me settle up with you first." He glanced at the meter and gave the driver two twenties. "Keep the change."

Curious, as soon as they were out of the cab, Kara tugged at his arm. "What were you about to tell me?"

"Ryan just found out—" he began.

"Good afternoon, sir and madam," a voice boomed.

Both Kara and Ryan turned and looked up. And up. The man smiling at them appeared to be nearly seven feet tall. His lined dark skin placed him in his late fifties or early sixties.

"That's right," he said. "I'm tall. My name's Tyrone Templeton. I used to play pro basketball a few decades ago. I just told you that to keep you from asking. Everybody asks. Now, what can I interest you in today?"

Frustrated, Kara followed the two men as they went to look at a pickup truck. As they walked off, the cab driver waved and left.

While Eric and Tyrone haggled over the price, she wandered the lot and checked out the other vehicles. A bright red Camaro caught her eye. "Eric," she called out, impulsively. "I really like this one."

Both Eric and Tyrone came over to see.

"That's pretty new," Tyrone said. "I think it's a 2012."

Which meant it would be a lot more than Eric had to spend.

"Never mind," she told the men, struggling to hide her disappointment. When all this was over, she planned to get her own car. Especially if she was going to stay in Oklahoma.

When the walked into the small office to finalize their deal, she continued checking out the red car.

"Are you ready?" Eric asked, emerging with car keys and a manila envelope. "We're all done."

Casting one last longing look at the Camaro, she turned to follow Eric to the pickup. Instead, he gave her that confident, sexy grin and held up a remote key fob. "Here," he said, tossing it to her. "Unlock the doors."

She caught it, wondering, but pressed the unlock icon anyway. To her surprise, the bright red sports car's lights flashed as the doors unlocked.

Stunned, she looked from the car to Eric and back again. "You bought this one?"

"Yep. You're going to need your own car and since you liked it so much…"

"But I know this cost more than a thousand dollars. How?"

The heart-rending tenderness in his gaze made her breath catch. "Just get in and drive. I'll tell you all about it once we get on the road."

So she did. When she turned the key, the engine started with a satisfying roar. "I'm not sure of what direction to take," she said. "You'll have to tell me."

He laughed. "I had to ask before we left. But I'm pretty sure I can remember it."

Concentrating on handling the car, she followed the directions he gave her, turning left, then right, until finally she saw an entrance ramp to a freeway up ahead.

"Now, are you going to fill me in on what Ryan said? And how you managed to buy this car?"

"I don't know," he said, following up his teasing tone with a devastatingly sexy grin. "How are you at driving when you're excited?"

"Now you really have me intrigued."

"Well, for starters, you don't have to testify," he said.

"What?" she yelped, swerving a little—just enough to hit the raised pavement markers separating the lanes.

He sighed. "Pull over. Take the next exit and we'll park. I should have told you before we left the car lot."

Not sure whether or not he was joking, she exited and parked at a McDonald's. Leaving the engine running, she turned in her seat to face him. "What do you mean, I don't have to testify?" she asked carefully. "Don't tell me Samboliono escaped or managed to reach some sort of plea bargain agreement."

"Nope. Ryan said Samboliono is dead, killed in prison awaiting trial. Apparently one of his nephews decided to stage a coup and had him murdered."

"What?" She gaped at him. "I'm really glad you had me pull over. He's dead?"

"Yep. And as a result, the US Marshals don't feel you need protection. No trial, no witness." He watched her closely. "That's how I was able to buy the car. I have a high-limit credit card or two, so I used one of those."

Stunned, she sat back in her seat, completely at a loss for words.

"Now you can resume your normal life," he continued. "Go back to New York City if you want. Or…"

When he didn't finish, she met his gaze. "Or what?"

The amused look disappeared from his green eyes, replaced by one of tenderness. "Or you can stay in Tulsa and open your own restaurant."

Her heart skipped a beat. Struggling to hide her disappointment, she nodded. "That's one possibility," she said, wondering if she'd been a fool to hope for more.

"Of course, if you do that, you'll have to agree to marry me." His expression fierce, he leaned over and kissed her. "I don't have a ring, but we can take care of that once we get back to Tulsa. I love you, Kara. Will you do me the honor of becoming my wife?"

With a glad cry, she launched herself at him, her heart singing with happiness. Or at least she tried to, but her seat belt stopped her short. Hands trembling, she managed to unlock it.

"Yes," she said, kissing him, letting her joy bubble up in her laugh. "I will."

He kissed her back with so much passion he made desire sing in her blood. When he released her his eyes smoldered. "If we weren't sitting in a fast-food restaurant parking lot, I'd show you how much I love you," he declared. "But since we are, that'll have to wait until later."

And later, that's exactly what he did.

\* \* \* \* \*

*Don't miss the next book in*
THE COLTONS OF OKLAHOMA *series*,
*PROTECTING THE COLTON BRIDE*
*by Elle James,*
*available September 2015*
*from Harlequin Romantic Suspense.*

*And if you loved this novel, don't miss other suspenseful titles by Karen Whiddon:*

*THE RANCHER'S RETURN*
*A SECRET COLTON BABY*
*TEXAS SECRETS, LOVERS' LIES*
*THE MILLIONAIRE COWBOY'S SECRET*

*Available now from Harlequin Romantic Suspense!*

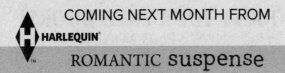
### #1863 PROTECTING THE COLTON BRIDE
*The Coltons of Oklahoma* • by Elle James
Megan Talbot needs money—fast—and the only way to get
her inheritance is to marry. Her wealthy rancher boss has his
own agenda when he proposes a marriage of convenience,
but as Megan is targeted by an assassin, family secrets must
be exposed.

### #1864 A WANTED MAN
*Cold Case Detectives* • by Jennifer Morey
Haunted by his past, Kadin Tandy moves to Wyoming to open
his own investigative firm. His new client, Penny Darden,
suspects someone close to her is a killer. As they hunt for
answers and she falls for the rugged PI, they both learn the
depths of healing, love...and true danger.

### #1865 AGENT ZERO
by Lilith Saintcrow
He's the most dangerous man terminally ill Holly Candless
will ever meet—and he'll do anything to keep her safe. But
it's a race against time, since only a top secret government
program stands between her and a slow, sure death....

### #1866 THE SECRET KING
*Conspiracy Against the Crown* • by C.J. Miller
After a tragic loss and an ensuing royal battle, the princess of
Acacia must choose between her heart and her duty. But the
man who comes to protect her and whom she starts to love
has a dark, twisted secret that could destroy them both.

# REQUEST YOUR FREE BOOKS!
## 2 FREE NOVELS PLUS 2 FREE GIFTS!

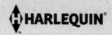

## ROMANTIC suspense

### *Sparked by danger, fueled by passion*

---

**YES!** Please send me 2 FREE Harlequin® Romantic Suspense novels and my 2 FREE gifts (gifts are worth about $10). After receiving them, if I don't wish to receive any more books, I can return the shipping statement marked "cancel." If I don't cancel, I will receive 4 brand-new novels every month and be billed just $4.74 per book in the U.S. or $5.49 per book in Canada. That's a savings of at least 12% off the cover price! It's quite a bargain! Shipping and handling is just 50¢ per book in the U.S. and 75¢ per book in Canada.* I understand that accepting the 2 free books and gifts places me under no obligation to buy anything. I can always return a shipment and cancel at any time. Even if I never buy another book, the two free books and gifts are mine to keep forever.

240/340 HDN GH3P

---

Name _____ (PLEASE PRINT)

Address _____ Apt. #

City _____ State/Prov. _____ Zip/Postal Code

Signature (if under 18, a parent or guardian must sign)

Mail to the **Reader Service:**
**IN U.S.A.:** P.O. Box 1867, Buffalo, NY 14240-1867
**IN CANADA:** P.O. Box 609, Fort Erie, Ontario L2A 5X3

**Want to try two free books from another line?**
**Call 1-800-873-8635 or visit www.ReaderService.com.**

\* Terms and prices subject to change without notice. Prices do not include applicable taxes. Sales tax applicable in N.Y. Canadian residents will be charged applicable taxes. Offer not valid in Quebec. This offer is limited to one order per household. Not valid for current subscribers to Harlequin Romantic Suspense books. All orders subject to credit approval. Credit or debit balances in a customer's account(s) may be offset by any other outstanding balance owed by or to the customer. Please allow 4 to 6 weeks for delivery. Offer available while quantities last.

---

**Your Privacy**—The Reader Service is committed to protecting your privacy. Our Privacy Policy is available online at www.ReaderService.com or upon request from the Reader Service.

We make a portion of our mailing list available to reputable third parties that offer products we believe may interest you. If you prefer that we not exchange your name with third parties, or if you wish to clarify or modify your communication preferences, please visit us at www.ReaderService.com/consumerschoice or write to us at Reader Service Preference Service, P.O. Box 9062, Buffalo, NY 14240-9062. Include your complete name and address.

SPECIAL EXCERPT FROM

**H** HARLEQUIN®

ROMANTIC suspense

*Can this Colton cowboy save his wife—and his
beloved ranch—when a killer threatens everything
they hold dear?*

*Read on for a sneak preview of
PROTECTING THE COLTON BRIDE
by* New York Times *bestselling author* **Elle James**,
*the fourth book in the 2015*
*COLTONS OF WYOMING continuity.*

"Why don't we get married?"

Even though she'd known it was coming, it still hit
her square in the chest. The air rushed from her lungs
and a tsunami of feelings washed over her. A surge of joy
made her heart beat so fast she felt faint. She crested that
wave and slid into the undertow of reality. "A marriage of
convenience?"

"Exactly." Daniel reached for her hands.

When she hid them behind her back, he dropped his
arms. "It wouldn't have to be forever. Just long enough
to satisfy the stipulations of your grandmother's will and
save your horses, and that would help me get past the
Kennedy gauntlet. We could leave tomorrow, spend a
night in Vegas, find a chapel and it would be over in less
than five minutes."

With her heart smarting, Megan forced a shaky smile.
"Way to sweep a girl off her feet."

He waved his hand and Halo tossed her head. "If you want, I can make an official announcement in front of my family."

Megan shook her head. "No."

"No, you won't marry me?"

"No." She pushed past him to pace down the center of the barn. "Your plan is insane."

"Do you have a better one?" he asked. "I'm all ears."

The plan was the same as the one she'd been thinking of before Daniel had woken up. Only when she'd dreamed it up, it didn't sound as cold and impersonal as Daniel's proposal. Somewhere in the back of her mind she'd hoped that marriage to Daniel would be something more than one of convenience.

After yesterday's kiss, she wasn't sure she could be around Daniel for long periods of time without wanting another. And another.

*Don't miss*
*PROTECTING THE COLTON BRIDE*
*by* New York Times *bestselling author Elle James.*
*Available September 2015*

www.Harlequin.com

Love the Harlequin book
you just read?

Your opinion matters.

Review this book on your favorite
book site, review site, blog or your own
social media properties and share
your opinion with other readers!

# JUST CAN'T GET ENOUGH?

Join our social communities
and talk to us online.

You will have access to the latest
news on upcoming titles and special
promotions, but most importantly,
you can talk to other fans about your
favorite Harlequin reads.

Harlequin.com/Community

Facebook.com/HarlequinBooks

Twitter.com/HarlequinBooks

Pinterest.com/HarlequinBooks

# THE WORLD IS BETTER WITH

## *Romance*

Harlequin has everything from contemporary, passionate and heartwarming to suspenseful and inspirational stories.

Whatever your mood,
we have a romance just for you!

Connect with us to find your next great read,
special offers and more.

f /HarlequinBooks

@HarlequinBooks

www.HarlequinBlog.com

www.Harlequin.com/Newsletters

**HARLEQUIN**

A *Romance* FOR EVERY MOOD™

www.Harlequin.com